OLIVER

BOOK FOUR
THE TIDES SERIES

PENELOPE AUSTIN

This book is a work of fiction.
Any references to historical events, real
people, or real locations are used fictitiously.
Other names, characters, places, and
Incidents are the product of the author's
imagination, and any resemblance to actual
events locations, or persons living or
dead, is entirely coincidental.

OLIVER
Book Four
Of the Tides Series
Copyright © 2023
by Penelope Austin
All rights reserved.

No portion of this book may be reproduced
in any form without written permission
from the publisher or author.

THIS STORY CONTAINS TRIGGERS—YOU
WILL FIND SCENES OF VIOLENCE, GORE,
VILLAINOUS CREATURES, MONSTERS FROM
HELL, DECAPITATIONS, ABUSE, TORTURE,
EROTIC SCENES WITH DESCRIPTION, AND
DEATH. IF YOU HAVE AN ISSUE WITH ANY
OF THE ABOVE THIS BOOK IS NOT FOR YOU.

DEDICATION & THANKS

"I'll take a break at the end of this book."
It's a common refrain, and I think my very
patient and loving husband got wise to
the truth two books ago. There won't be a
break after the next book or the one after.
Thanks for your incredible patience, my love.

Thank you again, Flirty Quill, for helping me
me polish my story and for listening to my
crazy ideas with enthusiasm and absolutely no
judgment. Your helpful critiques help me shine.

Thank you to my Beta readers, who comb through
my work to find all the boo-boos. Your efforts
are much appreciated. You help my kids shine!
And for the readers who reached out to me and told
me how much they loved the Florida Keys gang
and the stories! (this goes double for you, Susan)

~ THANK YOU ~

Special thanks to Annie, Charmaine, and Paige
for wonderful guidance with Oliver and Phoebe's
emotional issues. Their troubled souls bloomed
under your experienced therapeutic guidance.
My sensitivity readers were an amazing help in
crafting Sybil's character. Thank you so much!

You'll see a ton of pink in Oliver's book. I
want to dedicate this story to a good friend,
a staunch supporter, and a cancer survivor.
Even with the inevitable changes in her life,
she always finds time to support my writing.
She is a reminder that courage and tenacity
will take you further than expected in this life.

Side note! Charleston is one of my favorite
cities in the US. Sorry I picked on you, Charlie.
Don't let a host of dangerous paranormals keep
you from visiting this amazing stopover. It's a
phenomenal place if you ever get the chance.

PROLOGUE

Long braids battered her skull as the witch leaned into the blast from the Hellgate gaping before her. Five feet in the air, blinding blue and white light assaulted her eyes, a violent, otherworldly wind ripping at her skin. Squinting, her hands moving in organized but frantic patterns, she chanted between the gasping breaths that burned her lungs. The breach *must* close before things got any worse.

Heat seared her palms as the exhausted witch shoved every ounce of her power behind the spell, the gap gradually narrowing. It wasn't enough. Through squinted eyes, she watched as three more demons charged toward the opening, blue gems gleaming on their chests, their fangs clicking together with excitement. Frustration lashed through her even as panic spurred her to action. She redoubled her efforts, calling on the last ounce of her strength.

Falling to her knees, the witch tipped her head back in defeat, tears streaming from her eyes. She couldn't do it; she was about to die. Then, she remembered her reason for being here, and rallied.

With a guttural roar, she tapped into the depths of her soul, hurling one last, desperate incantation at the fissure. A golden bead of energy snaked upward from the ground, racing to meet the one slithering down from ten feet above. Sluggish, the two glowing arcs headed for each other, the rip shrinking. It was too late. The demons had reached the gate. One stuck a hand through and grabbed onto the edge of the rift. The raging wind drowned any sounds it made, but she saw its eyes. Yellow. Slitted. Hungry.

The sorceress had nothing left. On her knees, her chest heaving like bellows, she watched, wide-eyed, certain this was the end for her. The spell crackled, and with a final burst of energy, the fiery orbs shot for each other and merged with a hissing pop, mending the tear in the fabric of the world. A hand tumbled to the ground, the long, narrow claws ticking as the fingers eased closed into a morbid fist.

Sagging with relief, the witch raised a trembling hand to wipe her forehead, struggling to catch her breath as her ears rang in the silence. Glancing down at the break in her salt circle, her eyebrows clenched together. Staggering to her feet, she whirled, scanning the gnarled brush surrounding the small clearing.

On one side, a trampled path through the tall grass led to the turquoise ocean; on the other, a gaping tunnel through the dead mangroves disappeared into the impassible mess.

Her heart sank. No, this wasn't over. Not by a long shot.

CHAPTER 1

~ OLIVER ~

I came to my senses to find water lapping at my hip bones. Yep, I was naked. In the ocean. At night. *Fuck.*

Rummaging through blurry memories for what I'd been doing the last few hours, I drew a blank. My breath reeked of whisky; no surprise there. Checking my arms for bite marks, I didn't see any, but the bottle in my hand was an unexpected bonus. I took a sip, then glanced over my shoulder—too fast—and the universe swooped. I caught myself, then spotted the jumbled pile of clothing on shore. At least they were above the waterline this time.

With a curl of my lip, I glared down at my erection, the rebellious bugger bobbing at the water's surface. "So you're resisting arrest tonight, are you? You're a fighter, I'll give you that." The damn thing didn't answer, but it did keep bobbing. At least someone was happy tonight.

Listing like a marker buoy, I pulled it together, then splashed water on my face; something caught my eye. Lifting my hand, I struggled to focus on the thin metal band determined to rub the white-blonde hair from my wrist. Conspicuously dull, the cheap gold no longer glimmered pink.

No pink, no magic. I toasted with a swig of my half-empty bottle, nearly capsized, but somehow stayed on my feet. The seeping burn of whisky lowered my voice an octave.

"*Ahh*. Hints of heat, spice, and desperation. I smell our early retirement in there, Chubby." He bobbed and winked, saying nothing.

"Would you like some? Seeing as it's late and you're still up?" My constant companion didn't answer. I started to laugh and couldn't stop.

My crazed laughter echoed over the dark ocean. I laughed so hard I cried, lost my balance, and sat down in the Atlantic with a sploosh. The hatchwork of scars across my back pulled tight, sending needles of pain through me. I buried my face in one hand.

Ugly. I was goddamn ugly, inside and out. Thank God she'd never see the monster I'd become. I hissed when a warm smile flashed into my thoughts. *Phoebe*.

My lips pulled back in a tearless grimace. Images flickered, a silent film of all the things I'd lost: her tanned, athletic curves, those soft hazel eyes, and my fingers spread wide as silky brown waves tumbled through them.

I wept, hating the pathetic sound of it. Struggling to breathe through the vice on my chest, I raised my bottle in the moonlight and watched as tremors shook the coppery liquid against the glass.

Eight years. Eight miserable years since I'd felt Phoebe's soft curves against my skin. All that remained of our time together were ghostly memories. Before the lab.

Before the torture. Before I lost myself to rage. Tears poured in earnest, but they didn't bother me as much as the pathetic whine coming from my throat.

"Weak. You lost everything because you're so *fucking* weak. You should have resisted, you piece of shit."

I threw my head back and roared my rage at the stars, the anguished sound rolling out to sea. We could have been great together. We had a good thing going. And all it took was a side trip to a convenience store for my life to swerve off the tracks and straight into a living hell.

Pulling myself together, I scrubbed my hand across my face and slurred, "At least I've had you for company all these years, Chubs. You're a pillar of strength, pal." I jumped when someone spoke.

"I've never heard anyone talk to his penis before."

The baritone voice echoed in the space between my ears. I struggled to my feet, whirled around, and promptly fell on my ass again, my arm raised to keep the salt water out of my next swig of atonement. I waved the bottle at my tank-sized visitor.

"Hello, Gideon." I frowned, wondering how much the Gryphon heard. The Enforcer's telepathic voice tickled my brain.

"Good evening, Oliver. Are you ok out there, or do you want help before a shark takes a nibble?"

"I'd never be so lucky." Scratching my head, I found my feet and sloshed to shore. After another swig of Jim Beam, I tumbled onto the beach. Beside me, the majestic paranormal cop settled like a Sphinx on the sand, his long tail flicking beside his muscular tiger-striped body.

A hollow, rumbling purr filled the air as the Gryphon extended one enormous paw. Stretching his six-inch black talons, he licked between them with a forked tongue, then curled his feet beneath his chest. Gideon ruffled his wings and tucked them close, the sea breeze fluffing the feathers on his eagle head as he gazed at the galaxies above. The view and the soothing sound of waves should have cheered me. It didn't.

"Therapy not going well, Oliver?"

"Just dandy. I haven't tried to kill anyone for months," I snorted.

Gideon didn't laugh. He cocked his head and blinked. *"That's no way to talk, Oemar."*

"Don't call me that!" Heat sparked behind my eyes, and, for an instant, they lit the space between us before I reeled in my magic. The Enforcer would discover I'd slipped my leash if I didn't sober up. The last thing I needed was my wristband recharged and my powers snuffed—*again*.

"Sorry. My bad." I lay back on the sand and closed my eyes. The world swam in fast circles, so I sat up again, brushing sand from the hard curves of my chest. The Gryphon watched, unblinking. His silence unnerved me.

"I'm doing the best I can, alright? You'll have to forgive me if I'm a little indisposed. It's the only way I can function these days." I tipped the bottle at him. "I may need a second round to relieve my little problem this time. Or should I say, *big* problem?" I winked, and the fleshy corners of Gideon's beak turned down in a birdy frown.

"Phoebe asked about you tonight. She's worried and wants to know if you're alright. Reach out to her, Oliver. The girl cares about you."

I took a long pull from my bottle, ignoring the ache in my chest at the sound of her name.

"Tell her I'm fine and to stop worrying. She should go back to Georgia. Key West is too expensive, and I'm fine now."

The Gryphon said nothing, his golden eyes following me when I heaved to my feet, dusted the sand from my ass, and fumbled for my clothes. I managed to dress without falling again, but my cargo shorts wound up crooked, and the holes of my button-down shirt were off by two. I needed to beat it before Gideon realized Phoebe's bracelet ward had fizzled out. The pressure of his eagle-eyed stare annoyed me, but I stifled the anger coiling beneath my skin.

"What? You don't like my sense of style? No one's gonna die from my crooked buttons, Gideon. Your work is done here. Nice talk." I gave him a two-finger salute, then turned and staggered down the beach toward the sidewalk.

Behind me, feathers rustled as the Enforcer stood to follow. With a snarl, I whirled to face him, wisps of shimmering air wafting from my skin. Sucking in my magic, I hoped he didn't notice the slip. Phoebe's spell had reached its expiry date, but he didn't need to know that. One more stint of confinement, and I'd hit the end of my rope and wrap the damn thing around my own neck.

The only thing moving on the Gryphon was the furry tip of his striped tail, which jerked and twitched. *"Is there something you aren't telling me, Oliver?"*

"Yes. The Succubus that did this to me"—I pointed down—"should have finished the job and cut it off. It would have saved me a lifetime of misery."

"Don't do anything foolish. You must give yourself time to recover."

A bitter laugh spilled from my throat. "Ronan was under her thrall for what, five days? It took him a month to recover, Gideon. A month! *I did eight fucking years!*"

Spit flew from my mouth, and, breathing hard, I wiped my hand across my lips. "You are too optimistic, *Gryphon*. I'm stuck with this for life, and you know it."

Gideon sighed, his gaze flicking down to where my loose shirt covered my eternal embarrassment.

"Leave me alone, Gideon. I've broken no laws, and your paranormal citizens are safe from me. In fact, maybe you should get back to policing the *Others* and not me. Save your babysitting for the bad guys."

Turning to resume my forward stagger, the snap of giant wings over my head made me duck. I slanted a look at the black sky in time to see him sweep past and blink out of existence. If I didn't have the powerful senses of a Djinn, I would have missed the subtle sound of his wings as he flew away, invisible to prying human eyes.

"Sneaky bastard. How long do you think he watched us?"

My throbbing friend didn't answer. I should have known better than to venture away from my sailboat. The liveaboard was comfortable, the marina quiet, and no one bothered me there. I'd barely seen the Gryphon since he rescued me from the hellhole in Charleston, and now look—his beak poking into my business at the precise moment I had something to hide.

As I stood there, weaving in place, I stifled the urge to walk back into the Atlantic and keep right on going. There wasn't enough whisky on the planet to drown my problems, but the ocean …

Sighing, I stuck my hand in my pocket and tucked the throbbing menace against my hip. The salt water soak hadn't eased my discomfort, liquor no longer worked, and even a visit by the Enforcer couldn't scare the thing into submission. There was only one avenue left.

I dumped the last swig of flaming beverage down the hatch and headed for the Vampire Club.

***

My not-so-stable stroll down Duval Street blended right in with the revelers partying at the bars in the lively tourist town. Pausing at Key West Collectibles, I used the window's reflection to finger-comb my wavy white-blonde mess into a semblance of order.

The loose clothes hanging from me were a reminder—my sanity wasn't the only thing I left in Charleston. It would take forever to recover the muscle I'd lost in that cell. My silver eyes flared, and I growled, swallowing the magic itching to break free of my feeble hold.

Movement caught my eye, and I stiffened. Over my shoulder, a blurred reflection appeared, then drifted away. A face? I whirled, my skin prickly at the sensation of wrongness, my shoulders twitching as if caressed by a languorous hand.

"None of that, *Oemar*," I snapped. It wasn't the first time I saw things from my past that weren't there. When the Gryphon used my true name after a lifetime of running from it, my blood ran cold. How the hell did the Enforcer know it? I hadn't used that moniker since fleeing my family's desert home for the relative safety of Augusta, Georgia.

My thoughts drifted back to a sea of sand and the cold nights spent misting over it in happy exploration. I'd taken everything for granted back then. The sting of a dust storm on my skin, the hot breeze on my face, the freedom—the memories scattered as jagged pain chased them away.

With a long sigh, I turned from my reflection, stumbling a few steps before righting myself. Checking my shirt flap for coverage, I trudged to the lineup at Munchie's. As I crossed the street, a human stepped from the alley and waved a slip of microdots at me. *Fucking drugs.*

"Hey, man. Can I interest you in a boner you'll never forget?" The greasy piece of shit chuckled to himself. "I've got some of the last remaining doses of *Gush* right here, pal, and they're all yours for—"

His nose crunched beneath my knuckles. As he reeled backward into the darkness, I snatched the paper slip of horrors from his fingers, and with a flash of my eyes, it burst into flames. I dropped it to the street and watched it burn, flapping my bloodied fist and hissing at the pain. The dealer appeared from the darkness, his hands clutching his bleeding face.

Before he opened his mouth, I whispered, "If you don't want to die in the next three seconds, you'll turn around and disappear without another word."

Thankfully, he took my advice, and I continued on, the throb of my bloody hand matching the one in my shorts. *Ouch.* Fucking cretin. You'd think the damn humans would have learned after *Gush* nearly destroyed the southeastern seaboard six months ago. Leaving the asshole nursing his broken nose, I reached my destination.

The Vampire club looked like a shack; *Munchies* was anything but. Lord Luther's bar operated on the waterfront north of Mallory Square. Eerily lit by a single lightbulb, a heavily warded door led through a tear in the fabric of the space-time continuum. I had no idea what that meant, but paranormal patrons enjoyed the vast club beyond that door while hidden from prying human eyes. The doorway looked like any other, but an evening filled with badassery waited on the other side.

Invisible to all but *Others,* Munchies had a reputation, and it wasn't necessarily good. As I reached to pull the door open, Stan stepped outside and put his fat gray fingers on my chest.

"Where do you think you're going?" he snapped.

I held my hands out to the side and said, "For a drink. What's the problem, Stanley?"

The monstrous Gargoyle narrowed his beady eyes at me, the gray skin of his somewhat human face crinkling around the eyes. He sniffed, his lips curling down in a thick pout. I almost laughed when it made the fangs in his lower jaw poke free, reminding me of an overgrown bulldog. Stan's grumbling, stone-on-stone voice gave off a vibration that tickled my ears.

"Last time you were here, we had to use an extinguisher to put the fire out. Lord Luther said it was your last strike, *Djinn.*"

Shit. "Are you sure? I saw him the other night at Walgreens—your boss seemed fine then."

The Gargoyle cocked his head, his scowl deepening.

"Yeah. Luther bought a greeting card. Isn't your birthday next week?"

With an about-face, Stan's frown flipped into a thick smile, the fangs disappeared, and the Gargoyle looked less like a bulldog and more like a happy gray garden gnome.

"Luther bought a card? For me?"

I shot him a beaming smile. "Yes! I saw it myself. It was one of those musical cards, you know—they play a song?"

"Oooh. I love music," Stan whispered, his eye wrinkles angling up. After humming and hawing and scratching his rocky chin, the Gargoyle turned and opened the door.

"Fine. Have a wonderful time at Munchies. No biting without permission. And stay out of trouble, or you'll be dealing with Luther this time."

With a smile, I slipped past him and disappeared into the darkness. Sobriety threatened, so I headed straight to the bar, weaving through the crowd of patrons in the foyer and circling the packed dance floor. I squinted against the glare of the strobing lights, the thumping boards beneath my feet, and the ear-shattering music doing nothing for my stability. When I reached the bar, I pulled out a stool, but a long, thin arm snaked out to catch my wrist in a cold grip.

"It's taken."

I looked into the red-ringed eyes of a dark-haired vamp, his cold expression pinning me with icy precision.

Someone needed a snack. I couldn't afford a throw down exposing my unrestrained powers, so I moved over one seat, smiling at him from the corner of my mouth as I waited for Priscilla.

Working at the other end of the bar, the pretty blonde bartender noticed me and dropped her rag, her hands finding her hips. She glared.

Giving her my most apologetic smile, I raised my eyebrows and mouthed, *"Pretty Please?"* With a sigh, she headed my way, grabbed a tumbler, and poured me two fingers of scotch. At the sight of my boot lip, she snorted and added another. Priscilla slid it down the bar with a resigned smile, then turned to serve her next customer.

Enjoying the smooth warmth of decent whisky, I settled on my stool and peered through the gloom to see who came tonight. The dance floor pulsed beneath heavy feet, the sweaty, intoxicated bodies grinding together like a school of drunken sardines. Through the open doors at the far end, the waterside patio overlooked the ocean; tonight was standing room only.

Catering predominantly to vamps, only adventurous *Others* frequented the club. Most stuck to the front of the house, where semi-respectable things went down. It was the one place in Key West where *Others*—Shifters, Vampires, Paranormals—mingled freely. I wasn't here to socialize. Smiling into my drink, I jumped when someone tugged on my collar.

"That will be twenty bucks."

Choking on the liquor I inhaled, I gasped, "WHAT!?"

"Prices went up yesterday, Ollie. Pay up." With a knowing smile, Priscilla held out her hand.

"Put it on my tab, Luv."

She shook her head. "Uh Uh. Luther's orders. Anyone who makes the *shit* list gets on the *hit* list. There's a surcharge for troublemakers now." She flicked her fingers.

With a sigh, I reached into my pocket—the one not currently occupied by my aching tag-along—and pulled out a cash roll. She took it all.

"Hey!" I yelled after her. Prissy turned, shot me a little fang, and said, "That's for the table we replaced last week when you almost set the club on fire."

"Yeah, sorry about that," I grumbled, then turned to finish my drink. I wouldn't need further numbing after my next stop anyway.

As I tossed back the burning liquid, I watched Luther prowl across the far end of the club. The brooding, dark-skinned Vampire Lord pushed seven feet tall and probably bench-pressed cars. I'd have to behave if I didn't want to die tonight, which was a debatable subject.

The festive scene reminded me of the night I took Phoebe to a club. An image of her exhilarated face flashed behind my eyes—bouncing, waving, and circling me like a moon in orbit. Glistening skin, a radiant glow, and her breathless laughter took my breath away; it was the first night we made love.

At an angry throb from my hitchhiker, I gasped and swallowed the rest of my drink. "Alright, alright," I grumbled.

Standing, I sent Priscilla a grateful nod, then headed through the swinging doors beside the bar. As darkness enveloped me, the cool air pumping through this section of the club did nothing to sober me up.

The Dark Room was exclusive, expensive, and open only to depraved lunatics with a death wish. I smiled and headed down the dark hall toward the dim lights of my salvation.

***

~ PHOEBE ~

Dabbing at the sweat on my lip, I checked my makeup in the backlit mirror, snapped the compact shut, and popped my lips to freshen the rosy color. As I fluffed my brunette waves, I admired the beautiful marble sinks in the spacious executive bathroom, featuring top-of-the-line everything. Opening the door and stepping into the air-conditioned corridor, I ignored the butterflies trying to escape my tummy.

After a short wait at the modern reception desk, my heels made no sound on the soft rug as the smiling secretary ushered me into Mr. Griswald's office.

A balding gentleman behind the desk stared back at me with rheumy eyes, his lips turned down in a perpetual frown. *"I watched them building pyramids"* could have been this guy's LinkedIn caption.

"Have a seat, Ms. Peregrin."

As I pulled up a chair and smoothed my skirt, my eyes drifted to the regal Witch sitting very still beside Griswald. Bottomless espresso eyes stared back at me from a luxurious ebony face. Beautiful, but deadly. I smothered a wheeze as she inspected me, an icy sensation brushing across my skin. I smiled. She didn't.

Nodding at the Witch beside him, Griswald said, "This is Ms. Metroyer. She will observe our interview today."

It was hard not to stare at the Witch. Lush lips and oval features lent the tall, athletic woman a fashion model beauty. Her sable skin radiated pure champagne, her effervescent power tingling on the tip of my tongue.

Holy horse feathers, this was one powerful Witch. A tight-lipped one because, when she nodded in greeting, the rows of ceramic beads on her thin black braids ticked loudly in the deathly silence. I wondered if Griswald feared the force of nature beside him.

"So, the task," he stated, peering at me from behind his round spectacles. "We are looking for a ward witch with a specialty in binding powerful spells to subsurface limestone."

"I specialize in bindings and grounding—above *or* below the surface." I licked my lips, nervous at the intense stare from the brooding Ms. Metroyer.

"What is the nature of the job, Mr. Griswald? It might be helpful to know what you wish me to accomplish?"

The archaic geezer gave me a haughty look, then turned to the Witch beside him and raised an eyebrow. When she spoke, her evocative voice shocked my arm hair to attention.

"That will be disclosed at a later date. All you need to know is you will be working with me. Closely." Her voice and lips moved at slightly different rates. It was a power play; she was posturing.

Disconcerted, and with my attention glued to her mouth, I realized the room had gone silent. The pair stared at me, waiting for me to say something. Squaring my shoulders, I met the Witch's eyes.

"As you know, *Ms. Metroyer*, a Witch's reputation defines her value. I have the skills you seek, but I will not enter into a contract with you until I understand your expectations and the potential pitfalls."

Wow. That sounded professional. *Go me*. I resisted the urge to dab my lip sweat while I waited to see what she would say about *that*. After what seemed like an eternity, Ms. Metroyer answered, "I understand," and sliced a pointed look at Griswald.

Shuffling his papers, the man stood stiffly, motioned at the door with one hand, and said, "Thank you for your time, Ms. Peregrin. We will be in touch if you are selected to assist Ms. Metroyer. You may see yourself out."

Stiff-faced but determined not to falter, I stood and nodded to them both before sweeping as gracefully as possible from the room. I strutted past the receptionist, who watched me all the way to the elevator. As I waited for the ding, I glanced back. Through his open door, I saw Griswald still standing behind his desk, watching me leave, his eyes gleaming like a slavering dog waiting for a bone. I shuddered.

Stepping onto the lift, I hit the button without giving away the turmoil sizzling beneath my skin. When the doors closed, I fisted my hands and pounded them against my scrunched forehead.

"Shit, shit, shit!" I needed that job. Without it, my stay in Key West was over. I'd have to pack up and catch a bus back to Augusta. My metaphysical shop needed me, but so did Oliver. I couldn't leave. Not yet.

Texting my assistant Elli, I asked for the shop statements to review. I'd find a way to make this work or starve trying. Biting my lip, I added a request to fax a few specific pages from my grimoire. If Ms. Metroyer hired me, I had the feeling I'd need them.

"Disclosed at a later date," I grumped. "Fuck you, you animated corpse. I'm not putting my reputation on the line no matter *how* good the pay is." *Especially not with a witch who could turn me to dust with a whisper.*

As I stepped into the heat of a typical Key West day, I thought of Oliver and my heart sank. He wouldn't speak to me. I'd barely seen him since Gideon moved him here a month ago. Every time I stopped by his sailboat, he made excuses and disappeared.

Oliver's eyes no longer sparkled with laughter. On the rare occasion that his gaze met mine, they were dull. Lifeless. Thoughts turning inward, I remembered his long, passionate kisses, his silvery irises inches from mine as they flared with desire: the ghostly image of him throwing me over a shoulder and tossing me, giggling, onto our bed; his muscular arms hemming me in as I drank in the masculine scent of his skin; his smiling face so close that his breath tickled my cheeks. Tears threatened, and I struggled to breathe under the onslaught of emotion.

With a shuddering sigh, I dabbed my eyes and glanced toward the marina. Oliver was still in there somewhere, buried under years of hellish captivity. He'd come so far. I couldn't give up. Not yet.

"You're pathetic, Phoebe. Why are you wasting your time?" Biting back my defeated whisper, I picked up the pace. Oliver's liveaboard was around the corner from this interview. A visit would reassure me that he was alright. Then, I'd grab some groceries and invite him for dinner. If he said no, I'd try again next week. I refused to give up on him.

Careful not to break my ankle on the uneven boards, I made my way along the pier, then tapped on the side panel of Oliver's 40' Nordic Sailboat. When he didn't answer, I called his name a few times. The clothes strewn across the deck told me he was home.

With a sick feeling, I climbed aboard, careful not to lose my balance. I peeked through the open hatch. Someone stirred in the small bedroom under the bow.

"Oliver, are you there? It's Phoebe."

Soft mumbles and a thump made me feel better, but when he didn't answer, my desire to see him got the better of me. Clicking across the living area, I reached the open door to his berth and gasped.

Oliver sprawled naked on the mattress and tangled in the sheets around his legs. Restless, his muscles glistened with sweat as he panted. A bottle of scotch lay on the floor, the contents still draining onto the area rug. At least he'd somehow gotten relief from his constant arousal—I narrowed my eyes. *What the hell?*

Bright red puncture marks pocked his entire body. My hand flew to my mouth.

"Oh, Oliver. *What have you done to yourself?*" My whisper roused him, and his head lifted from the pillow, one bloodshot eye peering at me.

"Phoebe? What are you doing here?" he croaked.

I swallowed the urge to lash out at him. "I'm here to see you. I'm sorry I woke you. I'll come back later."

Oliver thumped his head back on the pillow and moaned. "Give me a minute."

Stepping back and closing the door, I felt like a fool for not knocking harder. Climbing awkwardly onto the deck,

I sat on the small seat beside the hatch. Above me, the seabirds squawked with throaty laughter, making me feel even worse. Even the seagulls knew trying to reach him was a waste of time.

Oliver appeared in a white t-shirt and shorts. He popped up from the hatch and attempted a smile, but the dark circles around his eyes painted his face an ugly color. Handsome, even at his worst, Oliver's morning stubble softened his appearance. His platinum hair lifted on the morning breeze, and the urge to run my fingers through it punched me in the gut.

Climbing stiffly through the hatch and sliding onto the bench opposite me, Oliver rubbed his knees. "What can I do for you?"

"Nothing. I ... I wanted to check on you. It's been so long. Are you alright?"

He frowned, running a hand through his hair. "Never better. Thanks. Sorry I worried you." Oliver looked everywhere but me, his eyes drooping with fatigue. An awkward silence filled the small deck.

"Ollie. Talk to me."

His silvery eyes flashed. "What do you want me to say, Phoebe? That everything is grand? Look, ma, no erection! No more blackouts!" He laughed, a cold, bitter sound. "The nightmares are to die for."

I ignored his outburst, my eyes trailing over the bite marks on his legs. Oliver's lips tightened, but I stiffened my spine and met his hard look.

"It's nothing, Phoebe. I'm fine. You shouldn't have come here." He stared up at the robin-egg sky, his chin pulled tight. Then he looked me square in the eye and said, "I don't think you should come to see me anymore. You need to go home to Augusta. Move on from this ... *mess*. Live your life."

Ignoring the agony in my chest, I stood, but when I stepped toward him, Oliver scrambled over the railing onto the dock and held out his hand. I stared at it, knowing that if I took his fingers in mine, that would be it for us. Being shoved away sucked, and I wanted to cry, but I didn't. I hiked up my skirt, climbed off the boat without a stumble, and turned to face him.

"Oliver. Let me make this clear—again. You are *not* alone. When I give up on you—*on us*—it will be *my* decision. I'll go home when I'm damn good and ready."

I turned and walked down the docks with as much poise as I could muster, my heels tapping on the wood. Thank the Gods, I made a graceful exit. When I looked back he was gone.

CHAPTER 2

~ PHOEBE ~

"Fuck my life," I hissed to myself. I stepped out of my shoe and bent to inspect the spider web of fishing net gnarled around the heel. That would teach me to be distracted while wearing instruments of torture on the docks.

"Thank you for not embarrassing me, but you're coming home today. I can't afford another pair, so just give up already, you piece of—" I lost my balance and tipped over, catching myself with one hand.

"Need some help?"

I looked toward the husky voice, but the sun shone behind my rescuer. A tanned, masculine hand reached down, and I took it, finding myself on my feet in a flash.

The good samaritan stooped and, using both hands, backed my heel through the fine mesh of the net, then hoisted my shoe in triumph. I would have taken it from him, but I was too busy ogling. Thirty-ish, the guy was about my age and insanely good-looking, his collar-length brown hair and wavy bangs styled by magical fingers. *My God*.

He stood, holding my shoe out to me. Embarrassed, I took it and mumbled, "Thanks. You're a lifesaver." His megawatt smile spurred a visceral reaction as my heart fluttered like a Fourth of July flag.

"May I?" He indicated my arm, and I nodded. My skin tingled where he grasped my elbow, helping me to the slatted bench beside the docks. Speechless, I watched as my brown-eyed rescuer took my shoe and slipped it on, then buckled the ankle strap. Yes, I was freaking Cinderella, the Prince had my foot in his hands, and I resisted the urge to look over my shoulder. Was my carriage in the parking lot?

"With my luck, it would be a pumpkin," I muttered, then covered my mouth when I realized Mr. Hot Pants heard me.

He chuckled. "You look like you could use a drink, *Ms …?*"

Laughter bubbled to my lips. "I'm Phoebe. And you are—?"

And there it was, a panty-burning smile. "Gabriel, or Gabe if you prefer. Can I buy you a cocktail?" He pointed toward McNally's, a popular bar at the end of the jetty.

"It's so unlike me to get angels," I murmured, wondering where the shut-off was for my mouth. I shook my head, chasing away the confusion. "I'm in!" My breathless words sounded desperate, and I flushed red.

When I stood and his warm hand pressed against my back to guide me, I resisted the urge to purr. An image of Oliver flashed into my mind, and I straightened. It was a drink. One drink. A busy bar and a non-stalker-ish guy. *Perfectly fine, right?*

An hour later, the sun started its descent, and my cheeks hurt from smiling at my charming new friend. Wine and the tangerine glow of a Key West sunset sent contentment curling through me. It turned out that Gabriel had a wonderful sense of humor, entertaining me with stories of his time in Italy.

"You've lived my dream vacation," I sighed.

"I'm sure you deserve one." Gabriel took a sip of his Glenfiddich, his soft brown eyes on me. This guy's moves were as smooth as the drink in that tumbler. There was no accent, but the timbre of his voice rumbled in a way that made me think of ancient buildings, cafes on corners, and eating grapes from someone's belly.

I shook my head. "Listen, it's been fun, but I should head home." Casting another look across the harbor, I watched Oliver's lifeless sailboat bob in its slip. No lights lit the windows, even though the sun had set.

Gabriel said something that I didn't catch.

"Sorry?" I asked, a bit too breathless.

"Would you like me to walk you home? It'll be dark soon."

"How do I know you're not the dangerous one?"

Gabe lifted one eyebrow comically. "Who, me? You can trust me, my dear," he teased, trying for creepy and looking cuddly instead.

"My apartment isn't far—but that would be nice." Guilt gnawed as I said the words.

After a lovely walk along the docks, warmth filled me. Spending time with the man was everything I'd longed to experience with Oliver. I didn't realize how lonely I'd been until Gabe treated me to friendly smiles, the scent of expensive cologne, and a warm hand touching the small of my back. For eight years, I'd longed for stability. This guy oozed it from every pore.

When we arrived at the red door of my apartment, I turned to find him close enough that I scented the subtle hint of scotch on his breath. And his cologne … *oh dear.*

"It's been delightful, Phoebe. Thank you. Can I see you again?" He eased in as if to kiss me, and my limbs turned to jello. I held my breath, emotions tumbling through me like Yahtzee dice.

The hum of the crowd one block over faded as the scent of fine cigars from Pepe's Bistro tickled my nose. Heat swept down my spine as Gabriel's lips lowered toward mine; a car backfired, jarring me to my senses.

"*Shitburgers,*" I whispered, breaking the spell. I stepped back, panting. "Thank you for rescuing my shoe." A sudden urge to flee hit me and I opened my door without answering his question. "It's been lovely, Gabriel. Goodnight."

Nearly slamming the door, I ran up the stairs, flopped onto my bed, and cried into my pillow.

***

~ OLIVER ~

Seeing Phoebe on my boat had been a shock. So close, so warm, and giving off her witchy cinnamon heart aroma, I'd nearly lost it. My little problem would have reared its ugly head had I not been completely sated.

I scowled at the thought and pulled open the door of Handy's, the convenience store near the marina. I was out of my liquor of choice, and the night was young. Thinking of spending time with her caused a stir downstairs, and I planned on a pre-emptive strike before things got out of hand.

As I browsed the shelves back near the coolers, I heard the door tinkle, and instinctively, I used my Djinn hearing to gather information. Years of living on the run had honed my senses to their finest.

When I heard a metallic click, I froze. Glancing into the corner security mirror, a black hoodie and a snarling face told me that trouble had arrived. At the glint of a gun, I couldn't help myself. I misted, blinking out of sight. I almost blew my cover when I sighed at the heady sensation of my atoms scattering.

"You have two seconds, pal. I'll take everything in that register. NOW."

The thief wore a black nylon buff pulled up to his eyes. I didn't need to see his face to know he was *Other*. From the smell of wet dog wafting my way, I knew he was a Shifter, most likely a wolf. Awesome. The tough-to-kill bastard was about to spice up my night. Mentally, I rubbed my hands together.

Invisible and spread against the ceiling, I watched the clerk throw everything on the counter and stand back with his hands up. The wolf shoved the money in his pocket and ran. As he disappeared through the entrance, the thrill of the hunt swept through me. It reminded me of home and stalking gazelles through the desert with Father.

After a jaunt through several alleys, the Shifter darted between a pair of dumpsters behind Munchies and slid through a gap beneath the docks. Creeping along the shoreline, the thief plunked down on the cement foundation.

Counting his loot, the Shifter's throaty chuckles grated on my last nerve. When I showed myself, slowly misting back to solid form, he glanced up, then resumed counting. When he finished, he shot me a dirty look.

"Hello, *Djinn*. It's mine. Now fuck off."

I kept quiet, quickly assessing the small space and my options.

"I said, FUCK OFF."

Slipping closer, I whispered, "You better hope the Enforcer doesn't catch you."

His laughter rang through the damp air, the human sound ending with a throaty growl. As the Shifter's body swelled and his rumbles deepened, I pushed on my magic. Striking while he was in human form was my best option. Another few seconds and I'd have enough power gathered—

With a grunt and a whole lot of popping bones and wheezing, he shifted. A jet-black, furred monstrosity swelled into the small space, and a clawed hand shot out, grabbing me around the throat. I went limp, dangling in his hold as I spooled more magic. The bracelet had stifled my powers for so long that it was slow in coming.

"You don't listen very well, do you, *Djinn?*" The garbled words sounded like he had a mouthful of marbles. The wolf's grip tightened, cutting off my air as he rose to balance over powerful haunches. My eyes rolled, watching his ears fold against the dock above us. This bastard was huge. He pulled me closer, his dog breath blasting my face as my feet swung in the air.

"Do you have a death wish, BOY?" He shook me for effect, and my teeth clacked together. I gurgled, resisting the urge to lift my hands and provoke him. *Come on. Come on ...!* My magic stuttered, then rushed into my fingers and toes.

Crimson flashed in the wolf's narrowed eyes, and he opened his mouth wider, his fangs gleaming white in the shadows. "Your submission is accepted, seeing how I forgot to grab myself a snack. And I can't have you running back to the Enforcer now, can I?"

Choking in his grip, I smiled into his face as thick white fur sprouted along my arms. This asshole was about to meet something that would crush his head like a ten-cent gumball. The wolf's teeth closed over the top of my head to tear it from my shoulders.

Before I could sweep through my change, something splashed in the ocean beside us. A pair of eyes, one white, one green, popped up on my right, the newcomer's bare, muscular chest gleaming with seawater. His short, dark hair and human features looked familiar.

A Syreni. NO. *A Servus*. What was the fucking hybrid doing here? With a growl, I pulled back my magic, the fur disappearing with a whisper.

"You'd be wise to stand down, wolf," Felix rumbled. His bi-colored eyes flicked over me, then focused back on his target. My rescuer's bulging thighs tensed for action, the shimmering green scales that covered them winking in the faint light from above.

I groaned. He recognized me. If I changed forms now, Felix would run straight back to Gideon. The Servus, a Djinn-Syreni hybrid, had been a pawn in the same facility that held me captive. He and his friend Jovi were liberated during the ferocious battle that freed me. They wound up in the Keys like many others from the demon's psychotic breeding program.

Releasing my head and snapping his jaws together, the wolf snarled. "Stand down? *Or what?* You'll drag me out to sea? You and whose army?"

Another Servus appeared from the shadows. Built like a runner with iridescent blue leg scales, his green eyes gleamed with excitement. "We don't need an army, *BOY*."

Jovi smiled, a small pair of fangs poking from between his lips.

My flaming face was about to explode, and spots filled my vision. I wouldn't need saving if my rescuers didn't get on with it. Tension crackled in the air, and then everything happened at once.

The wolf grabbed the top of my head to twist it off like a bottle cap. His eyes never left the two Servus as he snarled. It didn't help him.

Faster than the eye could track, the pair leapt forward. Felix grabbed the furry arm holding me up and snapped it in two—Jovi kicked the wolf's muscular hind leg from the side; it buckled with a crunching snap.

The wolf went down, yowling at the top of his lungs as he released me. I tumbled down the small bank and landed in the Gulf with a splash. Gasping for air, I rubbed my throat.

Before you could say, *"Here, boy,"* they'd snapped the thing's neck, and its shift back to human form began. Felix's bi-eyes roamed over me as he reached down and hauled me from the ocean, standing me upright and stepping back.

"Thanks for the save, guys. I remember you from Charleston."

The word caused a flinch, but the Servus smiled and raised a hand. "Yes. We visited you in your cell." My heart ached at Felix's sad expression. It wasn't too long ago that a warded door was the only thing that kept me from killing the pair.

Jovi hauled the Shifter up and heaved the now human body over one well-muscled shoulder. He frowned at the blood trickling down his bare chest.

"Where are you going with that?" I asked.

"We'll dispose of him and tell Gideon," Felix said. "The wolf would have been dead either way. You know the Enforcer's policy on *Others* who dare to break the law."

Now that the excitement was over, I shifted uncomfortably. Two pairs of eyes trailed to where my erection pressed against my shorts. Their sympathetic stares flicked over my glowing red face as I reached into my pocket and rearranged things. Did every *Other* in the Keys know my business?

"Are you in town long?" I asked.

Felix nodded. "Gideon asked us to stick around Key West. There have been some thefts, and he thought we would enjoy a vacation while helping him out."

I frowned at the unwanted complication. "Well, nice seeing you again. Thanks for your help. I don't know what I would have done if you hadn't come along."

Yeah. Turn into a 2000-pound polar bear and kill myself a Shifter—but I didn't mention that.

I stood to gather the scattered bills, and at their inquiring stare, I said, "I'll take it back to Handy's. I was there when this idiot robbed them."

The two Servus shrugged, pulled the dead shifter into deeper water, and transformed. I caught a glittering swirl of green and blue before they disappeared with a thrust of their dolphin-like tails. Watching them go, I marveled at how quickly they changed forms. Slightly smaller than full-blooded Syreni, they were still intimidating.

Scrambling up the bank, I hit the store before the owner had a coronary. He thanked me with a magnum of Glenfiddich. I returned to the sailboat, pulled out a lowball glass, and settled into my favorite spot to drink.

The only problem with the liveaboard was a slippery bow. Some knucklehead must have sunbathed up here on the regular, and sprayed sunscreen everywhere in the process. Despite many scrubbing sessions, it remained a boobytrap for the unsuspecting. One day I'd get some textured paint for it.

I enjoyed sitting in front of the mast in a lawn chair with extra padding. Watching the ocean at night was one of my favorite pastimes. Peaceful and mesmerizing, the dark water reflected the colorful lights coming from the cluster of vessels in the marina.

Putting my feet up, I thought about Phoebe. She saw the bites and didn't railroad me into explaining them. I looked down and realized—now that she knew of my wounds, I would need to steer clear of her for a while. My Djinn powers healed any wound in hours. If she noticed, she would know my bracelet no longer bound my magic.

Swallowing a burning mouthful of spirits, I decided that Gideon sent Felix and Jovi to keep tabs on my behavior. Not counting last night, I hadn't seen the Gryphon since he dropped me in Key West a month ago. Yet, somehow, he always knew where to find me. Clever bastard.

Gideon's boss, the Sovereign of the southeastern seaboard, was a virtual ghost. No one knew his identity, but he cared for his people. Ruling from the shadows, he ensured I had a home and cash in my pocket. The Sovereign was our leader, but Gideon was his muscle and, apparently, responsible for whatever shit I got up to in Key West.

Music drifted across the water, and I smiled as I sipped my drink. Darius Rucker's *Wagon Wheel*. One of my favorites. Tapping my foot, I thought about tomorrow. My therapist had no idea what she'd signed up for. We played a weekly game of cat and mouse. She pried, and I hedged.

"Talk about your feelings," I mimicked, my voice a nasal squeak. If Darla managed to get me down the rabbit hole of my past, neither of us would be the same again.

***

"What do you mean you killed it?" Darla was a Shifter, although I didn't know her species. I was determined to find out, though. She wasn't a Vampire, which made me wonder why our sessions were always scheduled at night. Fine with me. I was up all night anyway.

"Yep. It bit me. So I killed it." I reached my hands forward and mimed snapping something, my face scrunched and my eyes glittering with evil.

"Oliver! You can't go around killing people's pets!" Darla's face turned a bright shade of pink.

"I'm fine, sweetheart—thanks for asking. And that thing was nobody's pet. It's water under the bridge now. Speaking of water, do you mind?"

I raised my eyebrows at the crystal pitcher on the oak sideboard, and she waved her fingers, struggling to hide her irritation with me. Mentally, I rubbed my hands together. Only ten minutes to go, and I could head to Munchies. When I sat down, she resumed her probing.

"Have you always felt anger toward creatures weaker than yourself?"

"Darla, that thing was not defenseless. We're talking about something the size of a black bear. It went for my throat! What should I have done? Take it for dinner?"

"Get inside? Call Animal Control? You had options, Oliver."

I laughed. "I'm sorry, Darla. I'm kidding. I didn't kill it. I ran back inside and called Animal Control. Hello, yanking your chain here." I waved, and her face went pink.

Of course, I wasn't kidding, but I wouldn't tell her that. The thing was off the rails and would have gladly torn my head off. My therapist knowing that the Servus killed it and I may have exaggerated a bit wouldn't help me get out of here early.

Darla took a sip of the lemon water I poured for her and sighed. She rubbed her eyes. Yup, I was one smart-ass comment away from getting the boot. Mission accomplished.

"So how have you been managing your erections? And did you take the pills I prescribed to help with the blackouts?"

"No. My friends Jim and Jack do a better job on both counts." I mimed chugging a bottle while she stared, her expression blank—tough crowd tonight. I fidgeted, reaching into my pocket to ensure Mr. Happy was properly tucked.

"Hmm." She wrote something in her leather notepad. "Oliver, would you consider hypnosis? If we could get to the bottom of what was done to you ..."

"*No*. Absolutely not," I snapped. "Trust me, Darla. You don't want to know. And I don't want to remember."

"Have you seen the specialist that Gideon contacted about the scars on your back? We can reduce the severity of their appearance."

"No. Those scars remind me of what I really am."

"Oh? And what is that?"

"A pathetic piece of shit, that's what. If I had resisted harder ... " I trailed off, then caught her watchful eyes.

"Nice try, Doctor Busybody." I rubbed my finger up the side of my nose and pointed at her. "I'm onto you."

Taking off her glasses, Darla put them on her antique desk, rubbed her eyes, and sat back in her chair. Crossing her legs, she let out a long breath.

"Oliver. If you don't open up to me, I can't help you. We've been at this for weeks, and I'm no closer to understanding your situation than I was when we started. Right now, the Sovereign is paying for very expensive silence. You have to trust the process. I can help if you'll let me." She gave me her *kind, understanding eyes,* and a stab of pain lanced through me.

"I'm sorry, Darla, I really am. But what they did to me … It's too hard. Talking about it would make it real again. I'm trying to forget, alright?" She stared at me, her expression blank.

"You know Gideon *made* me come here, right? Partly to help but also to see what made me tick. And whether the ticking had a bomb attached." I spread my arms. "No bomb. I promise." I hastily dropped my hand into my lap before she noticed my bracelet no longer glowed pink.

"You've got scars, Oliver. And I'm not referring to the ones on your back. Talking will help. I've been a doctor for fifty years and have never met someone less willing to invest in their recovery than you." She put her glasses back on.

"It's not your fault. You've got PTSD and survivor's guilt. You've been abused, both emotionally and physically. You can't heal this on your own. You need help, son. It's staring you right in the face. Reach out. Meet me halfway, and take the gift you've been offered."

I frowned. *A gift?* It was more like a box full of explosives.

Darla sat up straight and asked, "How can I convince you to take that first step for yourself?"

With a sharp smile, I said, "Tell me your species of Shifter."

"No."

"Why not? You want this huge emotional reckoning from me, but you won't tell me your species. How is that fair?"

Darla's face turned red, and her lips formed a tight line. As I watched, her nose widened and turned up, and curly hairs formed around the oddly shaped nostrils. I slapped my thigh.

"I knew it! You're a pig! My God, Darla, don't be shy! Pigs are cute!"

Her face darkened, and I thought she might go full-on Miss Piggy on the spot, but Darla sucked in her power, and her face returned to normal. I was suitably impressed at her control.

With a haughty sniff, she said, "I am *not* a pig, Oliver."

I glanced at the fancy vintage clock over her head. Five minutes, and I was outta here. When Darla followed my gaze and saw the clock, a hard light shone in her eyes. *Uh oh.*

"Tell me about Layla."

I froze. I didn't move. I couldn't.

Pressing her advantage, Darla leaned forward. "The Succubus is still under your skin, even now, isn't she?"

My face reddened, and my lungs quit working. The memories came fast and furious. Her lips. Her hands. That fucking mist ... The erection in my pants roared to life, and I moaned. I glared at my therapist, biting my tongue until it bled.

"How many years will you waste, Oliver? It's time to move forward. Tell me about Layla."

Something inside me erupted, and in the glass of her framed diplomas, I watched my eyes flare to life. "You don't want to do this, Darla." My voice deepened as power stirred in my veins.

"Tell me about Layla." Her eyes challenged me.

The agony of my past flared to life like it hitched a ride on the Enola Gay. Inside, I detonated.

"You want to know? *Fine*. I'll tell you. That Succubus *bitch* dragged me out of my cell stuffed to the brim with her magic, three, four times a week. She cuffed me to a chair and rode me for hours—if I was lucky. If I wasn't, she hung me from the ceiling, pumped her magic into me, and turned me over to her male friends. They took turns fucking every orifice in my body. Layla kept me juiced as they whacked me off, took my semen, and used it to produce creatures, Darla. And now, those things are out in the world, doing God knows what. Even Gideon can't find them!

She held her stiff-backed posture, but her eyes widened.

"Oh, I'm just getting started, honey." I stood up. "Stephen was their controller—a *human,* if you can believe it. He carried a nice, long cattle prod; if you stepped out of line, you got it. And I'm not talking about your arm or your leg. No, I mean places where the sun never shines, Darla. Do you have any idea how bad that hurts?"

I leaned forward over her desk, my face inches from hers, and glared into her eyes. Her gaze flicked briefly to the antique desk phone, then her chin jutted.

"Do you know what they did after they finished with the prod?"

She shook her head, her lips tight, her fearless eyes meeting mine.

"They hung me from the rafters by my feet. On a pulley, so they could get *just* the right angle. They locked a metal mask over my face. It had a hole for the mouth and two for the eyes. But it had these tiny sliding covers that slipped into place so I couldn't see what happened."

Darla shook her head, and as I pressed forward, she was forced to lean back or bump noses with me.

"They fucked my mouth, Darla. My ass. Repeatedly. But that wasn't even the bad part. You know what was far, far worse?"

As she shook her head, my voice dropped to a whisper.

"I liked it."

I smashed my fists down on her desk, cracking it in two. My chest heaving, I panted through an open mouth, staring down at her. Darla tilted her head at me, her eyes soft. Even after what I'd done, she still cared. Remorse flooded through me, swelling to life like a candle in a dark room.

The rage sputtered out. I hung my head, tears trickling down my cheeks. "I'm sorry, ma'am. More than you'll ever know. I'll pay for the desk."

Spinning on my heel, I ran.

CHAPTER 3

~ PHOEBE ~

Festive crowds filled Duval Street, encouraging me to take a stroll. I changed into flip-flops—the official shoe of Key West. Ever since Gideon destroyed the Charleston facility, life was safer for all paranormals. *Others,* hidden safely amongst the human population, could once again enjoy the nightlife with a vengeance.

I smiled at the boisterous crowd as I passed Sloppy Joe's. As usual, partygoers spilled onto the street. Cold air conditioning blasted from the open doorway, and I stopped for a moment to enjoy some relief on my overheated skin. As I waited, a few tipsy guys offered to buy me a drink, which made me smile. When the crowd briefly parted, I could have sworn I saw Mr. Griswald staring at me from across the crowded bar. I blinked, and the image was gone. Weird.

Before I could investigate further, I glanced across the street, and my heart swelled when I saw two familiar figures. Jovi and Felix had joined our fight back in Charleston after learning their boss was a homicidal demon. I was shocked and excited to see the Servus here.

In their land-walking form, their finely scaled legs looked like a pair of expensive diving skins. Adding a casual shirt and a pair of sneaks, they fit right in with the blissfully unaware humans.

Felix waved, and when the pair jogged toward me, I laughed at their rooster t-shirts. The damn birds ran loose all over town and were the theme of many touristy items. Felix's shirt said, "Stop staring at my cock," while Jovi's had the word "HUGE" embossed over a fluffy rooster. Now, *that* was funny.

"Hello, fellas! I see you're blending in well. I'm so happy to see you." We hugged, and I pulled back to look at them. "You guys look great. Are you enjoying Key West?"

Jovi smiled. "It takes a bit of getting used to, but we're managing."

Felix poked him, adding, "He's had plenty of offers to explore human vaginas this week, but he's too shy and sends them to me." That earned him a punch in the arm as Jovi turned crimson.

"Where are you boys heading?"

The pair looked at each other and shuffled their feet. "We can't say. Sorry, Phoebe. Gideon's orders."

"Oh. I didn't mean to pry. I'm going in your direction. Can we walk together and catch up?"

The males looked uncomfortable, and Jovi shook his head. "I'm sorry. We were just …" he looked over his shoulder … "working."

I followed his glance to the end of the street and saw a shack with a small neon sign for a bar called Munchies. I'd always wondered about the hut. I'd never seen anyone coming or going, and it was too small for more than four people standing shoulder to shoulder. The single lightbulb over the rustic door screamed *horror movie*, yet the green, blue, and pink neon sign appeared welcoming. *Very strange*.

"Ok, then, you guys have a nice night." An insatiable curiosity filled me as they nodded and jogged down the street. Naturally, I followed them.

I didn't get far. As I passed a small side street, something moved in the shadows. With a gasp, I jumped back and raised my hands.

Being a ward witch without strong offensive skills, my father helped me build a few self-defense spells that saved me a time or two. Using it was second nature. My power sparked as something rushed at me from the darkness.

Sweeping my hands over my head, I clapped them together, pulled my elbows down, and hissed, *"Duratus!"* The figure halted, the dark form frozen from my spell. My heart pounded, and a familiar rush of excitement lit my veins.

Faster than should have been possible, a blue glow erupted from the middle of the shape to spiral outward, throwing a trail of sparks. Whoever it was broke my spell like it was nothing. A low chuckle from the darkness flushed my cheeks, my temper rising at the insult.

With a quick counterclockwise circle, I pinched my fingertips together and snapped, *"Ardeat!"*

Flames surrounded the figure, not burning but holding them in place. That's as far as I got because the light from my fire spell revealed who stalked me from the darkness.

"Ms. Metroyer!"

The Witch made a fist, and with a whisper, my fire blinked out. She stepped forward.

"Feeling a tad jumpy, *Ms. Peregrin?*" Her eyes glittered with wry amusement.

I let out my breath, my hand going to my throat. This uppity Witch wiped out my two most powerful spells without trying.

Dressed in black and blending with the shadows, her braided hair shone in the light of a nearby lamppost as she stepped forward. Familiar chills skated down my spine.

"Is sneaking up on another Witch standard practice where you come from, *Ms. Metroyer?*"

She nodded. "Touché." Glancing down at my hand, she paused. "I am pleasantly surprised, Ms. Per—"

"Enough of this formal nonsense. Call me Phoebe and state your business." Yes, she'd ruffled my feathers. Her deliberate pushing of my buttons wasn't lost on me. It was a standard power play common amongst competing witches.

"Then I must say, *Phoebe*, I would love to know where you managed to find a ring of pure Welsh gold."

She knew. Wasn't that interesting? "None of your business, Ms. Metroyer."

With a tight smile, she said, "Call me Sybil." As she stepped closer, the witch's black dress floated behind her, a delicate gold thread visible in the fabric. Woven into intricate patterns, the coppery color told me it was Welsh gold.

The witch frowned as she looked at my hand. "Those specialized constructs of yours combined magic and metallurgy. Where did you learn them?"

"With all due respect, I'd prefer if you explained the purpose of this visit."

Sybil tipped her head, her long braids swinging in the darkness. The rows of beads were gold as well, glittering brightly. *Interesting*.

"I'd like to hire you for my ... *project*."

"And my requirement to know more details?"

"A client contracted me to open a gateway similar to what you see behind you."

I looked over my shoulder, then glanced back at her, my eyebrows raised.

"Munchies." Sybil pointed to the neon bar sign I'd noticed earlier. As I watched, the dingy gray door opened and a giant of a man stepped out. You'd never know there was anything inside the darkened doorway.

"That is a paranormal bar cleaved into the fabric of another dimension. I will make a new one that is ... *similar*." Sybil's eyes glittered when her gaze met mine.

My head whipped back to stare at the shack. Not an entrance to a basement, then. Which, of course, made sense, with Key West sitting on solid limestone—*duh*. A tear in the fabric of our dimension. The power to make something like that would be extraordinary. *Amazing*.

I wasn't convinced. "You are a powerful Witch in your own right, *Sybil*. Why do you need me to do the bindings for this project?"

She hesitated, her deep brown eyes casting back and forth across my face. Her fingers twitched at her sides, and for a moment, I thought she was winding up to shoot a spell at me. I tensed.

"As much as it pains me to admit it, I am not skilled at bindings. Cross me, and you'll feel the full brunt of my power. But bindings ... no." The look she gave me bordered on threatening, and I bristled. Did I finally find her soft underbelly? Was the great Sybil Metroyer flawed? The thought cheered me.

"Do you have a contract for me?" I asked.

Sybil reached into a black leather satchel and pulled out an envelope. "If you agree with my terms, you will start tomorrow. The location is enclosed along with all the details you requested."

I looked down at the envelope in my hand and bit my lip. Tucked inside was something that felt like a wad of cash. I looked up to question her further, but the street was empty.

***

~ OLIVER ~

Darla's session had my hackles up, and by the time I hit Munchies, a feverish steam heated my blood. Despite my anger, when Stan met me at the door with locked fists, the Gargoyle's thunderous expression almost made me bolt for safety. Under the dim light of the single bulb, the shadows across his face looked creepy as hell.

"You said Luther bought me a card, but I got nuthin'! And when I asked Priscilla about it, she laughed. *Laughed!*" Stan took a menacing step toward me but stopped when I held up a pink envelope.

"I know, pal. I'm sorry. Desperation makes me do bad things. But I got you a little something to make up for it."

Stan frowned, then snatched the envelope from my hands. Paper fluttered in pieces to the ground as he scrabbled to open it with his fat gray fingers. When he looked inside the card, the Gargoyle's eyes widened and his lower jaw shot forward, exposing his fangs. Eyes bulging like a frog's, when it started playing, "You are the sunshine of my life," tears rolled down his dusty cheeks.

A hard arm squished me to the Gargoyle's chest. Sobbing so hard he couldn't speak, Stan motioned to the door without looking. As I stepped through it, I glanced back. He stared into his card, tears dripping from his chin. The Guardian's lips mouthed the message while the music played, the tinkling sound quiet in the darkness. *A little sunshine to brighten your night. Happy fifteen-hundredth, Stan.*

With a grim smile, I stepped into the bar and headed straight for The Dark Room. My mood didn't improve when a pretty, very drunk Vampire blocked my way and wrapped her arms around my neck.

"Let go," I hissed through clenched teeth.

"Aww, come on," she slurred. "I've been watching you, and I've noticed you watching me. You can't hide it, hun. You're hot for me."

She reached down and grabbed my hard cock through my shorts and squeezed.

Violet washed across my vision, and I stopped breathing. White light flooded her face, my eyes burning with power I couldn't control.

"That's enough of that, *lover girl,*" Priscilla said, peeling the vamp from my neck. There was a minor struggle until a male co-worker stepped in, and they hauled the female away.

I slammed through the doors into The Dark Room and released the breath struggling to leave my lungs. Pressing my forehead against the cool wall, I sucked in air. When my pulse returned to normal, I headed towards the light at the end of the hall.

Polly had explained once that the length of the entrance was to keep screams from reaching the club. I was too sober for the fucking length of it today.

Speak of the devil. Polly saw me and strode over. "Hello, Ollie. The usual?"

I nodded, my cock pulsing so hard in anticipation that I couldn't speak. The pretty Vampire pushed me down onto the padded entrance bench, and after a quick disappearing act, returned with a whisky. Watching me knock most of it back in one go, she chuckled. "Rough day today?"

I wheezed. "You have no idea."

Sliding onto the bench next to me, Polly lightly ran her fingers through my hair. At her glittering smile, I tipped my head to the side, and she leaned forward, her fangs slipping into my neck while her lips barely touched my skin. She knew, and I loved her for it.

An instant warmth joined the fire of the whisky, the swampy feeling of her venom pumping into my bloodstream. My engorged shaft throbbed with pain as she drank, and I tumbled head-first into the euphoric haze of her erototoxin.

Blessedly, the pain ebbed. My cock hardened more than should have been physically possible, but the pain disappeared. I sighed, and when she pulled back from my throat, I gave her a bright, unfocused smile.

"Thank you," I whispered.

"My pleasure, darling. A girl can appreciate a patron who keeps his hands to himself. Have fun tonight. And behave."

She smiled and clicked away on her towering heels, her fishnet stockings following her miniature shorts into the crack of her ass. Watching her splendid curves did nothing except remind me of Phoebe.

Shoving aside the memory of a similar pair of stockings bought *just for me*, I stood up, bolted the rest of my drink, and staggered further inside the room. Polly greeted the adventurous fools who wandered in; the real entertainment was inside.

As I got close to the first platform, I saw I was late to the party. An orgy unfolded on stage one, the moans and slick sounds making my cock jump. I bypassed the writhing partygoers and headed for the couches.

Tucked into a dark corner, the comfortable monstrosities of washable vinyl surrounded low-slung glass tables. I sank into the soft butt glove of the closest couch with an air-releasing thump, then lay my head back, surfing the wave of Polly's venom.

I didn't wait long. Riley clunked a drink on the table and flopped down beside me. He snuggled close, and I let him, closing my eyes to keep my heart rate down. If I didn't look, I didn't freak when his hands needed to touch me.

As he stroked the ridge in my shorts, Riley whispered, "Ollie, why don't you take care of this yourself?"

High as a kite, I barely registered his question. I squeezed my eyes tight and mumbled, "Doesn't work. Nothing works but this … "

A soft sigh left me as his lips found my neck, and with two sharp stings, his toxin joined Polly's. I moaned, my ass grinding deeper into the cushions as my cock throbbed.

"That's it," he muttered against my neck. "Another?"

I nodded and rolled my head the other way. My noggin swam with warm water, my smile leaking a bit of drool. Two more sharp stings and the bottom disappeared from beneath my feet. I dropped down the rabbit hole.

Vaguely aware of Riley's cock grinding into my hip as he sucked on my neck, I didn't care. He always gave me a little extra venom if he got his rocks off. Somehow, doing this with a guy felt less like cheating.

A bitter laugh whispered through my mind at the stupid thought that Phoebe would understand. I could never let her see how low I'd fallen.

After forever, Riley's fingers traced down my arm as he slipped away. My mind wallowed in a sea of bliss, my cock eagerly pressing against my zipper as if it knew what came next.

Lost for hours, a revolving door of squished cushions and psychedelic pricks filled my world with smiles and senseless fluff. Three or maybe four visitors later, my shirt hung open, and my head tipped forward, drool trailing from my lips and down my chest. Heaven spread before me, shimmering with whites and blues behind my closed eyelids.

I gasped when someone bit the inside of my thigh. I tried to open my eyes but couldn't. As my mind pulled me toward the surface, I relaxed. I didn't need to ask who it was; only one vamp dared. A garbled moan came from my throat as Riley's teeth sank deep, tapping the artery.

"It's ok, baby. It's me. You're fine." I relaxed. Riley licked his lips, and I sank deeper into the cushion.

That was the last coherent thought for some time. Someone brought me a shot of absinthe, which roused clients enough to continue breathing. I sipped at the vile stuff when I someone held a glass against my lips. My eyes opened, and Riley smiled down at me.

"There you are," he trilled. "Are you ready yet?"

I nodded and he kneeled between my legs. I lifted my hips, and he shucked off my shorts, his wet mouth sliding over my cock with a smooth glide. I hissed, my head pushing back into the cushions. Closing my eyes, I tried to relax.

Around me, I was vaguely aware of other moans, grunts, and soft sexy sounds. The odd scream shot through me like a hot knife, adding to the aura of danger. I never looked. I was here for one thing only and wouldn't leave until I got it.

When a soft hand cupped my balls, they pulled tight against my shaft. Riley used his long tongue creatively, wrapping it around the shiny head and then slurping me down, fast, wet, and firm. I hissed, my hips surging. Never letting up, Riley kept up a steady rhythm.

As I writhed beneath his sloppy mouth, a beautiful face joined me behind my eyelids, Phoebe's playful tongue lapping at my erection. Another place, at another time. Before my capture. Before *Layla*.

With a shout, I came. The noise from my throat was halfway between a scream and a groan and lasted a lifetime. Riley's mouth worked me. I spasmed, my cock jerking against the back of his throat. My fingers dug into his shoulders, the back of my head pushing the cushions into the next dimension.

When my hand reached to grab his wrist, Riley let my cock go with a wet pop. Still leaking, it strained against my belly. I opened my eyes. Still hard. *Shit*.

Panting, I shut out the sight of it and whispered, "Thank you. Riley, my God... *you have no idea.*"

Tears poured down my face, and the vamp rose to kiss them away. Softly, he whispered, "Glad to help, sugar. Don't worry. You'll get there." He slipped his fangs in once more for good measure, sending me back down into the well of numbing darkness.

After his bare feet padded away, I lay there, my eyes wet and my mind drowning. It wasn't over yet. The Succubus magic refused to dissipate. Taming the beast would take more than vampire venom and a blowjob.

When I eventually roused, I picked up the fresh shot of Absinthe and downed it. I needed to move, and to do that, I needed to see. That didn't mean I felt anything, though.

Oh no. The venom continued to work its magic. I could stand and move across the ground but had no sense of where my body was in the universe. My eyes struggled to control my feet as I managed a listing stagger. I reached the stretcher, grabbed a steel upright, and hung on tight. My cock pressed tightly to my belly as I focused on the waiting contraption.

"Ooh, hot stuff. You still have a ways to go yet, dontcha?"

I held out my wrists, and Bruin clapped the cuffs on. The bear Shifter loved his job, but it always creeped me out when he licked his lips as if I was on the menu.

"What's your safe word tonight, stud?" He finished buckling me in and slapped my ass, earning a weak growl from me. "OK then. No safe word. I like it. Up you go, then."

I crawled face down onto the padded framework, and Bruin cranked the leg holders wide enough to make me wince. Strapping my head down into the padded ring, the bear Shifter gave my ass a defiant swat. "Time to rock and roll, big fella."

Footsteps slapped across the floor, and I watched a pair of feet appear below my face, a ring on each toe. Velvet.

The unit, a glorified massage table, tilted as it spread-eagled my limbs. As it rose, the machine levered my arms out to the side and lurched into the vertical position, the scars on my back stretching to the point of pain. Bruin grabbed a paddle from his table and laced my ass with a few stinging slaps. I cried out, and he stopped, then motioned to Velvet. I closed my eyes.

My belly stung as the Vampire struck, sucked hard, and then moved on, striking fast again. My abs. My back, sides, and buttocks. Both shoulders. Up and down my thighs. Bite after bite, each one numbed me more and more, my cock swelling until I thought it might burst. Even stoned on venom, my balls were in a vice, but I knew. It would work. It always hurt before it worked.

I lost all concept of time. Velvet's stinging bites and the thunderous slaps of Bruin's paddle sent me into the stratosphere. I knew we were there when the shifter whispered something to Velvet.

Bruin dumped a bunch of lube on my ass, his fingers slowly sliding into me, first one, then two. Rasping breaths warmed my shoulder as he worked his digits in and out. The base of my spine ached, my balls throbbing. I danced with pink zebras as a python of a cock slid into me. I gasped. Velvet's lips slid over my shaft; I was lost.

Sensations fluttered into the numb recesses of my body, the slaps of Bruin's hips and the slippery feel of Velvet's lips tying me into hard knots of lust. Hot and wet came from both sides; my legs rattled the chains; I shook from the overwhelming onslaught. Tension coiled in my spine as hot licks of energy speared my groin. The need to climax became a roar beneath my skin.

With a scream, I came. On and on, my balls squeezed, my cock pumped and jerked, thick jets of cum hitting the back of the Vampire's throat. I cried out, and Velvet stopped. With a final lick and a parting nip on the hip, a soft hand patted my rump on the way by. As always, my eyes remained closed.

Feeling, but not seeing. In a sick way, it reminded me of the mask. The one from the lab. I shuddered. Images of burnished metal clicking into place, the cold iron against my face—my thoughts transported me to the cold darkness of the basement beneath the library.

"Are you alright? Breathe, Oliver. It's over." Bruin unstrapped and lifted my weightless form, laying me on a nearby couch before moving on to his next customer.

Stunned and stuporous, I dreamed of her, a Rolodex of color swirling in a sea of black. The market, picking out fresh fruits and vegetables. Jane Austen flicks and a sharp elbow when I snored. Phoebe sprawled on soft sheets, her naked curves inviting me in. I cried for the life that was long gone, burned to dust in the darkness of a basement. This was me now. I got what I deserved.

"There you are. I've been looking all over for you!"

I forced my eyes open to see the wasted female vamp from the bar. The one who groped me. And she had her hand around my flaccid cock.

My eyes flared, wisps of mist lifting from my skin. Snaking free, they rose, swirling in angry circles before lashing out to wrap around her throat.

"I said, *DON'T TOUCH ME!*" My voice came from nowhere and everywhere.

People screamed. A purple face stared at me, the eyes bulging. Dimly, I smiled, knowing this time I caused the screams. Not Stephen. Not Charles.

Bruin grabbed me by the throat and choked me, shaking me hard enough that my head slapped the couch. It took Riley pummeling my ribcage with Vampire strength to release my misty grip.

Everything went dark. I woke to feel my feet and shins dragging across a sticky floor. Seeing I was awake, Bruin whispered, "Sorry, man. Club rules. No killing."

The bear Shifter had me halfway to the front door when a deep voice stopped our progress, and a pair of booted feet came into view. My lips sent trickles of drool across the scuffed toes. Words were exchanged, and someone yanked me upright to peer into a dark, thunderous face.

"You broke the rules, *Djinn*. I am entitled to exact a penalty however I see fit—" Luther smiled, his fangs lengthening. "Compliments of the Sovereign's very own rule book."

Through an opaque haze, I turned my head to watch Polly drag the obnoxious female vampire out the doors.

"Not … dead." My head rolled toward the escapee.

"Close enough," Luther hissed. "Bring him to my throne."

More dragging, then Bruin dropped me on my knees before a massive oak chair embossed with golden eagles. When the giant of a man slid onto his throne, the Lord grinned at me, his enormous fangs dripping venom.

"Lord Luther, I should inform you that this guest donated considerable blood tonight. It might not be safe to—" At a look from his boss, Bruin zipped it.

"Bring it on," I rasped, my voice barely registering from beneath my hanging head. The furious Lord of The Dark Side heard me, though—vamp super hearing and all.

Luther struck, his fangs punching into an artery. Pain seared through me, then dulled as suction lifted my skin beneath his lips. His tongue warmed me, heat filling my veins as the Lord pulled in long swallows that flushed goosebumps over my skin. I sagged, the slow, weak thumps of my heart dragging me toward an all-consuming darkness. As Luther rushed me to judgment, the motherload of venom hit.

My limbs turned to water, and both lungs seized. My neck stopped working, my head flopped forward, and I smiled, welcoming the cold that swept through me. The receding flutter of my failing heart cheered me. I thought of Phoebe, sad I'd never see her wonderful smile again.

Tonight, I would find relief. I would finally be free.

***

"You've done quite a number on yourself, Oliver."

Gideon's hushed voice wafted to me through a haze. Filling my berth, the vague outline of an eagle's head and folded wings made me frown. Was I dreaming, or was this death? The weightlessness of my body suggested the latter, but the beading sweat on my cold skin meant I hadn't succeeded. I might yet. I smiled at the fuzzy thought.

The whispered words of a child slipped beneath my skin, two tiny hands and warm drops of kindness touching my cheeks. The sensations seemed dull, as if from a distance. I forced myself awake to a blurry world. *Was I awake?*

Hovering above me in the darkness was a child. Her emerald eyes overflowed with tears as she cried for me, pushing the hellish pain from my bones. With a sigh I slipped into a deep sleep, a comfortable warmth chasing the chills away. I dreamed, the soft words of the child sending me somewhere peaceful.

Time passed. I was happy. Warm sand tickled the bare bottoms of my feet as I ran, then misted into my mother's arms. She smiled and kissed my wispy cheek; it tingled. My mother's beauty filled my thoughts, and when my father slid an arm around her and their faces peered down at me, overwhelming love flooded my senses. They loved me, and I failed them.

The comforting blackness lifted, and I registered three voices. One was deep, and vaguely familiar. Quietly echoing from a distance, a scent whispered alongside it—

peaches and sunshine. *Who was he? How did I know him? So familiar ...*

Anxious chatter joined the soft murmurs of my mystery guest, but these were loud, and close. Jovi and Felix. They sounded worried, but I ignored them, keeping my eyes closed and drifting. A fourth voice shredded my weak grasp on peace.

"I know you are awake, Oliver. They carried you home. Without them, you would be dead." The words jammed into the space between my ears, pushing the cotton aside. Gideon was back, his revelation jarring me fully awake. I squeezed my lids together. I needed more time.

When I moved my hand over the sheets beneath my fingertips, my heart sank. I was alive. Speaking was out of the question, my dry tongue refusing to form words. The fog rolled in, and I dozed, waking to that soft, loving voice. The one that stirred both longing and regret in my heart.

Phoebe.

CHAPTER 4

~ PHOEBE ~

My heart shattered at the sight of Oliver's distress. Sweating and shivering under the sheets of his berth, dark circles painted his drawn face, the minefield of bite marks a horrifying contrast against the pale skin of his body.

This time, he went too far. Gideon said he nearly died. If Jovi and Felix hadn't found him in the alley behind the club, Oliver would be gone. Final, *dead,* gone.

Even muffled by a hand, my sobs made him stir. I looked into pale gray eyes that watched me with a sad calm. The morning sunshine filtered through the curtains on the porthole, giving his face a grayish cast.

"Oliver," I whispered, relieved to see him conscious. "Would you like a glass of water?"

He shook his head no, his voice cracking as he rasped, "You shouldn't be here. You don't need to see this."

He fell asleep when I didn't answer, and I pulled my footstool closer. Tossing and turning, the sweat poured freely as Oliver whimpered, his head thrashing.

Guilt tore mouthfuls from my flesh as I gazed at the man slowly self-destructing before me. I was a monster, because in the back of my mind, I thought of Gabriel. In town for work until the end of the month, he had asked to see me again.

Conflicted, I stared down at Oliver, who was desperate for my love and support. I shouldn't have spent time with a strange man. Shame burned my ears, then I laughed under my breath.

Oliver didn't want me. The bites peppering his skin made that abundantly clear. I was a fool. I had a good idea of what happened in that club. I had no claim on the male before me. We weren't together. Relationships weren't one-sided—a familiar refrain I shared with my bathroom mirror every morning.

The love of my life needed help but wouldn't take it. Like a pit bull, I'd ignored his wishes and sunk my teeth into him, refusing to let go. My heart ached for what we lost; I was desperate to reach him. Oliver was in there, somewhere, but what right did I have to force myself on him?

My mind drifted to happier times—our first brunch date a few days after we met in Savannah. When I opened my motel room door and Oliver said my name in such a warm, happy way, my heart stretched to breaking point. There was something about the Djinn that brought out the best in people.

He'd opened the door of his truck with a flourish, then helped me out again at the restaurant, his lopsided grin charming me all the way to my toes. When he opened the glass door to usher me into the restaurant, placing his warm palm on my back, my soft laugh startled him.

"Why are you laughing?"

"It's IHOP, Oliver. Not a five-star restaurant." He shot me a mischievous look and pressed his hand more firmly, sweeping me into the land of heavenly smells like a prince courting my affections.

"People should open doors for you everywhere, Phoebe. Treating esteemed women with respect is the way of my people." My heart fluttered at his boyish grin, and when he pulled out my chair with a grand gesture, I smiled until my face hurt.

Now, there was no smiling. There was only pain. Pain and the tenacity that kept me going, desperate for light in the dark corner of hell that held Oliver captive. Was I wasting my time?

My father always told me, "You're bull-headed, and you got it from me. The bravest witches are always stubborn." He died years ago. An iron will couldn't cure cancer.

Before he passed, Father gave me the Welsh gold ring on my finger, a family heirloom. It had been handed down for generations from Witch to Witch, amplifying my power in a time-honored tradition. I wore it always, but being a ward Witch, I had no idea how to use it offensively. Father taught me a few defensive spells using the ring for amplification, but they wouldn't help me against a Witch like Sybil.

Rubbing my thumb over the ring, I marveled at the rosy color. Nature forced traces of copper into the gold, and in its pure form, it was exceedingly rare. Rare, and powerful.

I looked at Oliver's wrist on top of the sheets, a jagged bite visible beneath his cuff. Wounds healed much slower with his magic suppressed. With full Djinn power, Oliver would have healed in hours.

"What the ...?" I squinted at the fully healed bite beneath the cheap band. Lifting his hand and squinting in the gloom, my fingers touched the metal, and I knew. There was no magic left in the damn bracelet.

Dropping his hand with a frown, I realized his eyes were open and carefully watching me. Unlike the other times he'd roused, Oliver saw me clearly this time.

"How long?" I asked.

He turned his head toward the wall. "A week."

"Oh my God. You've been running around Key West with full powers for a week? Why didn't you say something? I could have recharged it!"

With a sour look, he rasped, "I don't need it. I have more control now. I'm tired of having my power contained. It feels like cotton balls clogging my veins."

"Oliver! You nearly killed someone last night! She barely escaped with her life. You were lucky the bar owner didn't exercise his right to put you to death. It's clear—"

"I'm not doing it, Phoebe. If it's a choice between being restrained and dying, I choose death."

The cabin went silent; the only sound was waves lapping at the hull.

"You can't. No. I won't let you, Oliver. Gideon said—"

"I don't care what Gideon said." He turned to look at me, his bloodshot eyes reminding me of his close call last night. "He said I'd get over the effects of the Succubus in time. He was wrong. He said my mind would settle with therapy. It's not working. I'm done. If you take away my power, I'm tapping out." His eyes glittered, and a tear slipped from the corner of one eye.

"I'll talk to the Enforcer. Maybe I can do a limited binding, and you can retain at least some of your powers—"

"That won't be possible." I jumped at the smooth voice behind me, and Gideon's human form filled the cabin. The Enforcer appeared from nowhere, his shining blonde hair and athletic body painfully attractive. His casual clothes conflicted with the tense vibes rolling from him.

"Can we speak outside, please?" My eyes pleaded for mercy.

"No. Oliver needs to hear this, too. I've just come from a meeting with Lord Luther. He has agreed not to demand his death if we restrain his Djinn powers and he doesn't set foot at Munchies again. *Ever.*"

Oliver closed his eyes, his hands fisting where they lay.

Gideon crossed his muscular arms, his lips tight. "I'm sorry, Oliver, but I am responsible for the safety of the *Others* here. You are still a wild card. Work on things, stabilize yourself, and maybe in a few months, we can revisit—"

"Fuck you, Gideon. If you do it to me again, I'll disappear. I'm coping in the only way I know how, and—"

"*Coping?* Breaking the desk of your therapist in two and scaring her half to death is coping?"

Gideon looked at me and said, "Full strength, Phoebe, or he faces a tribunal. I'm sorry, but my hands are tied." And with that, Gideon disappeared into thin air.

That explained a lot, and left me wondering if he was still standing there, watching. Nervously, I glanced around the kitchenette, but saw no sign of him.

When I looked back at Oliver, his lips were a tight white line, and his eyes were shut, his hands trembling at his sides.

"It will kill me, Pheebs," he whispered.

"I'm sorry, Oliver. I can't disobey the Enforcer, or I'll be in as much trouble as you. I'll reactivate it tomorrow, when you're feeling better." With a reassuring smile, I reached out to take his hand and threaded my fingers through his.

"I'm not giving up on you, Ollie. I won't. And you can't force me to, no matter how you behave."

***

When Sybil met me before noon on Sugarloaf Key and pointed at the crumbling foundation of the Bat Tower, my mouth flopped open. The remote location had me questioning, *why here?*

The cleared area stood in the middle of a circular turnaround, the four cement piers the only thing remaining of the original structure. Built in 1929, the failed attempt at insect control blew down during Hurricane Irma.

"You want to form a tear here?" When the Witch nodded, I said, "How do you plan on hiding the constant traffic to this location?" The requested *details* in Sybil's contract had been sketchy at best. She mentioned plans for a paranormal bar. I didn't believe her. The humans living in this area would pick up on the activity all the way out here.

"That is none of your concern, Phoebe. I need the anchors. Four, one on each corner of the original structure. You have half of the money now and will receive the other half when your work is completed to my satisfaction."

Sybil looked down her nose at me, and said, "This project is vital to my client. I do not specialize in bindings, but you do. It needs to be done right. I must finish the tear within two days. I will contact you if I need your assistance when I fire it up. You will receive adequate compensation for the level of danger involved."

The Witch chose a perfect location for something shady. The only thing in the area, at least for now, was scrubby brush blocking the ocean's view. Biting my lip, I pictured the wad of cash I'd pulled out of that envelope.

Sighing, my eyes traveled over the site. I could use the existing foundation for my anchor points and wouldn't need to do much more than a simple binding piggybacked on a grounding. It was an hour, maybe two, tops.

"Alright, Sybil. But I need to do it tomorrow after some preparations. I pull power from the sun for most projects."

The Witch gave me a curt nod. "Text me when you have completed your work."

Swallowing back the fear that always rose while in Sybil's proximity, I waved goodbye as the Witch pulled away. Shaking my head, I climbed into my rental car. As I circled the site, I wondered what I'd gotten myself into.

***

When I arrived back at my apartment, a surprise visitor raised my spirits.

"Gabriel!" Guilt raced through me when I realized how happy I was to see him.

He leaned in and, grasping my elbow, kissed my cheek. "You look lovely today, Phoebe. I hope you don't mind my barging in like this?"

"Not at all. Did you want to pop up for a visit?" I pointed at my red door, but hehe shook his head.

"I wanted to take you sailing. I know it's last minute, but ..." He shrugged, a shy smile on his lips.

Excitement bloomed in my belly. Ever since Gideon arranged for a liveaboard sailboat for Oliver, I wondered what it would be like to sail through the turquoise waters of the Keys with him. A glass of champagne in my hand. Toasting his recovery. The salty spray sparkling across his hard, tanned chest ...

Shoving the fairytale away, I smiled at Gabe. "I'd love that. Let me get my things."

When I popped back onto the street in my dry shorts and a rash guard, my sunhat firmly in hand, he smiled. "That was quick."

"I'm excited! My friend owns a sailboat, and I always wondered what it would be like to sail away on it."

"Well, I hope your friend doesn't get jealous when he sees us sailing away together."

I frowned. "How did you know it was a he?"

Gabe laughed. "Phoebe, there's not a guy on this island who wouldn't give his eye teeth to take you sailing. Let's just say it was a mathematical probability."

The smile he gave me made my stomach flip, and I cringed. *Oliver. Remember Oliver.*

When Gabriel led me down the docks on the far side of Garrison Bight, I let out a relieved breath. I didn't want Ollie to spot me with another man. I was terrified I'd see a look of relief on his face and know he was truly done with us—or, God forbid, a heartbroken look if he wasn't.

Besides, today was a harmless outing. Today, I could skip sifting through the wreckage of my relationship with Oliver.

After piloting the Bluewater sailboat out of the harbor with the inboard motor, I soon learned my date was an expert sailor. My heart lifted as the ocean opened around us and he got to work. The wind was perfect—fifteen knots and minimal gusting, the light chop on the water making it a sailor's dream.

Soon we powered over the ocean, the wind snapping the mainsail as waves rushed past the hull with a calming effect. Once we cleared Key West harbor, Gabe said, "There's a tray in the fridge, if you don't mind. I took some liberties, hoping you'd come along this afternoon."

I scrambled down the teak ladder to the well-furnished belly of the boat. The brand-new stainless fridge held a tray of grapes, cheeses, assorted cured meats and crackers. There was a bottle of bubbly beside it. I didn't know whether to laugh or cry. In that fridge was my dream date with Oliver.

Smearing the moisture from the corners of my eyes, I popped back into the cockpit. My heart swelled at Gabe's megawatt smile as he watched me. *Relax. Enjoy the afternoon. You deserve this.*

It seemed I had found myself a model captain. He made sure I had everything I needed, kept up a lively banter, and at one point, he leaned over and slipped his arm around my shoulders. I raised my face to the sun, feeling the wind on my cheeks, and for the first time since finding Oliver alive, peace settled over me.

I sipped my champagne, snacked on Gabe's clever offerings, and relaxed. The afternoon passed with a blissful lack of drama, and when he stopped on a shoal and dropped the sails, I helped him set the anchor.

A short swim from the boat, a paradise worthy of a postcard spread before us. Excitement filled me as I took in the beauty of the reef, the amazing shades of blue over the sand and coral making me feverish to snorkel.

"Western Sambo," he said, smiling. His tanned face lit up as he saw my expression. "You like it?"

"Oh my God, it's beautiful!"

His brown hair fluttered in the breeze as Gabe flipped open the stainless marine grill attached to the railing.

"Are you hungry? I have steak, but if you're still full from our snacks, I can grill some fresh shrimp I bought this morning. Key West Pinks."

"Oh, definitely the shrimp," I said, rubbing my belly. Suddenly glad I wore my dive shorts instead of a skimpy bathing suit, I sat back and sipped the cocktail he handed me.

As I watched, Gabe shucked off his shirt, the tanned expanse of his broad chest sending nervous flutters through my stomach. The urge to touch him overwhelmed me, then guilt hit like a knife to the chest.

"Fork," I hissed to myself. *I shouldn't be looking.*

"What's that?" He raised his eyebrows.

"Oh, nothing." I smiled, sipping my drink to hide the flush of my cheeks. Training my eyes on the beautiful water, I tried to decide whether to swim and cool off.

"Would you like to do some snorkeling before eating?" When I nodded, Gabe reached into a storage bin beneath the seats and pulled out fins, snorkels, and masks, handing some to me. It was a high-quality set of gear worth hundreds of dollars.

When we jumped over the railing and the expanse of coral opened up before me, I gasped into my snorkel. Finning along the surface as I gazed at the colorful wonders below, I tilted my head to Gabriel. His smiling face focused on the coral. and without thinking, my hand found his. Glancing at me, he threaded his fingers with mine, his eyes smiling through the glass of his mask.

My heart sang as we swam slowly over the purple fans, brain coral, and ocean whips. Colorful fish dotted the reef, and Gabriel stopped to point every time he saw something interesting. When a long Moray eel slithered by, I shivered.

Warm brown eyes smiled at me as Gabe squeezed my hand. The things were huge, and their mouths were always open. They were creepy and snake-like, their bright green bodies undulating as they swam. When the eel disappeared into a gap in the coral, I relaxed.

An hour later, Gabe helped me up the metal ladder, and I grabbed a towel. His relaxed smile added to the peaceful calm spreading through me after our snorkel.

Firing up the grill, he turned to me with another glass of champagne.

"Only one more. I can't get silly, I have a big job tomorrow afternoon," I said.

"Oh? What sort of job is that?"

Too late, I realized my mistake. Gabriel, as far as I knew, was human.

"*Uhh* ... a survey. I'm considering buying some property and want to look around." I cringed inside. I hated lying, but honestly, I never thought I'd see him again after that first pleasant evening at the bar. Before Oliver, humans weren't on my dating radar.

He dropped the subject, and we spent the rest of the late afternoon enjoying delicious grilled shrimp and champagne. More than one glass, unfortunately, and soon, happiness fizzed through me. Slightly tipsy, I allowed myself to forget about Oliver and our problems.

The day was over too soon, and as Gabriel pulled away from our little oasis, I felt a stab of pain. I shoved it away. He was a lovely person, polite, capable, and attentive. Combining that with his astonishing good looks was a recipe for disaster. I had to keep my wits about me. Lining myself up for a relationship with a human was a bad idea, and I had to consider Oliver.

"What are you thinking about? Your face got all crinkly there for a minute," Gabe chuckled.

"Oh, just a friend." I smiled. "He would have loved this."

He took my hand and pulled me closer, easing me against his side. His arm slipped over my shoulders. "Is this a friend I need to worry about, Phoebe?"

As he gazed into my eyes, I saw only smiles there. He didn't seem bothered. Then again, no one said we were getting married this week. I needed to tap the brakes and skip the next glass of champagne.

"I'll be honest," I said. "If you're looking for something serious, that *friend* is my focus right now. If you want to have some fun and enjoy this"—I waved my arm at the ocean—"and have some laughs, then I'm your girl."

He frowned. "Well, I'm not sure what to make of that. I had sort of hoped—"

I raised my fingers and laid them across his lips. "Don't. Let's enjoy the rest of the afternoon. I want to forget about everything but this sliver of time, if that's ok?"

Teeth appeared in a big, bold smile. "Of course. I'll take you however I can get you."

I sucked in a breath. At his concerned expression, I said, "I'm sorry. I used to say that to my friend all the time." I looked out at the ocean around me. "Ignore me. I'm a bit emotional these days."

He snuggled me in closer and tipped his cheek to rest it on the top of my head. "Well, you're safe with me. And if we're lucky, the sun will set as we get home. We'll be able to enjoy it from the water."

He was right. As Key West appeared on the horizon, the sun began its fiery drop to the sea. There was nothing more spectacular. The sun set quickly and the orange, mandarin, and magenta hues took my breath away. Seeing it from the water would have been even better if Gabriel hadn't insisted I view it from the bow. He manned the wheel at the stern, and I barely had time to throw a smile at him over my shoulder because I was so busy hanging on. The ocean swells gained some height as we pulled into Key West harbor and passed a cruise ship heading out to sea. The whole experience mesmerized me and, sadly, made me long for Oliver.

An indigo sky twinkled with the first stars as we finished tying off the sailboat and he walked me home. When we got to my door, he turned me to face him. Before I could say a word, Gabriel kissed me.

His soft, warm tongue swept between my lips, and after a brief hesitation, I relaxed into his arms. His breath smelled divine, a mixture of champagne and sunshine. When I didn't resist, he deepened the kiss, his hand coming up to grasp the back of my neck and tip my head back so he could explore more fully.

Sighing, my hands slid up the firm curves of his chest, smoothing out over the hard muscles there. My breath came faster, matching his, and I drifted away beneath the soft caress of his lips.

Oliver was an excellent kisser, too. Pain ripped through me, and I pressed my hand to Gabe's chest.

"I'm sorry," I breathed. *"I just ..."*

"You don't have to explain, Phoebe. It's alright. I understand." He smoothed the back of his fingers across my cheek gently, then tucked a strand of my hair behind an ear. "There's no rush."

With another small peck on the cheek, Gabe let his fingers slip from mine before slowly turning to walk away.

"Good Night! Thank you for a lovely afternoon," I called after him. He didn't hear me, slipping around the corner and out of sight.

CHAPTER 5

~ PHOEBE ~

Oliver wouldn't look at me. Instead, he stared off at the ocean while I recharged his bracelet. The sun blazed in a cloudless sky today so the wards I set would be strong. When I twisted my ring three times and said the words, "Potestas tenet"—*power holds firm*—his gold wristband sparked to life with a pink glow.

"I'm sorry, Oliver." I leaned forward to hug him, but he shrugged me off, and I winced. "You know I had to do this. I would have found an alternative—"

"Don't cheapen yourself by apologizing, Phoebe. I know how it works."

At his biting words, anger seared through me, hot and sharp. Maybe it was the lovely day I had on the water with Gabriel, I don't know. But I stood up, dusted myself off, and gave it to him straight. He deserved no less.

"Oliver. I'm thinking of leaving the Keys."

His head jerked, his light eyes boring into me as they silvered to life. They were bloodshot, and his hands still trembled from his near disaster. As Oliver stared intently into my eyes, his mouth drooped.

"I understand. I think you should."

"So that's it, then? I scrambled back and forth between the Keys and Georgia for six months trying to break through the walls you've built. Now you're saying it was all for nothing?" I bit my lip for giving in to my inner *Karen*.

"Pretty much. You deserve better, Phoebe."

"Oh, stop wallowing, Oliver! You are one of the luckiest males on this planet right now."

He faced me, his brows lifting. "Oh? And how is that?"

"Because a ton of people out there have *no one*. You, on the other hand, have a strong support system. People who love you. People who want to see you get back on your feet. Many don't have anything even close to that, *Oliver*."

My last words came out snappish. It didn't seem to sink in, though. Oliver turned back to the water without saying a word.

Sighing, I said, "I'll let you know what I decide. I'm working on a job right now that might take a few days, but Elli needs help at the shop in Augusta. Things aren't going very well."

Oliver huffed. "See? You wasted all this time down here trying to help someone who doesn't deserve it, and now you've gotten yourself in a jam. And that's not supposed to make me feel guilty?"

"The only one making you feel guilty is *you*. I have never, nor would I ever, lay my problems on your shoulders."

I stood to go. "You'll come through this, Oliver. I know you will. But I'm seriously questioning whether or not you will ever be able to love me back. And I need ... I need someone who can ..." My voice trailed off.

"Never mind. Take care, and I'll see you soon. And for the record, I didn't want to do that to you." I nodded to his bracelet, then climbed off the sailboat.

As I walked away, I glanced over my shoulder. Oliver stood on the bow beside his lawn chair watching me go. His expression blurred at this distance, but his shoulders drooped, making me hope that inside, he was sorry I planned on leaving.

Pathetic, Phoebe. When will you learn?

A few hours later, I headed to the site of the old Bat Tower to complete my anchors. I'd begun at my apartment, mixing my herbal elements there. Using vervain and stinging nettle ground into a paste, I put on a mask when adding the highly toxic henbane. After mixing everything with red dye for a visual, I coated the four metal rods I'd picked up at the hardware store.

I arrived at the location mid-day. Using a sledge to pound the rods in, I dropped it in the tall grass and lifted a camera every time a human drove by. I was lucky because the few residents out this way were at work.

Leaving a foot of rod protruding from the ground in all four corners, I painted a complex series of runes on all four sides of each thick steel bar. It took forever, but I was happy with my handiwork when I was done. I used old-fashioned Tremclad paint mixed with Angelica, Anise, Agrimony, and Cinquefoil.

A sly smile played on my lips. My father always told me—*never trust a Witch*. I took it to heart for this job by inscribing a failsafe. Most of my herbal elements were meant to protect against evil or dark magic.

Sybil would never see the runes I selected. Each one increased my power and gave me a measure of control over the future use of the binding. If the witch decided to turn her project into something dark, she would be in for a surprise.

After the runes dried, I used another short stake to pound the steel rods well below the surface. I planted a small daisy over each anchor to mark the locations. Then, standing back, I did a rotational spell calling on the sun and chanted the final words.

"Caelum ad terram, tenetur in aeternum"—*heaven to earth is bound forever*—then I stood back and watched.

When a car appeared down the road, I experienced a brief moment of terror, knowing a light show was imminent. Luckily, the guy was a lead foot and tore past as circular sparks began in each corner of my binding.

Rising higher and higher, swirling in a blue cloud of magic, the expanding power of the anchors brushed over my skin. Finally, with a loud crackle, magic blasted outward with an eruption of fireworks. This spell always manifested prettily; judging by the bright blue color, my casting was a success.

I pulled out my cell phone and texted Sybil.

It's done. Your rift should anchor easily to all four of my bindings. Let me know if you need anything further.

I didn't mention payment. She obviously had money to burn, so I wasn't worried.

After dropping off the rental car, I decided to walk back to my apartment. Happy Hour wasn't over yet, and Mallory Square, a few blocks from my unit, was a great spot for a celebratory drink. You were never alone in Key West.

When I found myself watching for Gabriel, I mentally slapped myself. As I passed Sloppy Joe's, I noticed the shack at the end of the street. Munchies. The small neon sign over the door glowed in welcome. A morbid curiosity pulled me in, and I passed the human bars, my jaw tight.

Walking up to the man at the door, I realized he wasn't a man at all. He was a Gargoyle, trying his very best to look human. When he smiled at me, and his bottom jaw jutted out, I almost laughed out loud. He looked like a bulldog.

"Hello, lovely lady," he rumbled. "Are you interested in some entertainment tonight?"

As he gave me a good once over, I answered, "I'd like to have a peek inside, if that's alright?"

He nodded. "Every paranormal is welcome at Munchies, and I can see clearly that you are a Witch. An exceptional Witch." His eyebrows wobbled up and down, and again, I nearly laughed.

"How do you know—? I'm sorry, I didn't get your name."

"Stan Hildebrand Esquire, at your service, my exquisite lady." He swept into a generous bow, dust sifting from him to land on the ground.

"Well, that's quite a moniker!"

He rose, giving me a jaw-jutting smile. "It means a Battle Sword of Rock." He thumped his chest with a jarring sound. "That, I certainly am."

"Well, I'm Phoebe. Happy to meet you, Stan. I've never been to a paranormal bar. Will I be safe in there?"

"If you don't go into The Dark Room, you'll be fine," he smiled, his jaw pushing his fangs up and making his speech slur.

As Stan turned to open the door for me, I noticed his back, smooth except for two large lumps. "Stan, don't most Gargoyles have wings?

His entire face drooped, the sorrow projecting from him almost bringing tears to my eyes. I was immediately sorry that I asked.

"Alas, that's a story from another time, mistress. I have none where there should be two." He sighed, his rocky shoulders drooping. "They were beautiful, my wings."

Biting my lip, I said, "I'm sorry, Stan. I had no idea."

Shoving his chin forward, he straightened and motioned to the door with a sad smile. "Welcome to Munchies. No biting without permission. Have a wonderful evening."

Nodding, I stepped into the dark foyer, then followed the sound of music. Loud and booming, it started a throb in my head. Earplugs would have been ideal. I headed around the dance floor to the bar. A bartender named Priscilla served me, her vampire teeth freaking me out when she smiled.

"So, what's this I hear about The Dark Room? It sounds intriguing." I took a sip of my wine.

Priscilla frowned. "If I were you, I'd stay out of there. Last night, we had an incident, and the workers are on pins and needles."

"Oh? What sort of incident?"

She looked me up and down, then, with a shrug, said, "One of our regulars almost killed a girl. She got handsy with him, and he flipped."

I froze, my glass halfway to my lips. "Oh, that sounds awful. Why on earth would he do that?"

Priscilla frowned. "Ah, he's ok. A good guy, really. But he has some issues. He uses The Dark Room to work some of them out. She grabbed him when he was high as a kite, and he overreacted. I thought Luther might kill him, but we all went to bat for the guy."

"Where did he end up?"

"I don't know," she sighed. "We're all worried about him. He was Polly's favorite—always so polite. After his punishment, Luther had Stan dump him ... " As if realizing she'd said too much, she pursed her lips and returned to wiping glasses.

"No one knows how he fared, but the odds say he boffed it. He was as white as a sheet when Luther finished with him. The Lord can be a hard vamp if you cross him."

Priscilla nodded to another patron and disappeared. A sick feeling spiraled through me when I realized she spoke of Oliver, the serpent around my chest squeezing tighter and tighter as she relayed the story. Now, I struggled to keep my Merlot where it belonged.

"Work out his issues?" I whispered to myself. Then, it dawned on me. The two times Oliver returned covered in bites, he didn't have an erection. My mind imploded.

I slapped the bar, nearly choking on a mouthful of wine. Anger flared, and I decided to have a look at this *Dark Room*. I might even have a visit with *Polly* while I was at it.

Looking around the room, I didn't need to search hard. A doorway beside the bar flapped the entire time I spoke with the bartender. The stupefied look of the patrons that came and went told me all I needed to know.

Nothing prepared me for what I saw when I walked through the door. At the end of a long, dark hall, the room opened up, and dim sconces lit the true entrance. A male faced me on a bench, a pretty female sprawled across his lap. With her fangs locked in his neck, she gripped his cock, stroking up and down, his grunts and sighs stirring me in unintended ways. As I watched, the

Vampire changed sides, the male sighing with an erotic moan as she bit him again.

She lifted her leg across his lap and slid down onto his shaft. He groaned, reaching up with shaking hands to grab her by the ass. His fingers dug in deep, his throaty grunts of appreciation getting louder as she slid up and down, the slick sounds fueling the rage burning in my belly. He let go of her ass and pulled her blouse away, fondling her breasts as her hips worked him up and down.

A growl rumbled from my throat, and she startled, turning to see who watched. Blood dripped from one fang, and she licked her lips. Her eyes traveled up and down my sundress, and she smiled. "Be with you in a minute, sweetheart."

When I glanced down at her name tag, my insides water bombed into nothingness. My fire snuffed out and tears stabbed at my eyelids. *Polly*.

I whirled on my heel, slammed through the swinging doors, circled the dance floor, and blasted through the entrance hard enough that it smashed poor Stan on a full swing. Wood cracked, and the Gargoyle grabbed the door before it toppled over.

"Whoa there, mistress. Where are you going in such a hurry? You didn't like our little oasis on the ocean?"

"I'm sorry, Stan. Are you alright?" I dusted him off as he gave me his bulldog smile, yanked the broken door free, and leaned it against the wall.

"I'm fine, miss. Hard as a rock," he grinned, tapping his arm with one hand. "What's got you riled up so quick?"

I let out the breath I held. "I heard someone almost died in there last night. A patron."

"Ah, yes, Oliver. Wonderful guy, really. Lots of troubles, though. Luther nearly killed him. He was past his last strike, anyway."

"Last strike?"

"Yes, he caused a few issues recently but managed to get in again. If he's still alive, I don't know what he will do now that Luther banned him."

"Banned. Yes, I heard." Spite splashed my insides like lava.

"Probably for the best. A loose cannon, that one. I'll miss him. He brought me a birthday card," Stan said with a wistful sigh. "A musical card."

Fat tears rolled down his cheeks, and I covered my mouth to hide a sympathetic sob. I wasn't exactly stable at the moment.

With a goodbye wave I stomped across the cobblestones and headed for my apartment. When I got to the street leading to the marina, I hesitated, then swerved toward Oliver's slip.

Fury straddled me like a rodeo clown, the image of Polly riding Oliver's lap coloring my vision white. It hit a spot so deep that wildfires raged uncontrolled in my belly. If they made the surface, Key West would burn.

When I reached my target, Oliver lounged on his deck watching the stars. Panting from my foxtrot down the docks, I didn't hesitate.

"Phoebe?" His shocked gaze took in my red face, and his eyes shot wide, his hands coming up as if to protect himself.

I was angry enough to put it all on the table. "I *know*, Oliver."

"I'm sorry, what?"

"The Dark Room. The bites. Stan. *POLLY!* I know it all, and I want to hear what you have to say for yourself."

Oliver sighed. "It's not what you think." His eyes traveled over me, a faint glow lighting their depths.

"Oh, I bet it is *precisely* what I think. I *saw*, Oliver. I went into the Dark Room and got a good *hard* look at what Polly *does* for you. How could you do that to me? *To us?*"

Oliver frowned as if trying to make sense of my words. "Yeah, about that. It won't happen again, I've been banned. Even bringing Stan something musical won't get me in now." He shoved his fingers through his hair and closed his eyes.

"Yes, I'm aware you've been banned. And what exactly will you do now? Your little therapy sessions won't bear fruit. You've not done the work to get better, and you've found some godforsaken shortcut. Now, you don't even have that."

He paled, his feet restless. "Phoebe, listen to me ... "

I held up my hand. "No. You listen to *ME*. We are done, do you hear me? I can handle the issues you're having, and I can support you through just about anything. But I won't stay with someone who cheats. I need someone tearing open my lingerie, not my fucking heart!"

Oliver opened his mouth to say something, but I cut him off.

"I loved you, *once*. You were everything to me. I waited for you. I tried harder than anyone could ever expect of a Witch. But I can't do it anymore. I can't. When I finish the job for Sybil Metroyer, I'm gone."

I whirled and ran; the tears poured. Branded "L" for loser, that was me. How could I be so stupid? All the way home, that fiery letter worked its way through me, burning like a bitch. But I didn't look back. Oliver would never know how much he hurt me.

CHAPTER 6

~ OLIVER ~

When Phoebe confronted me on the boat, white-hot anger licked inside my skull. *How dare she!?* She knew nothing about what I went through.

My irrational rage eventually sputtered out, calm descended, and I came to my senses. I blew it. Phoebe was the best thing that ever happened to me, and I was so busy navel-gazing that I let the love of my life slip out to sea. My behavior was worse than pathetic.

After a good dose of self-pity, anger returned, and I went a second round with rage. Phoebe cuffed my wrist to keep me from hurting anyone with my power. But that couldn't stop me from wreaking havoc in human form.

I broke everything. Glasses, cupboard doors, dishes, picture frames ... it all wound up on the floor. Soon, I ended up there too, my head in my hands, that odd disembodied voice echoing in my head once again. The smell of peaches and sunshine wafted to me, and I looked up. No one was there.

Rising, I put my fist through a cupboard door, and renewed my attack on my sailboat. When I was out of breath, I picked the glass from my bare feet and slipped on my shoes, marching up the docks and stopping at the bar where Phoebe drank with *the guy*.

Pot, meet kettle, I thought, seething inside. Phoebe had no idea that I knew about her *new squeeze*. She didn't waste any time snuggling up to him, even with my boat a hundred yards away.

I ordered a drink, and at ten bucks a pop, I nursed it. I'd stop at the variety store again. The guy gave me great deals on liquor after rescuing his money.

Seated at the beautiful oak bar, my reflection glared back at me from the mirrored backing. As I nursed my drink and stared at my pathetic self, a mist appeared behind me, barely visible in the bright room. Whispers in my ear made me shiver. *"I'm coming for you, Oemar."*

Spinning my stool, my wide eyes darted around the bar. Nothing was there. When my pulse slowed, I rotated back and buried my nose into my drink. Blackouts, seeing things—fun times. When two large bodies plopped down on either side of me, I jumped.

"Hi, Oliver."

"Felix. Jovi. What brings you here tonight?" God, I was sick of small talk. I growled into my drink.

"Oh, this and that," Felix said. Jovi ordered a drink, but not until he spent ten minutes inspecting the colorful drink menu. It fascinated him, having spent a sheltered life at the facility where I'd been ruined. Jovi settled for *Something Blue*. I snorted into my whisky.

"That's quite a girly drink you got there, pal."

Jovi raised his eyebrows. "What? It matches my leg scales."

Well, he wasn't wrong. "Is Gideon paying you guys to follow me?"

The two Servus looked at each other, then nodded.

"Well, I won't kill you if you help me out," I said with a glittery smile.

"A threat that holds no water, Djinn. Not now." Felix nodded toward my glowing bracelet.

"Fine, you got me there. I need you to find someone for me. Sybil Metroyer."

Felix looked at his friend, then said, "We know of her."

"Tell me." I took a long pull of my drink and waited. Felix shrugged.

"She's a secretive Witch from Savannah. She's got enormous talent, strong offensive skills, and is known to be quite dangerous. She's in town for something, and Gideon asked us to watch her." His bi-eyes sparkling, Felix added, "You didn't hear that from me."

"A Witch, you say? Interesting. Where can I find her?"

"I can't tell you that."

"You owe me. You could have set me free back in Charleston, and you didn't."

"What!?" Jovi squeaked. His voice came out too loud, and people looked over at us. "You can't blame us for that! You were out of your mind and would have killed us where we stood."

The conversation trailed off, then Jovi asked, "Why do you need this information, Oliver?"

"No reason. But the Witch hired Phoebe, and I'm worried about her. I want to make sure Ms. Metroyer isn't a Dark Witch."

A look passed between them. Felix leaned over and whispered in my ear.

***

The next morning, I stood before the modern office where Sybil Metroyer conducted business while in town. I sat down on a bench and waited. Jovi and Felix probably skulked nearby, but I didn't care. I had to do this.

When a tall, dark-haired beauty stepped through the smoked glass doors, and her knowing midnight eyes found me instantly, I confronted her.

"I need your help, Witch."

She looked down her nose at me with an imperious expression. "And why would I do that, exactly?"

I faltered. *Why indeed?* Grasping at straws and angry with myself for not thinking it through, I blurted out, "My girlfriend is Phoebe Peregrin."

Her eyes darted down to the bracelet on my wrist. "*Ahh.* The Djinn who can't control himself. I remember. It appears you've been recently recharged. You must have worried your *friends.*"

I lifted my arm. "I need this removed."

She laughed. "Of course you do. *NO.*"

Brushing me aside, she continued down the street, and I followed.

"If you don't help me, something terrible will happen to Phoebe."

"No, it won't. The girl can handle herself just fine."

"I'll die if you don't get it off."

"No, you won't. And on the upside, neither will anyone else."

She reached the corner and turned toward the harbor.

"Ms. Metroyer. Stop. *Please.*"

It must have been the tears in my voice. She halted, then slowly turned to face me, one eyebrow raised in question.

"I ... I love Phoebe. More than anything. I've been a fool. I need to try harder. Things went great—okay, not great, but better—after my bracelet expired. I need that freedom back. *Please.*"

Did I imagine a guilty look flashing over her face? Hopeful, I watched as she stalked back toward me and flinched when she grabbed my wrist and lifted the bracelet to see it better. A few angry grumbles later, she dropped my hand. The bracelet glowed even brighter. *The bitch!*

"I can't help you. Now go away."

As I stood there, watching her stalk down the sidewalk, a depression darker than anything I'd known descended on me.

Numb, I headed back toward the boat but only got one block before stopping at a bench, sitting, and burying my face in my hands. My eyes filled with unshed tears as I pulled back and looked at the *extra* pink glow from the band.

"You suck. And so does that fucking Witch."

My shaft pulsed at the choice of words. I reached into my pocket to pull myself back into position. My constant companion was back with a vengeance now that I was healed. The benefits from my night at the club were long gone, and I hurt like hell. My balls squeezed in an invisible vice, and I knew if I didn't find a way to release soon, I'd be heading out to sea without a life vest before the weekend was over.

Phoebe was gone. She'd given up on me. Getting that bracelet off had been my only chance for redemption.

So distraught that tears blurred my vision, I almost didn't see it. I blinked, wiped my eyes, then concentrated. My skin shimmered, and when I tucked my fingers into my lap, I made them disappear.

I looked back the way I came and smiled through the tears. Maybe someone wasn't a hard-assed bitch after all.

***

~ PHOEBE ~

I tossed my phone on the coffee table. I'd just purchased the bus ticket home and wouldn't have to endure being close to Oliver for much longer. I would get back to my life, and Oliver could get back to—whatever Oliver did. Things would reach an even keel for me. Perhaps I'd hear from Gabriel once I was home. He told me he had a home near Charleston. It wasn't far from Augusta, a little under two hours. Stranger things had happened.

My phone buzzed. A text from Sybil.

Come to the Bat Tower tonight at midnight. I need your help to finish my job. I will double your pay.

Odd, but alright. Double pay was fine by me, and by my hasty calculations, the extra fees would be enough to solve the financial nightmare I'd created for my shop. You couldn't sell witchy items without money to fill the shelves.

I took a walk, then headed over to hire a rental car. I was almost there when I saw a familiar figure hustling down the busy street. What the hell? Did the Gods have no mercy?

Oliver saw me and approached with caution. I crossed my arms and turned to face the distant view of the ocean down the street. The shade of the palm trees above did nothing to cool the heat wafting from my skin.

"I'm sorry, alright? It's not what you think. Polly isn't … *doesn't* …" Running his fingers through his hair, Oliver blurted, "Don't give up on us, Pheebs. I swear. I'll try harder."

I glared at him, tears threatening. "It's too late, Oliver. When I saw the club—it broke something inside of me. You win. You've convinced me it's over. While you ran around trying to protect me from your horrible self, you killed the last spark of hope keeping me going. I'm sorry. I can't …"

When I tried to push past him, Oliver reached out and grabbed my arm, turning me to face him. His silver irises sparkled. I'd swear his power wasn't bound if I didn't see the bright pink glow on his wrist.

"You mean everything to me, Phoebe. I may not have told you this since my rescue, but my feelings haven't changed. I still care for you."

A void yawned inside me at his words—the bleak future for me if I stayed with Oliver. I yanked my arm away. "Too little. Too late. Goodbye, Oliver. My bus leaves tomorrow and I'll be on it. *Don't follow me.*"

At his crestfallen expression, I nearly changed my mind. But then I pictured Polly, with her perfect ass and smiling face, sliding up and down his shaft as he moaned. Something snapped, and sparks danced across my skin.

"Stay away from me, Oliver." As I stormed away, I heard him call my name, but I didn't look back.

CHAPTER 7

~ PHOEBE ~

When I arrived at the Bat Tower location, I parked and was surprised to see Sybil wasn't alone. My headlights shone over a drool-worthy guy with dark, curly hair standing nearby, a sly smile on his face. I hated him instantly. An Incubus.

Fairly common as far as paranormals go, the male demons fed from the power of their victims to stay young and vibrant. Incubi weren't easy to spot in a crowd. Usually athletic and painfully handsome, like Vampires, they lived centuries if well-fed. As a Witch I spotted them easily by the oily smell wafting from their skin, and after I climbed from the car, my nose confirmed it. This Incubus looked eerily familiar.

Sybil ignored us both, working away at a level of witchery far above my pay grade. Chanting and twisting her fingers while smudging the entire site, I knew something big was about to happen. The moon cast enough light to see, and when I peered through the gloom and spied the enormous circle of salt around the entire Bat Tower foundation, I freaked. That circle had only one purpose—to contain a demon.

"Oh, no, you don't! I won't stand by and let you open the gates of hell to summon a demon, Sybil. What the hell are you thinking!?"

She paused, peering down her nose at me. "It's merely a precaution, *Ms. Peregrin.*"

Returning to her work, Sybil shook her smudge in intricate patterns, her whispered incantation joining the smoke wafting through the air. The woody yet floral scent of dragon's blood set my nerves jangling. *Protection. Power.* A thickening storm of intensity poured from Sybil, the heavy blanket of her magic coating my skin.

"You can't! We've barely recovered from the last demon to hit the Keys. If you let out another, we'll all pay." I followed her, hoping to bring the Witch to her senses.

My pleas fell on deaf ears, Sybil's chants getting louder as she worked. That was one way to drown out my objections.

A hand on my arm sent warmth spreading through me, a tendril of power circling my nipples and one sliding straight to my core. I looked into a pair of dark brown eyes and frowned at the curly-haired dude.

"Take your hand from my arm this instant."

The Incubus smiled. "Call me Charles." Buzzing tickled the back of my throat, a cloying sweetness coating my tongue. Heat tingled into my fingers and toes.

"Perhaps we can keep each other busy while the Witch finishes her work?"

Charles' oily smile relit the rage churning beneath my skin since meeting Polly. *Fuck you, you freaky Casanova piece of shit.*

I mumbled harsh words under my breath and twisted my ring. The Incubus hissed and pulled his hand from my arm.

"That's your only warning, asshole. The next time you touch me or invade my privates with your power, you better have a tourniquet." My smile was vicious, anger at Oliver making me bold. I didn't know the strength of this Incubus. I should tread carefully.

Sybil worked with him. There was no telling what their connection might be—and damned if I knew whether or not she was on the dark side of this thing. Sybil just crafted a demon containment circle. Any rookie would know that.

For now, the Incubus backed off, his hands in the air. At his cutesy smile, I decided not to turn my back on him until we parted ways.

I strode over to where Sybil worked. "You want my assistance, fine. But you'll tell me what this is all about, or I won't help, and you can go screw yourself, *Ms. Metroyer*."

She paused, then tilted her head to look down at me. Her cold smile blew in straight from the Arctic Circle.

"I would watch the attitude if I were you, *Ms. Peregrin*. She resumed her work, and I followed. After another few minutes of chants, smudging, and spells, the four bindings began to sparkle, lighting up the daisies I'd planted to mark the corners.

Sybil turned to me. "It's ready. When I say *now*, I need you to lock down the doorway after I open it. It needs to be properly grounded, or it will keep growing. We don't want that, trust me." She glanced at my ring. "You'll use that if you're wise."

I frowned. "And what's to stop me from saying no?"

Her gaze flicked to the guy with the curls. "Then Charles will step in, and we will *convince you*. He's not the pussycat he pretends to be." Sybil's eyes glittered, her chin set in stone. Hot air wafted across my skin as she turned up her power in a deliberate warning.

"Right. Well then, I need to think about this and get back to you." I turned toward my car, but the Incubus blocked my way.

"Not so fast, sweet thing." His magic swept through me, my vagina threatening to abandon ship and join team bad guy.

I ground my molars and, under my breath, whispered, *"Mortuus es, motherfucker,"* then bit my tongue. Sweeping my fingertip into my mouth, I gathered some blood and rubbed it on my ring. His gaze tracking my movements, Charles' magic rose. Dark, glittering eyes drilled into me.

I smiled. *"Repleti harenae—NUNC!"*

Wind sprang up from nowhere, a tiny sandstorm starting at Charles' feet. Forming an inverted tornado, it shot straight up, spiraling fast and high as he watched—

then curved and raced straight for him. Charles opened his mouth with surprise, his eyes going wide.

"Bad move, Chuck. Don't say I didn't warn you."

The sandstorm narrowed to magic marker thickness and shot between his open lips, filling his trachea with sand. With no time to sputter, his hands went to his throat, and his eyes rolled back in his head. As his lungs filled with sand, his screams became muffled whines; my tornado throttled him. In less than a minute, he lay on the sand, unconscious.

When I was sure he was out cold, I whispered, "*Revertere ad terram*" and as quickly as it came, every grain of sand retreated, leaving Charles sleeping like the dead.

I glanced at Sybil, who gaped at me. Her eyes flicked over my face with what I hoped was admiration and not a "*you're so dead*" expression.

She dropped her tools, in this case, a feather and a bottle of ink, and clapped.

"Well done, Phoebe. I see you've been practicing. Don't make the mistake of thinking your parlor tricks will work on me, however." She brushed her hands off. "I'm done here anyway. Stand back. And be ready. I can start the tear, but if your magic doesn't anchor this thing, it will keep right on going—as in, unstoppable."

Apparently, my approval was no longer required. Sybil stepped out of the circle, clapped her hands, and tossed a handful of black powder. It sparkled against the moonlight, and the earth rumbled beneath my feet.

HOLY SHIT.

Moaning filled the air, but it wasn't a human sound. It was the noise a skyscraper made before it fell on your head.

Light sparked over each of the daisies, a galaxy of stars gathering between four rising pillars of energy. The ground rumbled, the air moaned, and something that resembled the bead of a welder's torch appeared. From six feet in the air, a glowing orb of energy burned a line slowly toward the ground. As it lengthened, it parted, a bright blue light beaming from within the tear.

"NOW!" Sybil yelled. I hesitated, and she hissed, "If you don't lock down the ends of this thing *right fucking now*, we're all going to die."

I rubbed my fingers, chanting the spell I'd hastily shaped in my mind when Sybil told me I'd be helping. As the rip extended upward, I chanted louder, and it stopped spreading, the bottom edge of the seam pausing a foot above the ground. We had a doorway, and it was ten feet tall.

Noises came from within—grotesque, guttural noises. A clawed hand reached through the slit, gripping the edge and pulling it aside like a rubbery shower curtain. A head appeared, a pair of horns sweeping back from above pointed ears. A brilliant blue gem gleamed above glowing yellow eyes, nearly blinding me. The thing curled its lips back with a wet snarl, exposing long, pointed teeth.

Sybil was insane. I had to stop her. She'd opened a freaking gateway to hell. Whispering as quickly as I dared, my safety spell over the four corners responded, tickling my palms.

Faster and faster I cast, pulling the power together to form invisible lines connecting the four corners. Using my ring and quickly depleting its stored power, I didn't hesitate. I finished my spell, a loud crack sounding as the lines converged.

Stepping into the salt circle, Sybil held a knife as she headed for the demon, its upper body now leaning into our dimension. Startled by the sound of my safety spell locking into place, Sybil yelled, *"NOOO!"*

I clapped my hands over my head, and with all the power left in me, I yelled, *"Defendat Nos!"*—then dropped my arms and whispered, *"Defend us."*

Power shot from beneath my daisies, the leaves and petals exploding outward. With a sizzling bang like a transformer exploding, the rip snapped shut, the demon screeching as it pulled itself back. It wasn't fast enough. One scaly forearm dropped to the ground with a thud.

Sybil's face rippled with fury. "What have you done!? You *FOOL!*"

The Witch came at me, her hands out, her steps sure. Wind sprang up from nowhere, her beaded hair and billowy wrap floating behind her as she powered toward me. I would be dead in seconds if I didn't think fast.

I had nothing. My ring was spent, and the sun long gone. There was no way to recharge. I turned and ran. Five useless steps later, a thunderclap nearly broke my eardrums as a hot boxing glove hammered my back, slapping me face-first on the ground.

Burning pressure wrapped my ankles, hauling me backward, my hands grasping at the dirt and scrub as it tore at my bare skin. Shrieking, I reversed with painful speed. When I stopped sliding, the unseen force flipped me over, and I stared straight up Sybil's nose.

Surprisingly quiet, her hushed voice oozed death. "You're going to pay for that," she whispered.

***
~ OLIVER ~

Holy shit—my girl had stones! Invisible, I slipped from the back seat of Phoebe's car and hovered around the clearing, chewing my nails as I circled the fighting witches and debated getting involved.

If I joined the fray, Phoebe would cuff me once it was over. If I pissed off Sybil, she'd bury me, and I wouldn't need to worry about being cuffed. There was also a slight chance of death if I got between one of the spells flying back and forth. Either way, it was a losing proposition.

How ironic that the Witch who freed me would tangle with Phoebe so soon after the happy deed.

Phoebe held her own, so I watched and waited, my heart in my throat. When the demon almost stepped through the portal, I came pretty close to crapping my drawers. I had no idea how she did it, but Pheebs rocked their world. One detached arm later, and we were safe, at least for now.

When Phoebe ran, I almost threw caution to the winds. Instead, I moved closer, looking for a chance to help her. When Sybil reached out a hand, grasped at nothing, and pulled, I cringed as Phoebe slid backward through the brush. When she cried out in pain, fury shimmered through the mist around me.

I didn't think. I acted. As Sybil loomed over Phoebe and threatened her, I sent a speedy tendril of my power around her throat. I squeezed. Sybil choked. My girl hauled ass.

Phoebe couldn't see me, but she knew something was up. She pulled herself to her feet and ran for the cars. I had my hands full, choking the Witch with everything I had. Somehow, I heard Sybil's voice in my head.

"Djinn, let go right the hell now, or I'll fry you like the insect you are."

I was so busted. I let go and quickly slipped away before the Witch got her power-slick fingers on me. As I dropped and sailed over the ground, I found a pile of tools, smiling at the massive mortar and pestle. I grabbed the long wooden pestle, hefting it into my cloud where it disappeared from view.

Sybil was already halfway to the cars. Phoebe scrambled to open her door, and when the dark Witch moved faster and raised her hand, I gave up on stealth and launched.

She never saw the swing coming. I gave her a pretty good tap on the back of her head and Sybil went down, her eyes rolling back. Whoops.

Panting like a greyhound as she yanked her door open, Phoebe looked over her shoulder. She paused when she saw Sybil on the ground. Confused, her eyes tracked around the brushy clearing. Luckily, my makeshift bat lay hidden in the grass where I dropped it.

Phoebe stared at the unconscious Witch, chewing her nail. Charles still lay where she'd dropped him, and she grimaced as she cast a look his way. But when Sybil stirred, Phoebe hopped in her car, slammed the door, and—planned or not—covered the Witch in a spray of stones as she fled.

Laughing into my sleeve, I moved into the bushes and waited to see how things played out. Sybil sat up, rubbed her head, and narrowed her eyes in my general direction.

"I know you're there, you rotten little bastard. You have no idea what you two have done. This gate will open if it's the last thing I do. If you're smart, you'll convince your Witch to see this through, or suffer the consequences."

Sybil stood and walked over to stare down at the Incubus, her lips set in a thin line. I nearly choked when she kicked him in the ribs. Charles groaned, and at her angry snarl, he rose, the pair getting into her car and speeding away.

Charles was lucky. I recognized the demon from the Charleston facility. He'd even left me a memento. The slimy prick would be dead now if I hadn't been concentrating on Phoebe. If the bastard wanted to stay off my radar, he shouldn't have burned his initial into my ass.

Having lost my ride, I morphed back to human form and took a lengthy look at the gateway. Someone had planted four daisies at the corners. I chuckled at the carnage of leaves and petals. Daisies were Phoebe's favorite flower.

I reached out a hand, and layers of power hummed over each shredded plant. Phoebe's magic tickled my fingertips. When I picked up a few white petals, I tasted her on my tongue—*cinnamon*. God, I'd missed her.

When I moved to the center of the salt circle, the flavor of peanut butter and motor oil coated my mouth. I stuck out my tongue, trying to rid myself of the thick taste.

The rip had faded, now invisible to human eyes. I held up my hand before the faint scar and its vile pulse made me ill. How in the world did Phoebe manage to cap the gate?

Pride swelled until my chest hurt. With a slow smile, I misted, then swirled toward Key West. The next sixteen miles would be painful, but *totally* worth the sight of Phoebe kicking some witchy ass.

CHAPTER 8

~ PHOEBE ~

There went my new job. I blew my bangs up and turned back from the apartment window. The wards on my place protected me for now, but I didn't doubt that if Sybil wanted in, she would make short work of my barrier. Luckily, the Witch expended tremendous power at the gate. It should slow her down.

My father, a respected ward practitioner, taught me everything he knew. In Witch families, power was genetic, the knowledge accumulating between generations throughout history. I tried to keep my talent concealed, as my father taught me.

Witches with power also had egos and a thirst for more juice. Under the right circumstances, Sybil Metroyer could make a snack out of my powers, knowledge, and, if she was batshit crazy, my physical body. Cannibalism at its finest.

I squirmed when I thought of my friend's stepmother's cousin. The poor woman wasn't powerful, but she'd wound up on the menu in a throwdown with a scrappy, less-than-sane warlock. They found parts of her in his freezer after he was arrested for public intoxication while whizzing on a statue in their small town. Things escalated when they found her defrosting finger in his pocket. I'd prefer to avoid freezer burn at all costs—and pocket lint.

Never expecting this trip to require the use of magic, I'd left my family grimoire locked in a safe at home. Oliver needed help, not witchcraft. It was a good thing I'd learned to think on my feet. Thanks, Dad.

I won the throwdown with Charles because I had my assistant Elli fax me the pages from the 1890's section of my grimoire—my great-great-uncle Alistair's battle spells. I crossed myself and pulled out my phone to text her again. I needed every remaining section she could find on offensive spells.

Rubbing my aching chest, my thoughts boomeranged to the Djinn who held my heart. For eight years, I'd feared for Oliver, knowing something terrible had happened to him. Almost a decade of pining for him, and for what? I was a fool. My father always told me I gave my heart too easily and should hold out for a prince.

It shredded my soul when I realized Oliver had sex with that lovely female Vampire. In hindsight, I brought it on myself. When he insisted that I leave Key West, I didn't listen, because he never said those final, horrible words. Or he did, and I refused to listen.

Oh boy, it was *crystal clear* to me now. We were no longer together. My skin burned with shame and anger at the thought of him touching her. He no longer wanted me. I jutted my chin, wrestling the tears into submission.

There was stubbornness, and there was stupidity. I nailed both in one go. Hope sprung eternal alright—then promptly circled the drain behind foolish love and good intentions. *GAH!*

My hands trembled as I poured myself a whisky. Being a successful businesswoman and a somewhat talented Witch, I wasn't used to falling on my face. A powerful Sorceress wanted my head, my business was in shambles, and the male of my dreams lost his mind and cheated on me—all splendid additions to my resume.

After ten minutes of debating whether he actually *cheated*—apparently, we were no longer a couple—I slapped my face and questioned my sanity. Oliver never gave me a reason to believe he was the unfaithful sort. Like a dog with a bone, I wanted—no, I *needed*—the truth of what happened in that bar.

Looking in the mirror, I whispered, "Ready for another dose of foolishness, Phoebe?" With a last cautious look out the window, I chugged my drink and let my restless feet find some answers.

I couldn't sit in my apartment and stew. Imagining the loud crack of my wards and my blood splashing the walls during Sybil's assault, I decided I was no safer inside than out.

"To Hell with this!"

Hastily stuffing two weak spells into a pair of chopsticks, I shoved the makeshift wands into my sundress pocket and headed to Munchies. If Sybil attacked, I could catch her hair on fire, then take her for Pho. I nearly turned back twice, but the bar wasn't far, and determination replaced melancholy somewhere along the way. When the Gargoyle saw me coming, he beamed.

"Hello, lovely Witch!" It was impossible not to like Stan.

"I brought you something, big fella!" I opened my hand, and with a glittery puff, a butterfly appeared, gently opening and closing its cobalt blue wings. Stan gasped, and the butterfly took to the air, circling his head while he watched in wonder. The Gargoyle held out a hand, and it landed, its wings giving off an iridescent shimmer.

"It's beautiful," he breathed.

"You love music and miss your wings, so I thought you might like it. Have a listen."

Stan tilted his head, his stony ear scraping as it swiveled forward. After listening for a moment, he smiled, his fangs popping as his pink tongue glistened between them.

I grinned. "It's Beethoven. If you whisper your choice, it will play whatever song you like. It's spelled to last for at least a month. Here." I handed him a small wooden box that I fished from my dress pocket. "When you aren't using it, keep it in this to protect it. It's very delicate."

"Delicate," he whispered, his eyes huge. The tiny box disappeared into his enormous hand, a tear tracking down his face. "Thank you so much, my loveliest of all ladies. I will cherish it always." He sniffed and opened the door for me with a theatrical bow. "You are more than welcome at Munchies. No biting without permission, my lady."

Booming techno something or other assaulted my ears, and I squinted. I hastened through the dark foyer and skirted the dance floor to find Priscilla at the bar. She pulled a glass from the rack over her head with a pointy smile.

"Wine, right?"

"Whisky. Neat." With a wry smile, I smoothed my skirt, and when she handed me the tulip glass, I nodded in appreciation. After a nice sniff of the shot of Four Roses, I asked, "How can I get in touch with Polly?"

"Our Polly?" When I nodded, her eye flitted to the door of The Dark Room, one corner of her mouth twisting as she thought about it. "Give me a second." She put down her rag and walked through the door. She returned with a flushed Polly, who stared at me with curiosity, then slid onto the stool beside me.

"What can I do for you—?" she asked.

"You don't know me, but I have a question about a … client."

Polly shook her head. "Nope. That's strictly against our policies. I can't tell you anything." Looking a tad angry, she slid off her stool. I reached out to grab her arm.

"It's about Oliver. Do you know him?"

She paused, her eyes on my hand. The sharp points of her fangs left dents in her lip.

"You're Phoebe."

When I nodded, there was more lip chewing, then Polly peeled my fingers from her arm. I thought she would leave, but she slid back onto a stool.

Lowering her voice, the pretty vamp said, "Look, Oliver is ... well, he's a sweet guy, but he's in a ton of pain. He came here to relieve—she looked at me and frowned—well, I'm pretty sure you know his issue. The poor guy. I can't imagine going through life aroused twenty-four hours a day."

At my stricken expression, she sighed. "He doesn't like to be touched. He's here for the venom. I've had to develop a new technique to bite him without touching anything, but we made it work."

I gasped.

"Exactly," Polly said. "You understand the nature of what goes on back there?" When I nodded, she pursed her lips and measured her words. "Oliver only lets *men* finish him. Well, except for Velvet. But they don't identify either way." When I looked confused, she added, "Velvet is gender-neutral and prefers the pronoun *they*."

Polly saw my pale face and paused to order a drink from the bartender. She took a sip, her eyes finding mine over the rim of her glass.

"Phoebe, you must understand, the vamps here don't care about gender; they're 'into' whatever gets them their next meal, and honestly, our staff enjoy their jobs. What's not to love? We can't get diseases, and it's fun. Vampire toxins are euphoric to *Others*, and the males—*and females*—who come to The Dark Room are chasing relief from something. We help people."

At my raised eyebrows, she laughed. "*We do!* You'd be surprised how many people have issues that wash away after they come in. Vampire toxin isn't addictive; it gives them a buzz, and usually, they go home, straighten things out, and we never see them again. And if we get a client that doesn't understand the rules, Stan takes care of them."

"Thank you. I know you could get in trouble for helping me." I sipped my whisky and felt her eyes on me. She smiled, her fangs on full display.

"He loves you, you know." At my surprised look, she rushed on. "Once he's really snowed under, Ollie says your name. *Often.* We all know he has someone he cares about, so we keep it professional. Well, as professional as one can keep these things." With a wink, she slipped off the stool.

"Nice chatting. I can see why he loves you. Your aura tastes like cinnamon hearts. Snappy and sweet."

Polly grinned, blew me a kiss, and strutted away, her firm ass cheeks eating her thong. I saw why Oliver liked her enough to allow her inside his tiny circle. I rubbed my throat, jealousy strangling me at the thought of someone else handling him. No one should touch him but *me*.

For the love of God, why wouldn't he let me help him!? Banging my head on the fancy oak bar briefly crossed my mind.

I sipped my drink and thought back to the beginning. We had such a promising start. Tears threatened, but I shoved them away. Waterworks wouldn't help me now. I wasn't sure anything could help us, but at least I knew Oliver hadn't been with another woman. Well, not literally.

Oh my God, was it better, or worse, now that I knew the truth? My face flamed. Not a woman. *Not. A. Woman. Jesus, what a godforsaken mess.*

I paid my tab and slid from my stool, feeling only marginally better as I slipped out the front door. Seeing Stan holding his hand to his ear, his butterfly playing music just for him—grief hit me. Hard. I wished a butterfly spell would make me happy. Then I could self-medicate.

As I walked home through the muggy night, I skirted the crowds of revelers enjoying the Duval Street bars. Everywhere I looked, couples kissed and hugged, the festive mood in the air bringing me down in flames.

Being outside the apartment right now was a bad idea. I hustled home to pack. I had my ticket, and the bus pulled out at suppertime tomorrow. Now that I'd nuked the bridge with Sybil and confirmed she was up to no good, it was time to leave town. I'd be lucky if she didn't track me to Augusta, Georgia, and turn me into hors d'oeuvres for her next party.

***

~ OLIVER ~

"Darla. I'm so sorry. I shouldn't have threatened you like that. I lashed out. It won't happen again."

She sniffed, and a few hairs sprouted from the edge of her nose. God, it would kill me now if I didn't figure out her species.

"I promise, Dar. Ask me anything. I'll open up."

My therapist gave me a suspicious look, her eyes darting to the pink glow of my bracelet. Then, jutting her chin, she grabbed her pencil and notepad and said, "Tell me about Layla."

"Oh. Shit. Of course, you'd go there. Well played, madam."

She looked at me expectantly and clicked her pen.

Sighing, I closed my eyes. "Layla was their most powerful Succubus. She did all the heavy lifting. If they had difficulty handling a male … " I stopped at the look on her face. "You don't know anything about what happened in Charleston, do you?"

She shook her head, so I gave her the short version.

"A demon hatched a scheme to breed Djinn-Syreni … basically mermaid … crosses, then train the male offspring as a military force to take over the country. At the same time, they extracted nectar from their fangs—the resulting hybrids are called *Servus, by the way*—"

At her confused look, I simplified it. "They made a powerful drug called *Gush* from the erototoxic secretions of the male hybrids. The young males were brainwashed from birth. They thought the collections were for a noble cause." I pointed at my canines, and she nodded.

"The nectar from their bite is highly addictive to humans. The goal was to enslave the population using addiction. The demon had enough stashed that I heard the next step was putting it in the water supply." Darla gasped. "I was their Djinn sperm donor for eight years. I fathered who knows how many."

My stomach rolled at the mention of the lab. I closed my eyes against the images that flashed through my mind. The shackles. The vibrating collector. *Layla's magic* … When I opened them, Darla held a tissue under her eyelashes.

"Anyway, Layla and her pals weren't content with taking my semen. They used me for a little sex play on the side."

Sweat beaded through my skin, and I rubbed my forehead on my sleeve. I wasn't sure how much more I could say without cracking, so I showed her instead and hoped we could leave it at that.

"They loved twisted games. They gave me some mementos."

I stood, turned around, and dropped my shorts. There was no sound, but Darla stopped breathing for a moment. My head hung in shame; tears threatened. I didn't need to see the initials burned into my ass to remember the days it happened with horrifying clarity.

"Oh, Oliver. I'm so sorry."

I pulled my pants up and sat back down. "Ya, well, save the sympathy, sister. As I mentioned in our last session, I didn't complain. At first, yes. I fought like a maniac. But they wore me down. I finally gave up and got right into it."

"I stopped thinking about—*about freedom*. I knew I'd never see the sun or stars again. So I handled it as best I could." I looked into her white face and shrugged. "If you can't beat 'em..."

Darla plucked another tissue from her box and discreetly dabbed at her eyes, trying not to smear her makeup. "Whose initials are those?" she sniffed.

I held up my hand, counting on my fingers. 'Layla, Hex, Boris, Stephen, and Charles. I don't know who the "Y" is. They never let me see his face, but it was a male. He smelled like cedar."

Darla frowned. "I'm so sorry, Oliver. It must have been horrible." Pulling herself together, she scribbled a few notes, took a deep breath, and said, "I can help you, but you must do the work. Get your shovel in the ground as they say. Emotional recovery is dirty work."

I groaned. "I figured as much."

"Gideon tells me you're still having a problem with ongoing erections. Is that right?"

I nodded, feeling around in my shorts to make sure I was properly tucked, then fluffed my shirt.

"Oliver, what you are experiencing is called sexual compulsivity, or hypersexuality, brought about by your abuse. It can cause—*what?*"

Waving my hands and shaking my head, I stopped her. "No, it's not that. It's the Succubus. Their power is residual. I know of someone who took a month to recover after five days of Layla's magic. She blasted me with it for eight fucking years." I looked down at the hands twitching in my lap. "This permanent boner of mine could take decades to dissipate. I have to learn to live with it."

I looked up at her, my eyes wet. "I lost the best thing that ever happened to me because of it. Phoebe finally gave up on me."

Maybe it was Darla's sympathetic look, I don't know, but tears came and wouldn't stop. I covered my face, sobbing into my hand. Darla's chair scraped across the floor, and she gently gripped my shoulder as she placed the Kleenex box on my lap.

"It's OK, Oliver. Go ahead and cry. It's part of healing," she whispered.

A puddle of pathetic later, I sucked in the last of my messy display and smiled at her, my face hot and puffy. "I'm sorry," I whispered.

She squeezed my shoulder. "Oliver, you have nothing to be sorry about. This is the first step. It's good news. Now, I can help you."

Our eyes met, her expression brittle. "Unfortunately, this is not the first time I've helped someone recover from sexual abuse. Recovering starts with letting go of the guilt. Your reaction to their physical stimulation was a biological and emotional response. Do you understand? You had no control. You can't blame yourself for any of it."

When I stared at her in surprise, she nodded. "You're incredibly brave, Oliver. You handled things the best you could for as long as you had to. You found a way to deal with your situation. It wasn't perfect; it's haunting you now. But you're still here. You're alive. And where there's life, there's hope. Remember that."

After Darla prescribed something to help me sleep and gave me some reading material, I left. Sharing with her lifted a suffocating weight from my shoulders. For the first time since my rescue, I felt hopeful.

As I trotted down the stairs and stepped into the darkness, downtown sprawled ahead, the bawdy racket of the bars stirring something inside of me. Key West nights hummed with excitement, and it was contagious.

CHAPTER 9

~ OLIVER ~

Invigorated, I headed back to the sailboat, changed into some clean clothes, and fired up my grill. I tried not to think about Munchies and being unable to relieve myself there. Those pointless thoughts stirred my panic. So I tucked Chubbers and grabbed a pan—because everything was better with bacon, even in the wee hours.

The scent of peaches and sunshine rose over the delicious smells in the kitchenette, and I saluted my ghost with greasy tongs.

"Greetings, friend. Feel free to show yourself anytime." No one answered. As I plunked the crispy goodness onto a plate, I had a real visitor.

A lamp post on the docks lit up the tall, athletic blonde male striding toward me like a muscular runway model. Startled to see him, I waved the Enforcer on board, and motioned down the ladder to the small kitchenette.

"What brings you here tonight?" I asked, sliding into the bench seat.

Gideon looked at my bracelet, his lips a firm line even though it glowed pink. I glanced at my wrist, wondering at his expression.

"I'm here to check on you and pay a visit to Phoebe. I felt a disturbance on Sugarloaf Key a few hours ago. I wondered if you knew anything about it." The Enforcer gave me a look that made my pulse race. I scratched at my itchy ear.

"Nope, nothing. Not sure why you think I'd know anything, but the answer is a big fat no."

After a long, quiet spell, Gideon sat back and put his hands behind his head, his open shirt showing off his eight-pack. He watched me intently as he spoke.

"Jovi and Felix reported odd things happening in the area. I wondered if you knew anything about them?" At my shrug, he continued.

"A few days ago, they killed a wolf shifter after he robbed a general store. Shifters are usually mellow, especially down here. We have no idea where he came from; he was bigger than usual for a wolf. It might be a random incident, but it has piqued my curiosity."

I raised my eyebrows—no mention of my involvement. Felix and Jovi kept my secret, which I appreciated. "I don't know what to tell you, Gideon."

Gideon stared into my eyes and said, "Darla mentioned your progress and suggested that staying busy might do you some good. I've had the Servus set up patrols to watch for suspicious activity around town. The Sovereign provided resources for a truck, but neither Jovi nor Felix knows how to drive."

"You want me to chauffeur them?" I rolled my eyes.

"Felix and Jovi like you. It is a good fit, and you need a distraction."

I realized he was right. When Phoebe made good on her threat and left, I'd lose my marbles.

"Fine. When do I start?"

Pulling some keys from his pocket, Gideon shoved them toward me. "Tomorrow. Your truck is in the parking lot, and Felix and Jovi are anxious to get going."

"And we'll be going where—?"

"Saddlebunch Key. I need the Servus to clear a residence there. We suspect rogue vampires have taken over a house and killed the owners. Lord Luther wants them brought in for punishment."

I swallowed. "Yeah, about that. I'm not exactly high on his list of favorites at the moment."

Gideon pinned me with a stare. "I am aware." At my nervous look, he said, "Let me deal with Luther."

***

At noon the next day, a strange excitement shot through my bloodstream, almost drowning the pain in my balls. I tucked my friend, fluffed my shirt, and headed up the jetty. When I jogged into the parking lot, I burst out laughing.

Standing next to a white Ford pickup were two fashion disasters. Felix and Jovi wore pink hightops, which would have been funnier had they not matched their blue and green legs so well. Both wore silver metallic button-down shirts opened to show their tanned chests. But the ball caps and sunglasses sent me into a laughing jag.

"*Uhh*. Guys. If you're trying to blend in, that's not how to do it."

Jovi scowled. "We picked out this clothing ourselves. It came highly recommended by the pretty salesgirl."

I rolled my eyes. "Let me guess. Was she young?"

Felix nodded. "Yes, a human youngling. She gave us these too, but we can't figure out how to wear them." He held up a handful of gold chains.

"She wanted us to pull our 'pants' lower and tried very hard to grab the top of our leg skins. It was difficult to dissuade her. I'm not sure what we would have done if she discovered they're permanent. We were almost revealed as *Other*," he said with an anxious frown.

"Well, unless you're into rap, you can leave those chains in the glove box. Let's go."

"What is this rap thing?" Jovi asked. He rummaged around in the glove box and pulled out a set of fake diamond grillz. "She sold us these as well. Are they to help us chew?" I choked when he slipped them over his teeth and grinned at me.

I put the truck in drive. "Rap is music. And you can put that bling in the glove box with the chains." I smiled all the way to Saddlebunch Key.

It was lunchtime because, well, *Vampires*. After driving forever down the desolate Old State Road and finding nothing but miles of mangroves and mosquitoes, we hit a dead end. I checked the address, wondering if we'd gotten it wrong.

After investigating, we found a house hidden by the mangroves. The two-story home overlooked Geiger Key, visible across the glowing turquoise water of the channel. The property appeared deserted but was too new and well-kept to be a seedy Vampire hole. I looked at my partners and swallowed another laugh at their clothing.

"OK, guys. Let's go poke around and see if anything flies out." I turned to see them already heading for the house. *Ok then*.

I followed the Servus across the dry, brittle scrub that passed for grass in the Keys. Darting across the spacious yard, we peered in the first window we came to. It was an empty garage filled with fishing rods, nets, and spare parts for what looked like an old Yamaha motor. Each window yielded the same results. There were typical signs of human life: laundry, a workout room, and an empty office. No one built main-floor living areas in the Keys because couches made great sponges during hurricanes.

The office told us all we needed to know. Blood. Lots and lots of blood. And a few bones—probably too big and crunchy for whatever ate the rest of the body. Something lurked in this house, but it wasn't a vamp. We retreated to the truck.

"This is bad, boys. Whatever is in there probably gives zero shits about the sun. We need to call Gideon."

Felix scowled. "We don't need the Gryphon's help. We will handle this." Felix reached over the seat and pulled a helmet from behind me. It was a metal hunk of ancient history, one of those medieval helmets with a "T" cut out for the eyes and leaving a strip of metal to cover the nose. A galloping horse embossed in gold adorned the sides of the clunky thing.

"What the hell is that!?" I snapped.

"It's a Barbute," Jovi said with a proud smile. "You don't remember? These were our helmets at the compound in Charleston. I wasn't a fan at first, but since the battle, I've become a believer." He removed his ball cap and glasses and slipped the clunky metal thing over his head.

My cheeks hurt when I saw the helmet next to his fashion faux-pas. "I'd lose the shirt," I damn near giggled. "You'll get blood on it."

With a shrug, the two Servus tossed their clothes through the truck window. I remembered nothing of the battle in Charleston. I was imprisoned in the basement beneath the library, so had no idea whether these males had any fighting skills or if they were clueless. This could go very badly.

"Gideon supplied us well," Jovi exclaimed, his face bright. Climbing into the truck bed, he opened a stainless job box behind the window and pulled out a smorgasbord of weapons. He started with throwing stars, then added three short swords, a short-handled pole ax, three knives, various leather sheaths—each piece landed on the crispy grass at my feet with a thump. I watched in horror, not being a weapons guy and all. When Jovi pulled out a bow and a quiver of arrows, I stopped him.

"What the hell do you plan on doing with that? If we find ourselves in this up to our butt holes, it's gonna be hand to hand, pal."

Jovi bit his lip, put the bow and arrow back in the job box, and pulled out three brass knuckles, his eyebrows raised in question. I nodded, and he jumped down, beaming.

"Do you guys know how to use these things?"

Felix paused, his silvery eye glowing back at me. "We're trained in the use of every weapon, excluding guns," he said, resuming the process of strapping the arsenal to his body.

"You don't know how to use guns." My expression flat, I resisted the urge to hang my jaw in shock.

Jovi frowned. "We were meant as ocean fighters. Hello, *tails?*" He slapped his rump, which made Felix laugh.

"The Medieval period fascinated our Benefactor—*uhh,* the demon."* Felix looked down, embarrassed. Loyal to a fault, he'd thrown the full weight of his support behind Hex until he learned the truth.

The demon loved metal helmets—and masks. The one in the lab. *The one they clamped over my face* before they …

Swallowing the lump in my throat, I shook it off and headed for the house. The Servus males followed. The sound of our feet crunching on the dried grass snapped me out of the ghostly memories.

"Let us go first, Djinn. We are properly trained for these situations." Felix straightened his helmet and pushed past me, the *fresh from the ocean* smell of his skin jolting me.

The same salty fragrance wafted through the vents to my basement prison, reminding me of Phoebe. We met on a beach. I would lay on my palette in constant darkness, sucking in the tangy scent as I imagined kissing her. Before I forgot what she looked like. Before I lost my mind. Before my cock became the center of everything. Almost a decade of unwilling sperm donation ...

I shook my head. The males I followed weren't my offspring. Their father was the Djinn before me—likely dead, now. I'd fathered kids in this world I would never meet. The oldest would be eight ... I stopped, staring at nothing.

When Jovi glanced over his shoulder, his green eyes flashing through the helmet slits, my mind cleared. I caught up as Felix's broad shoulders filled the doorway of the house, his bare feet silent as he stepped inside. Jovi slipped in behind him, the athletic curves of his chest slick with sweat. Their short swords flashed in the gloom of the stairway, their curled lips revealing sharp fangs that reminded me—being at the back was perfectly acceptable.

Streaks of blood painted the walls as we crept up the stairs; the sight turned my stomach. Luckily, the fear coursing through me subdued the beast in my shorts. I made a mental note for future reference.

I squeezed the sword's braided grip with sweaty hands. If bad things went down, I'd have to use my powers, but I would cross that bridge later. Glancing at the sharp blade, I wondered if I'd cut my hand off trying to use it.

Before we reached the top of the stairs, it was clear we weren't alone. The smell of rotting meat filled my nose, but the horror movie sounds were far worse. Something enjoyed an afternoon snack up there; I was terrified to meet it face-to-face.

Felix peered around the wall separating the stairs from the carpeted living room. He pulled back and, judging by Jovi's nods, a mental conversation passed between them. Jovi motioned for me to stay back, and the two charged into the room.

At the rippling snarls and wet thuds, curiosity overcame my fear, and I followed. In the middle of a blood-spattered living room stood a Volkswagen-sized creature straight out of Hades.

Completely hairless except for a tuft on his chin, the demon's bluish skin glistened with moisture. An oblong, scaled head sat on neckless shoulders, the thing's small pointed ears folded back against its skull. Overly long arms tied into a chest corded with muscle, his taloned hands as big as his head.

The creature's oddly short, muscled hindquarters ended in clawed feet, the shape of the thing reminding me of a hyena. Balancing on his hands and swinging his chimp-like ass, the hunched form was surprisingly quick.

The demon's snarling face bristled with a mouthful of fangs, its glittering eyes matching a glowing blue crystal embedded in his chest. It reminded me of the blue gem on the monster that Phoebe forced back into Hell. When the thing before me howled, every hair on my body vibrated from the rippling sound.

Felix and Jovi engaged the demon, their swords held defensively before them, their feet constantly moving. As they harried it from all sides, it pivoted on those odd back legs, swinging its arms to swipe at them. He still hadn't connected, but the beast was fast. My boys needed some help.

I didn't think it through. Pulling my arm over my head, I put my back into it and threw the short sword like a knife. It whooped end over end through the air, landing with a resounding slap against the thing's ribcage before falling to the floor.

Two metal helmets turned in my direction, and Felix snarled. Apparently, that was not an approved Servus technique; the creature took that moment to flee.

Humping down the hallway at top speed, it stayed ahead of Jovi and Felix as they barrelled after it.

Our demon took refuge in a small bedroom at the end of the hall. A bloody, half-eaten carcass filled a small bed cramming half the room. I resisted the urge to gag at the stench.

The monster slid to a stop then spun to watch us, his face splitting into a toothy grin. It was in the perfect position to defend, squatting in the ten-foot square patch of available space, with a closet on one side and a wall at its back.

Felix looked over his shoulder and growled. "Oliver, you should stay out of this fight."

"Thanks for sparing my feelings, buddy." I saluted him with my sword, which I'd picked up before following. Miscalculating, the ultra-sharp blade tapped my forehead and opened a gash that immediately bled into my eyes.

Jovi shook his head, then moved into the doorway with Felix, the pair planning their attack in light of the current situation. Jovi turned, brushed past me, and scampered back down the stairs.

The demon must have decided he liked the odds. He launched at the doorway, tackling the Servus at chest height and knocking us both to the floor. We formed a Felix sandwich for a few seconds, and I got a face full of stinking tongue before my defender recovered and jammed a sword into the creature's side.

The freaky thing screeched as it scrambled backward, raking its claws down Felix's chest before hissing back into the room. Without hesitation, Felix pressed forward, pinning the heavy demon against the wall and stabbing at it with his blade.

The monster's leathery arms deflected his blows; it barely bled. I cringed when it wrapped long claws around Felix's wrist and swung him over a shoulder, slamming him into the closet. The demon was on him in a second, Felix's legs jerking and twitching as the beast tore into him. I wanted to help but couldn't, the thing's oversized body filling the room. Felix screamed, and I panicked.

During the fight, I'd noticed a bald patch on the demon's scaley back—too high to reach—but if I used the bed …

"DAMMIT!" No way. I wasn't climbing into that pile of goo—

Above the thing's snarls, Felix's screams of anger turned to howls of pain. I closed my eyes and jumped onto the mangled cadaver covering the bed. I promptly fell on my ass.

Ignoring the stench and my sopping clothes, I put my hand into the glop and pushed to my feet. Swaying over the demon's writhing body, I turned my sword and stabbed downward.

My hands slipped on the slimy sword, the tip glancing sideways. I tried again, but halfway through the second strike, cold, blue eyes stared into my face. Right. The head could turn 180 degrees. Good to know.

I swallowed, ready to go for the eyes. Before I could move, an arrow smacked through the thing's skull, the sharp point coming out the other side. A piece of brain dangled from the tip. Eyes rolling, the creature fell backward with a crash.

Jovi popped his head inside the bedroom with a triumphant shout. His tanned chest covered in scratches, Felix sat up in the closet, the dead beast pinning him down. I turned and heaved my breakfast onto the slippery pile beneath me, then promptly lost my footing and fell ass-first into it.

As labored pants filled the room, I gave up on moving, the sour stew soaking through my clothes. What did pukey glutes matter now?

Jovi and Felix looked at each other and roared, laughing so hard that tears poured. Jovi stepped forward and, with minimal effort, pulled the six-hundred-pound monster from his friend's lap. They turned to me, doubling over with laughter at my predicament.

"Funny. Very funny. Can you help me up?" Jovi reached out and dragged me from my slimy predicament, and we all retreated to the untainted air of the hallway.

When their mocking laughter faded and they wiped their tears away, Felix put his hand on my shoulder and said, "Oliver, you're very lucky we were trained to fight.

And don't take this personally, but next time, would you mind staying in the truck?"

CHAPTER 10

~ OLIVER ~

Thankfully, the house was on the ocean, and the three of us cleaned the gore off before getting in the truck. As I waded to my neck and scrubbed my clothes, I watched a pod of dolphins slip past. The biggest adult peeked at me with one dark, suspicious eye before diving, slapping its tail in warning.

"Yeah, you're a good judge of character, big fella." I rubbed my hand over my scruff as I watched them head out to sea.

Phoebe and I met in Savannah, spending time on the beach there. She went mental at the sight of the curious cetaceans. She'd run into the surf with a huge grin on her face, hoping that one would come closer. It never happened, and I vowed to take her to swim with dolphins one day. That never happened either.

Agony tore through my chest like a cannonball, and I slammed the door on the memory. My face flamed as I plodded from the ocean onto the sand. Jovi and Felix waited for me.

"Are you alright, Oliver?" Jovi scanned my face. "Were you injured?"

I shook my head. "Nothing visible, anyway. Let's get back. Is that the gemstone?"

Felix opened his hand, the intricate blue facets appearing dull in the sunshine. "It seemed important, so I cut it out for Gideon. I checked through the house. I don't think the demon has been there long."

"The creature turned to ash and disappeared when Felix took the gem." Jovi frowned. "Someone will have to clean up that cadaver, though."

Sighing, I wrung out my shirt and slipped it back on. "Yeah, that sounds like a Gideon problem. Where do I drop you guys off? Do you have an apartment or something?"

"A ride back to your marina would be helpful. Jovi and I sleep on the beach of a mangrove island in the Gulf of Mexico. Every day, droves of human females come in boats, take off their clothing, and frolic in the water. We keep an eye on them. For Gideon." He blushed when Jovi rolled his eyes.

After parking the truck near Garrison Bight, I waved goodbye, and the Servus males trotted down the street. I smiled, remembering my own energetic youth, and headed to my slip.

Gideon picked up the 40' Nordic for me to live in after selling the Spectre yacht they confiscated from Hex. As I approached the sailboat, I frowned at the bright gold letters emblazoned across the transom.

Every time I saw the name, I cracked a sweat. *Caught in the Wind* certainly depicted my current status. With a sigh, I climbed aboard, heading straight for the fridge. I got a surprise when I noticed a note pinned to it. I recognized the writing, and my chest constricted as I read it.

"Oliver. I owe you an apology. This doesn't change anything between us, but I know you didn't sleep with Polly. You know what they say about assuming. By the time you receive this note, I'll be on a bus home. I'm sorry for everything. I hope you find a way to live free and be happy. Love, Phoebe."

Staring at the paper in my hand, a tidal wave of grief hit me like a fist to the gut. I wheezed, covering my eyes and rubbing. How the hell did she know about Polly? When was she on the boat? I looked around, but nothing was out of place. I stuck the note back on the fridge as a reminder of my many failures.

"Where did we go wrong, Pheebs?" I whispered. Grabbing the bottle of cheap whisky from the fridge, I headed for my chair on the bow. As I sat there, sipping my drink and letting the sun burn me to a crisp, I struggled to breathe through the vice clamped around my chest.

Darla, Gideon, even Phoebe—they all said to give myself time. My time had come and gone. I was surprised Phoebe lasted this long.

***

~ PHOEBE ~

As the Greyhound pulled onto Highway 1, I struggled to hold back tears. In my heart, I knew I'd done my best and chasing after Oliver was a foolish use of time, energy, and emotion. I might be the same, but he was different now. How could he not be? And it certainly wasn't his fault.

Watching him self-destruct meant living with crippling fear. Would I find him dead on his boat one day? The threat was real, especially now that he wasn't focused on killing everything in sight. Having time to think wasn't a good thing for Oliver.

My thoughts went to his pink wristband. Oliver's Djinn magic had been out of control the night we rescued him. I quickly warded him into one of the rooms in the hold of the Spectre. I hated doing it, but it was for everyone's safety.

I had a cheap gold bracelet with me, and later, I fed power into it from my ring. I planned to use it once we freed him from the holding room. The room Hex used to torture creatures.

Memories assaulted me of our battle in Charleston. The night his polar bear saved so many lives. The night our forces defeated the demon, and we found Oliver.

***

~ THE SPECTRE ~

As the luxury yacht powered toward home, the Spectre left a living hell in its wake. For twenty years, the now-decimated lab had produced hybrid Djinn-Syreni crosses to take over the world. A grand scheme brought to life by a demon named Hex, it took our combined forces and a handful of defectors to overthrow the entrenched and well-trained military force.

The moans of our injured drifted from the medical rooms in the lower hallway of the yacht. Gideon stealing the vessel for the assault had been a brilliant play, with plenty of room to manage the aftermath of the battle.

Many of our allies died in combat, the Gryphon Enforcer narrowly escaping with his life. It was not all bad news, though. We won. We rescued one tortured soul—if that's what you called it.

Crouched facing the corner in his room, his arms over his head, the Oliver I loved was gone. In his place was a ruined shell—a dangerous one. The wards I'd laid around the doors and windows glowed a faint pink, a silly part of me thinking the color might cheer him up when—if— he came to his senses.

When the sedative that subdued his bear form wore off, Oliver scrambled into the corner and stayed there. Naked and squatting on his heels, the position exposed a small sample of what those bastards had done to him— thickly scarred letters covered his buttocks: S, H, L, C, B, and one I couldn't attach to his abusers—*"Y."*

Whip scars thatched the pale skin of his back, the blood of his enemies covered him, and his incoherent words rocked me with every garbled syllable. He had no idea who I was; his eyes didn't focus. When he did make eye contact, a rare occurrence, Oliver didn't "see" me. And his erection—my God, we still didn't know what that was all about.

My wards were a precaution so he didn't mist out and go on a killing spree. It wasn't safe to be on the same vessel with him, let alone in the same room. Felix and Jovi recounted their visit to him in the bowels of the facility, and it hadn't been good news. Djinn were notoriously unstable even in good situations. Oliver's mind had broken. Even his captors went to great lengths to keep him secure.

Luckily, we hadn't seen his polar bear since it saved our asses in Charleston. That would have ended badly for everyone on the Spectre. A Koala appeared for a few hours, but Oliver's soft and placid creature stayed curled up and unmoving in the corner until his human body gradually reappeared.

I called for help when Oliver roused and went berserk. His face lit with fury as he attacked the reinforced windows of the medical room, smashing his face on the glass and smearing blood all over it. Coming to my aid, Eddi's friend Cal pored over the breaker panel to the sound of Oliver's forehead slamming on the glass.

I was useless, holding back sobs as I watched Oliver destroy himself. At that moment, I realized my fairytale ending had burned to dust alongside the lab that did this to him.

A clever Octopus shifter, Cal found the breaker, and Oliver's room plunged into darkness. Keeping a careful eye on the reinforced glass, he brought a blanket to cover the window, and the roars stopped. My stomach never recovered. To this day, the sight of blood made me nauseous.

All these years, I thought everything would be wonderful if I could find him. We would pick up right where we left off. *Naive idiot.* Our relationship sank before it ever left the harbor. A bitter laugh burned my throat when I realized the pink didn't help.

***

When the bus parked at the Post Office in Big Pine Key, I shook off the memories and stepped outside for fresh air. As the driver loaded suitcases for the new passengers, I looked over the old stone post office. Tucked neatly beside a pretty yellow building with white shutters and gorgeous palms decorating the gardens, the two buildings blended old and new—typical for the Keys.

I looked around, but saw nothing, too busy holding back tears at leaving the most beautiful place in the country. Was I being hasty? Elli said she could handle the shop fine. Was I making a stupid decision? As a desperate gloom settled over me, I heard my name. I looked around the parking lot.

"Phoebe!"

I turned, my heart nearly pounding out of my chest. "Gabriel? What are you doing here?"

"Getting my mail. Where are you going? I'm so happy to see you, but ..." He looked at the bus. *"You're leaving?"*

I nodded, and when tears tracked down my cheeks, he pulled me into his arms for a fierce hug. His breath tickled my ear. "What's wrong, luv?"

As I shook my head, the concerned look on his face opened the floodgates. There was no stopping the tears. "I have to get back on my bus," I sobbed.

"NO. You are *not* getting back on that bus." The look on his face was a mix of frustration and fear. "You can't leave yet. I'm not ready to let you go. I'll pay for your replacement ticket. Stay. *Please.*"

With a wet laugh, I dabbed my red face with the tissue he offered. "I have to go. I hate to, but I've been gone for a while. I keep worrying about work."

"Don't you have someone helping you back in Augusta? What was her name—Elli?"

I nodded, and Gabriel gave me a toothy grin. "See!? It's settled. You can stay another week and go home then. Augusta is what, ten hours away? That's not even half a day."

My heart melted at his grin. God he was handsome—and a master manipulator, too. Gabe smelled defeat, and turned on the charm.

"Won't the grind keep for a *teensy bit* longer? I planned to take you sailing to the Marquesas. In fact, I was heading to your apartment next." He winked. "Meeting you here was fate. And I've even got a place you can stay free of charge."

Holy shit. He wasn't kidding. And the Marquesas … wow.

"You're serious?" I opened my mouth, then closed it. Maybe he was right. I had exactly zero *me* time while I was in the Keys. I'd spent the entire visit chasing after Oliver. A commercial sail to the Marquesas cost thousands.

Saving money was smart, right? I ignored the cold sweat coating my neck as I teetered on the razor edge of a hasty decision. Someone coughed, and the bus driver sent me a sympathetic look.

"I'm sorry ma'am but the bus is leaving. Are you coming?"

"No, she isn't." Gabriel grabbed my hand and hauled me to the steps. "Can you find her luggage for me, please?"

The bus driver smiled. He must have been sentimental because he reopened the belly panels and hauled out my bag, then ran inside and grabbed my purse for me. "Glad to see young love getting a chance. Ma'am." With a tip of his cap, he jogged up the stairs, and with a loud hiss, the bus pulled away.

I wasn't sure why I stood there letting Gabe railroad me. I should have been on that bus. The Florida Keys had that effect on people, though. Gabriel taking control felt good for a change. I got along so well with him. Staying felt—*right*.

"Now what?" I asked. "That bus just drove away with most of the funds left in my account." At my misty smile, Gabe took me by the shoulders.

"Don't you worry. It'll cost you zero dollars. You'll stay at my rental. I work all day with some late nights, so I'll stay at our satellite office to give you some privacy. It won't work permanently, but it should buy me a week to convince you I'm the only man for you."

He said it with a wry smile, but damn, it was so hot I almost threw my arms around his neck and told him no waiting would be necessary.

"A drink?" he asked, his face beaming. At my smile, Gabriel grabbed my hand, and as he trucked me down the sidewalk, I asked, "Why do you pick up your mail in Big Pine if you're staying in Key West?"

He shrugged. "When I first arranged to stay down here, I had a place lined up in Big Pine. It fell through, and the boss sprung for a hotel in Key West. I never bothered to change the mailbox." He shot me an award-winning smile. *"Thank goodness!"*

I laughed, and the sinking ship in my stomach bobbed to the surface with a splash. Damn the torpedoes, I'd figure this out later—after I enjoyed a bit of undivided male attention. For a brief moment, I felt guilty and shameless. Then, fun, spontaneous Phoebe pushed her stick-in-the-mud twin off the dock.

Luckily, the Big Pine Grill next door was air-conditioned. As Gabe pulled me into a small back room and settled me at a pine table, I fluffed my favorite blue sundress and my emotional trauma melted away. Plunking himself down on the bench seat opposite me, Gabriel looked exhausted. He reached out and took my hand in his.

"I shouldn't have done that, but I'm not sorry, Phoebe. I saw you standing next to the bus and got quite a shock when I put it together. Something came over me. I couldn't let you leave."

The worried frown on his face made me wonder if I misjudged the depth of his feelings. I had no idea he'd become so invested in whatever we had going on.

"I'm glad," I said, glancing at the menu. "Suddenly, I'm famished. I couldn't eat this morning. I'll be honest and tell you, I really didn't want to leave."

He laughed. "Have whatever you like. My treat."

When the waitress brought my Cobb salad, Gabriel grilled me on what I'd been up to. He was human, so I had to think carefully before answering.

"I've been … " I bit my lip. Shoot. What the hell could I tell him? "*Uhh* … I might open a new shop. It's very trendy."

"A shop. What sort of shop?"

"I'm embarrassed to say. It's a metaphysical shop."

"Like Witches and Warlocks, spells and hexes?" His eyebrows disappeared into his hairline.

I blushed. "Yes. Something like that. I own a store in Augusta." At the look on his face, I rushed to add, "It's very popular! People love having trinkets to pull out at cocktail parties—and many believe witchcraft is real. You'd be shocked, actually."

Reaching out, he took my hand in his. "Phoebe, if you're a Witch, I'm sure you're a very good one. Hell, if you were a werewolf, I'd still have lunch with you." His sincere look sent heat through me, and I melted.

After a snack and a few cocktails, Gabe paid the bill, and we left the restaurant, the blast furnace of the afternoon hitting hard after the cool restaurant. Lifting my face to the sun, I marveled that I was still in the Keys. I could stay. Ethereal happiness bubbled inside me.

We returned to the Post Office, and he stopped, rubbing his chin. His eyes darted around the parking lot. "Shit," he said, scowling.

"What's wrong?" I followed his gaze, and when he headed to the payphone, I knew something was up. "Is everything alright?"

"I forgot my cell phone." He motioned at the empty parking space. "And they towed me," he said, turning red. "I'll call a cab."

"Why would they tow you from here? It's a public lot!"

He pointed at the fire hydrant before us. "I didn't see *that* when I parked, is why."

"Welcome to my nightmare," I grumped. "My life is full of nasty surprises these days."

After he made the call, Gabe pulled me into the shade of some palms, and his arms slid around me.

"You don't mind, do you? I need a hug—for my wounded pride," he joked.

I squeezed him and pressed my cheek to his chest. "Consider yourself supported."

He murmured into my ear, "You're one of those women who puts everyone else first, aren't you?"

"So I've been told."

***

"Phoebe, I'm sorry, but I have a prior engagement," Gabe said. "I'll leave you here to get settled, is that alright? I'll be back this evening, and we'll have a drink on the patio bar—if that works for you?"

I smiled. "Of course. I'm sorry to take you from your work."

With a hug, he slipped out, leaving the key on the accent table near the door. As far as hotels went, this one was pretty posh. When we first arrived, he'd taken me to the small lobby bar, ordered me a wine, and spoke to the front desk about our arrangements. As I looked around at the bar's delicate accents and brass fittings, I realized Gabe's boss must have been loaded to afford this place. Key West was hella expensive.

After he left for work, I ran a bath in the white clawfoot tub, enjoying a long soak while trying to figure out my next move. It wouldn't hurt that I left my apartment with the pretty red door behind. If she hunted me, Sybil would look there first and assume I'd left town. I'd have to be careful on the street, but she'd never find me tucked away in Gabriel's hotel. Lady luck must have decided I needed a break.

As I sponged verbena-scented bubbles over my arms, I thought about Oliver. Leaving the Keys for good was the only way to let him go. Would I have the resolve to steer clear now that I'd returned?

I groaned. I'd made my decision. Oliver wouldn't care. That much was clear. But I was pretty sure Gabe wouldn't appreciate my ex being in town. Or that being near him was the reason I moved to the Keys in the first place. I needed to tell him about Oliver. It was the right thing to do.

***

The pretty burgundy dress clung to my curves as the ocean breeze whispered through the palms on the terrace. The table was perfect, the faerie lights a lovely touch. Tucked in a corner, it had an incredible ocean view, and the full moon lit the water all the way to the horizon. Gabriel, as always, was the perfect gentleman.

"So you're telling me your ex-boyfriend is in town, you've called it quits, and that's why you're leaving?"

"Well, that's a summary, but yes." I couldn't elaborate without dropping the *paranormal* bombshell.

"Oliver is a troubled male … man. He's gone through some terrible things. I loved him with all my heart, but now, he's someone different. I tried to reach him, but it didn't happen. I hate to dump this on you, but I thought I should tell you the truth. I would have told you sooner, but we weren't—*it didn't seem the right time*. I'm sorry."

Gabe mulled over my words as he watched the ocean, but when he looked my way, he smiled. "Fair enough. I did steamroll over you this afternoon. It's me who should apologize."

My mouth opened and closed. How I'd found the world's most forgiving man was beyond me. Laughter bubbled up in response to his soft, happy expression. Light-hearted was good. Fun times, and no brooding in sight.

"Would you like to go dancing?" I asked.

"I'm not much of a dancer, unfortunately."

Laughing at his pinched expression, I said, "It's ok. Oliver couldn't dance either. It doesn't matter, though. It's not that sort of dancing. Get drunk and jump up and down. You'll fit right in."

"Fine, but if I step on your toes, I did warn you."

The club down the street was new, with a nice mix of music, playing everything from country pop to hard rock. The lighting, decorations, and an open dance floor had a modern country chic feel. It was an instant hit with my date.

The drinks flowed, the music was perfect, and my partner danced much better than he'd let on. Soon, I was breathless, smiling and laughing at his jokes and snuggling close for the slower dances.

This patio looked over the ocean as well, and with a happy buzz from the dancing and drinks, we stepped outside to enjoy the view. Standing at the railing, the breeze cooled my flushed face. As we watched the sparkling ocean, Gabe stepped closer, slipping an arm over my shoulders.

"If there was one thing you could change in your life, what would it be?" I asked him.

He thought about it, then turned to me, lifting a strand of my long hair and staring at it. Mesmerized, he rubbed his fingers over it, then tucked it behind my ear as he spoke.

"Like you, I once had a partner I cared for very much. Life pulled us apart. Soon, we were like strangers and couldn't return to where we'd started. I always felt that if things hadn't come between us, we'd have been happy together. I vowed never to let that happen again. And here you are." The dazzling smile he gave me took my breath away.

"Good answer," I whispered, and when he pulled me closer, I sank into his arms.

His breath dusted my cheeks, the familiar scent of his cologne a tease to my senses. My lips parted under his, and his tongue dipped to taste me, my response eager. Our lips explored as his hands dipped low to smooth over my hips, the subtle squeeze of his fingers on my buttocks pulling me closer. I leaned in, pressing my breasts against his chest, and he moaned.

"Phoebe. The things you do to me." Panting, Gabriel pulled back, his hooded eyes sweeping over my lips. With a sigh, he kissed me again. I wrapped my hands behind his neck, my fingers tickling the hair at his nape and making him shudder.

His hips pushed closer, the urgent swell of his arousal sending heat through me. I moaned against his lips, my mind drifting as he showed me what he wanted, pulling me tightly against his thickening shaft.

Oliver drifted into my thoughts, his expression haunted. Something inside of me snapped and, breathless, I pulled back to look into Gabriel's eyes. Confusion marred his perfect features, and his sad look startled me.

"I'm so sorry. I can't." Grabbing my purse, I ran.

"Phoebe, *wait!*"

His footsteps tracked me, but I kept going, bursting out the front doors and onto the sidewalk. I hightailed it toward the hotel two blocks away. Heavy feet pounded down the pavement behind me, and before I got far, I felt a hand on my wrist. He pulled me to a stop and turned me to face him.

"What's wrong! *Tell me.*" His eyes roamed over my face, concerned, affectionate, and a tad frustrated. "What happened?"

"I can't. *He's still … I'm just …* Oh my God, this was a mistake." I covered my eyes and sobbed. "I still love him." Tears poured down my face. Gabe tried to pull me into a hug, but I resisted, pushing him away.

"God help me. He's a disaster, I'm a disaster, this whole freaking thing is a disaster!" I threw my hands in the air. "I'm an idiot. I hurt him, and now I've hurt you. I'm so sorry! What the hell was I thinking?"

I tried to shake off his hand, but Gabe stopped me, his expression tender.

"Phoebe, it's alright. I'm not a child. I assumed you were … *entangled*. When I stopped you at the bus today, I didn't care. I wanted to spend time with you. Can't we just share some fun? Maybe things will change. You might get over him, and then we can move forward. I know it's a dumb idea, but I can't stand the thought of losing you."

Looking into his face, I saw that he was sincere. The man was a saint. I wiped my eyes on the back of my hand and whispered, "I don't think I can."

"Listen," he said. "We'll take you to the hotel, get you settled, and I'll head back to the office. I'll give you some space, and we can meet for dinner tomorrow. Would you like that?"

I bit my lip. Time. Didn't it always come down to time?

"Tomorrow," I sighed. "That's a good idea. I need to decide what I'm doing. I'm so confused. I appreciate all you've done for me. We'll figure it out over dinner tomorrow—minus the drinks. Those didn't help whatsoever," I laughed, my eyes glistening.

"Good idea," he said, taking my hand.

CHAPTER 11

~ OLIVER ~

It was late, and Felix and Jovi stood beside me after hauling me to the beach to wait for Gideon. Their constant *protection* frustrated the hell out of me. Before they showed up, I enjoyed my self-medicated solitude. I sighed. At least they entertained me. As we waited in the darkness, I couldn't help laughing when Felix tried using the waterproof phone Gideon gave them.

His face lit by the glow of the screen, Felix growled at the device, cursing, then squeezed until the plastic creaked. When he snarled and pulled his arm behind his head as if to toss it into the ocean, I stepped forward to help, but the air stirred around us. Gideon had arrived.

The inky darkness hid the Gryphon until he landed on the sand with a thump, his wings cupping as he appeared from nowhere. I would never get used to his surprise appearances or the golden shine in his eyes that always made my brain itch. He was a game player, our Enforcer. When a familiar buzz rasped between my ears, I tried not to think about my powerless bracelet—just in case.

Gideon wasted no time. *"The demon you killed was a Charun—a guardian from the gates of Hell. We know little about the gemstone, but it is found only on a Charun demon. The theory is that the blue gem preserves their life, allowing them to breathe in the corners of hell without oxygen."*

"How does a demon wind up on the human plane?" Jovi asked.

"Witches call demons with a summoning circle. A creature that size would require something large to manifest in this dimension. A gateway—nearly impossible without a significant amount of power."

My legs turned to rubber. A gateway. Like the one at the Bat Tower. I remembered the severed arm and realized it resembled the monstrous front legs of the demon we killed at Saddlebunch Key.

"So. About these gateways. Are they permanent, or do they disappear?" I asked, biting my nail.

"Once a gateway opens, it doesn't close unless the practitioner reverses the spell, and it takes far more power to close them. I've seen up to five witches struggle to close a portal; in one case, they failed. Every Witch died, and many more when the demons poured into our world without resistance. It took a demi-god to shut the breach."

"Holy shit," I breathed. What the hell did Phoebe get herself into? Was the Bat Tower gateway still open?

Gideon cocked his head. *"Hiding a secret, Oliver?"*

I rubbed at the buzzing behind my ear. "Nope. Just curious, that's all." When I'd inspected the site in the aftermath, energy still hummed around the tear. That freaking gateway was probably still open. Did Sybil intend to use it again?

Gideon's long slender ears swiveled forward as if listening. "*We have someone looking at the gemstone now, although information about the Charun is scarce. On a more positive note, the carcass wasn't human. It was half a cow, and it's been cleaned up. The human homeowners returned from vacation none the wiser.*"

"You think someone was feeding it, then?" It made sense to me.

Gideon nodded his regal head. *"That demon wasn't there by accident. Someone put it there."* His giant golden eyes blinked as he cocked his head at me. The buzzing whispered away and I rubbed the inside of one ear. The Enforcer's power made me damned uncomfortable.

While Gideon spoke with the two Servus, I wandered down the beach. Felix's eyes followed me as he listened to whatever internal conversation went on between the trio. I wasn't imagining it, then. Gideon had appointed them as babysitters.

I thought about the horrifying creature I'd seen at Saddlebunch. No wonder Phoebe decided to leave. She wasn't just afraid of Sybil Metroyer. Somehow, she knew what was on the other side of that gateway.

After giving my pals the slip, I enjoyed a few hours of freedom before heading back to the sailboat. As the darkness closed in around me, restlessness gripped my mind. Phoebe cut me loose to fend for myself, and the Servus were out in the Gulf enjoying the moonlight together. Desperation licked at my senses, every muscle pulling tight. I was alone, and it hurt like hell.

Well, if you didn't count the throbbing pain in my groin. It had been days since I'd found relief. Every time I closed my eyes, I pictured Phoebe, and my God, thinking about her tore holes in me. It would be dawn in a few hours, but I still had time. I downed my drink and headed to Munchies.

Stan met me at the door, his stony lips grinding together. "Oh no, you don't. Lord Luther told me if I let you in again, I would be looking for a new job."

"Just a drink, Stan. Please? I'll stay out of The Dark Room, I promise."

"I don't believe you, Oliver. I'm sorry. I like my job."

With a sigh, I turned to leave. Stan sniffled, and I turned back to see him pull a butterfly out of a small wooden box.

"What's that, Stan?"

"My finest lady Phoebe gave it to me. It plays music," he sighed, holding the fluttering blue wings up to his ear. "She's wonderful. If I had a female like her, I'd find us a cathedral and never let her go," he sighed.

His words slid through me like a hot poker. I spun on my heels, picked up the largest bottle of whisky I could find at Handy's, then headed back to the beach.

I plopped down on the sand after I was sure Gideon and the Servus were long gone. It took me until sunrise to finish the bottle, but I did.

I lay back on the sand drowning in desperation and sorrow. I was too drunk to feel the pain between my legs, but it worsened the ache in my chest. Phoebe abandoned ship. She didn't want to see me again. I curled into a ball and sobbed, finally dozing off.

When I woke up, I wasn't on the beach. The cool damp chill of being underground filtered through the haze of the alcohol. My head pounded, and my throat was so dry my tongue stuck to the roof of my mouth.

With a groan, I sat up, inky darkness and the musty basement smell yanking me back to reality with a horrifying swell of nausea. Something metallic scraped along the ground between my legs. The cold sensation of metal around my wrists registered, and I froze. I didn't have to investigate further to know I had metal handcuffs around my wrists.

Closing my eyes, I called on my power. It didn't answer. Beneath the cuffs, my bracelet glowed the usual bright pink in the dark, but someone had recharged it.

A band tightened around my chest, cutting off my air. *I can't breathe. I can't fucking breathe!*

My eyes bulged, panic stampeding through me. Scrambling to my feet, I twisted my wrists, back and forth, yanking on the handcuffs in a wild-eyed frenzy. When that didn't work, I gathered a fistful of the thin chain and pulled like a madman, jerking until blood slicked my wrists.

It was useless. The pain stalled me out. Blinded, panting, and numb, I blinked at the wall of black around me. My mind whirled into a vortex of despair, and I whimpered, my chest heaving. Seconds turned to minutes. I stared at nothing.

Then I snapped with a jaw-cracking roar. Renewing the attack on my bindings, my pants and whines peppered the void. *Charleston. I was back in Charleston. I'd never escape. This was it.*

After twenty minutes, I ran out of steam, my chest a rasping bellows. The alcohol kicked back in, and I slumped to the ground, curling into a ball. That was how Sybil found me when she opened the door.

"I see you're awake." She slid me a plate with some food, then shoved over a gallon of water. "I suggest you drink this."

As she turned to leave, I scratched out, "Why?"

She paused in the doorway. "I need your Witch friend. Using you is the only way to get her here. You're a dangerous creature, Oliver, and I'm certainly no fool. Your restraints are a precaution."

"You're wasting your time. Phoebe went back to Augusta." I snarled. "She's gone and you can't touch her." The room spun on its axis.

Sybil laughed, a long, low sound that grated on my nerves. "Oh, she hasn't left. She's still here, and she's going to help me finish what I started."

As the door clicked shut, leaving me in utter darkness, something inside of me broke. Diving into the shadowy place beneath my skin, I disappeared into myself.

***

~ PHOEBE ~

Dark circles lined my eyes when I looked in the mirror. Morning had come and gone; I'd eaten breakfast, and nervous, I waited for Gabriel's return. He had my business card, but I never asked for his contact information. I would have to leave and hope he understood my reasons. It was time to head home. He knew it. Even Oliver knew it. The only one who took too long to figure it out was me.

My phone dinged. I opened it expecting to see a text from Gabriel. What I got was an image of Oliver. I gasped, my hand going to my mouth.

Handcuffs bound his wrists, and a long, thin chain snaked between his legs. He appeared to be asleep, but the image sickened me. When I read the accompanying text, white obscured my vision.

Meet me at the Bat Tower at dusk, or he's dead.

I paced back and forth across the room. Panic, anger, fear, back to panic—around and around, my mind raced in circles. Finally, it screeched to a halt.

Oliver was in trouble, and it was all my fault. He hadn't recovered from his last trauma, and now—I ran to the bathroom, my breakfast returning with a vengeance. I washed my face and sat down to stare into space.

Who would I call for help? Gideon? He terrified me. And he'd probably kill me for not reporting the tear, even though it was an honest mistake. I couldn't call Jovi or Felix because they would tell Gideon. Gabriel was human.

I briefly considered pleading to Stan, hoping Oliver's vamp friends might assist. But then I'd expose even more *Others* to danger. No, I created this mess. I would fix it myself.

Rotating my gold ring, I heaved a relieved sigh when my fingertips tickled at the power in it. The rest had recharged it. I sent a silent prayer of thanks to my Father for teaching me how to use it properly.

Oliver needed me. This was my fault. I gathered my things, left a note on the table for Gabe, and headed out the door, hauling my suitcase behind me. I had enough money for a rental car; after that, I'd find a way home.

Sybil outpowered me, but she wouldn't outsmart me. I'd been practicing my offensive spells while lounging in luxury. I was ready for her this time, and now she'd pissed me off. No one fucked with my people.

***

As I pulled up to the Bat Tower site, the sun set a bright orange. Sybil waited, her head high, her radiant skin dark against the coming twilight. If I thought she was powerful before, she was on fire with energy now.

"You're still angry about our little incident, I see." I sent her a snide smile. With not much more than guts and a death wish, I figured I might as well go all in.

Sybil didn't move. Her stillness unnerved me, and I fought the desire to fill the space with empty words. After several minutes of heated stares, I broke first.

"Are you aware that the Djinn you slapped in cuffs was recently rescued from years of torture by demons? Being my romantic partner when he disappeared, you'll *forgive* me for taking your little scheme personally. And for the record, releasing more monsters into the world is complete *fucking* insanity."

"I have my reasons. And the bindings are a precaution." Her voice was flat. Calm. *Chilling*.

That riled me. "Is destroying everyone around you part of the power generation you have going on there?" I circled my finger in her direction. "Because if it is, you will rot in hell, *Sybil*."

Her lips squeezing together, the Witch finally moved. She pointed at the remnants of the four daisies and said, "You'll help me open the gate, or your friend will die. Those are my terms."

"Yeah, well, screw you and your terms, *bitch!*" I hissed and ran straight at her.

Surprised, Sybil took a step back before reacting. Too late. I threw my hand at her, and a marble-sized ball of magic flew at her face, detonating as it reached her. Powder glittered through the air, coating her in a fine dust.

"Incendio!" I screamed, and a flash bang ripped through the air, her skin lighting up like the fourth of July. Sybil's lips moved, and the flames went out with a hiss.

It didn't matter because the next spell piggybacked the first. I tucked and rolled, closing the space between us, came up with another handful of fun and threw it.

"Duratus!" Ice crackled over her skin, surprising her. I leapt up, using the precious seconds I had to get closer. She snarled, and the ice melted, steam rising into the air as Sybil started toward me, her hands out.

Ok. Shock-and-awe was fun. Time to close the deal. I had three yards left to go, and I roared toward her, my fingers rubbing together as I cast through tight lips. Three steps, my fury fueling the fireball in my mind—

I grabbed my ring and, with a twist, launched my spell. It hit her so hard that the fine braids dangling from her head blew back with a crackle of power so fierce that they straightened behind her, suspended in the air. Everything froze. The only thing that moved were her eyes.

Panting, I rasped, "I knew you were trouble the minute I met you. Let's just say I've been practicing. Now, tell me where Oliver is."

Sybil's eyes narrowed, and I swear she laughed at me beneath her frozen face. Nervous energy tickled across my scalp. "Tell me where he is, and I won't kill you."

All my life, I'd been a pacifist. I hated weapons. But seeing what happened to Oliver changed me. Every day, anger simmered beneath my skin over what those bastards had done to the male I loved. I couldn't help him, but I could burn for him.

So when I pulled out the filet knife I'd nicked off a fishing boat on my way here, something dangerous roared to life inside me. Sybil's eyes widened. I held the blade to her throat and hissed through gritted teeth—"You have three seconds."

Our eyes were inches apart, so close that my gasping pants moved the stray hairs on her scalp at every breath. When she didn't answer, I pressed the knife tighter to her throat. "NOW."

Sybil reached up, her hand closing around my wrist. Her braids dropped, swinging back around her neck with a soft series of clicks. She smiled.

"Nice try." She squeezed so hard that something popped in my wrist, and I dropped the knife. "Help me open the gate, and I'll spare both of you."

Letting go of my wrist, Sybil stalked to her car. She opened the door and pulled a familiar lump from the backseat. Bound and gagged, his bracelet glowing softly against his wrist, Oliver tumbled to the ground and his eyes found mine.

I'd seen that wild-eyed stare before. Before Oliver got better, and learned to control his rage. Before our love stretched so far that it shattered into microscopic pieces. I laughed in Sybil's face.

"Well, you better hope he doesn't get loose. Because you don't have what it takes to stop what's boiling inside his head right now. You may have unleashed a monster with your *precautions.*" I spat the last word at her.

Oliver shoved himself backward, leaning against the car's side panel, his breath whistling in and out through his nostrils. A pang of guilt clanged through me for getting him into this, but I didn't have time to think about it. As Sybil pulled her tools from the car, I did a mental tally of what I had left for power in my ring and my core. It wasn't much, but it might be enough.

Sybil's angry glares were the only difference between this shitstorm and the last, but the results were quicker. The tear was still there, covered by a thin scab of reality. Sybil began chanting and smudging, and the long, thin slit soon appeared. The glowing blue rope spread vertically, shockingly bright against the night sky. It was a strange sight now that I had time to look at it.

"*Now,* Ms. Peregrin. Or have you forgotten the hazards?"

I hissed my spell through clenched teeth, and the fiery blue slit stopped expanding, hovering a foot above the ground once more. The world rumbled around us, and the tear gaped wide, a clawed hand appearing, followed closely by an ugly head covered in grayish-blue scales. Its small pointed ears hugged its skull as it snarled, glowing blue eyes peering around the clearing.

Keeping one eye on me, Sybil strode forward, her rhythmic chant growing in intensity. She hopped over the salt and into the circle. The demon saw her, and a strange, echoing laugh gurgled from its drooling lips.

I watched in horror as she marched up to the freaky thing. "Holy shit. You've got a death wish, woman!"

Closing in on the tear, Sybil ignored me, her chants loud enough that she nearly shouted them. She'd need to, with the racket coming from the rift. The ground trembled, the wind pouring from the slit picked up, and soon, it was all I could do to keep my hair from blinding me. I raised my hand before my eyes, dimly aware that Oliver no longer leaned against the car.

Sybil's hands moved like a world-class juggler, symbols and runes appearing on the air currents like glowing white etchings, then whisking away. Through the pulsing rip in the world, the torso of the demon came into view. Rows of long, sharp teeth filled the gaping mouth, saliva dribbling from them in thick strands. Its long taloned fingers reached for Sybil, and she quickly stepped back, the creature stumbling forward out of the tear.

Landing on its long arms, the demon glowed with a strange blue light from a gemstone on its muscular chest. Beneath the lean, hollowed-out belly, a loin cloth covered its privates. The thing's legs were so short they looked awkward; it could barely walk.

The demon didn't get much chance to try out those legs because, inside the maelstrom surrounding the pair, Sybil shouted, *"Ego Interficiom!"* I gasped when a knife appeared in her hand, and the Witch leapt forward and plunged it into the thing's glowing chest. It screamed, the piercing cry making me squint. *Holy hell!*

The witch's thin plaits blew back with the sudden energy pouring from the rip; Sybil leaned into it, her braids wrapping and unwrapping in the blast. Her feet slid backward, furrowing the dried grass as she struggled with the demon.

The thing looked down at the witch's hand buried in its chest and panicked. It pushed at her, but Sybil must have hit it with a spell—it froze, immobilized except for a wide set of rolling eyes.

Sybil pulled her hand back, the blue gemstone fading as she shoved it into a pocket of her blousy dress. Sucking in a breath, she held it as the demon bellowed, crumbled to dust, and disappeared in the raging wind.

The ground rumbled, the wind tearing at my hair as it hit me with the force of a hurricane. Struggling against the energy pouring from the rift, Sybil leaned forward, her cheeks flapping in the wind. She opened her mouth to shout a spell, but the words pushed back down her throat.

Wide-eyed, Sybil looked over her shoulder and screamed, "Help me!"

Her panicked expression spurred me to action. I jumped into the salted circle, grabbed my ring, and pushed with all I had. Standing behind Sybil, I got a full blast of the fetid smell pouring from the gap and struggled not to retch at the acid stench of it. I leaned harder, slamming my magic into Sybil's like a rear-end collision.

With a determined jerk of her chin, the Witch leaned forward, her hands thrusting out as a strange glow filled her palms. Her lips moved, and I heard her spell in my mind—

"IN ... PERPETUUM ... *CLAUSI!*"

Closed forever. The wind continued to rage, and at first, I didn't think it worked. And then, with a growing rumble, the wind reversed, sucking back into the tear fast enough that the two of us clung together, digging in our feet against the pull.

With a hollow snap, the seam healed, the glowing ends pulling toward the center of the rip until they became a solid bead of energy. It hovered in the air, flared bright, then blinked out of sight. The black wisp of smoke drifting into the quiet night was the only sign of the near disaster.

Sybil let me go and collapsed to her knees, panting, her chin resting on her chest and her arms hanging weakly at her sides. I looked over at the car. There was no sign of Oliver. He was gone.

Rising on shaking legs, Sybil stepped out of the circle and headed to her car, completely ignoring me. Exhaustion etched her face as the Witch grabbed the handle.

"Hold it right there, Sybil."

She paused, her eyes turning to stare at me.

"What in the ever-loving hell was that all about?"

The exhausted Witch didn't answer, her lips a thin slash in her face. She opened the car door, slipped inside, and drove away. As her tail lights disappeared, I shivered.

There was still no sign of Oliver, but when I walked over to where, seconds ago, a gateway had threatened all of humanity, the energy was gone. We healed the tear.

Nothing made sense to me. Why did she want that bloody crystal? What would be worth the cost of unleashing a hoard of demons?

I whispered, "Why did you want it, Sybil?" A familiar voice answered.

"I don't know, but there's another one just like it, and I know where it is."

With a yelp, I whirled to see Oliver behind me, close enough to reach out and touch him. And that's exactly what I did.

I threw my arms around his neck and pulled him close, sobbing into his warm skin. "Oh my God, Oliver. I was so worried about you! What she did to you is all my fault. I'm so, so sorry!"

My fear for him and the anxiety of the last few hours—no, the last eight years—came pouring from me in a rush of tears. Sobbing hysterically, I clutched his shirt, my head tucked beneath his chin.

It took me a moment to realize his arms had slipped around me, pulling me closer as his lips brushed against my hair so gently that I almost didn't feel it.

"Shh. It's alright. I'm fine." His arms tightened, and I closed my eyes, my sobs quieting as he held me.

Softly, he whispered into my ear, "The darkness almost ruined me—it was a basement—but I wasn't in there long. Thank you for coming to save me." He held up his hand, the bracelet I forced on him glowing pink. "If it wasn't for this cuff, I could have helped you fight her."

That was the wrong thing to say, because I fell apart as the tears poured again, my sobs bordering on pathetic. I was embarrassed as hell but beyond caring. His arms squeezed tight around me, and his heart beat beneath my cheek for the first time in—*forever.*

Oliver's scent filled my nostrils, a delightful mix of hot sun on warm sand and a hint of citrus, a swirling essence that was uniquely his. God, I'd missed it. I buried my face in his shirt, smelling him until his chuckles rumbled in my ear. He was here, *touching me*, and wrapping me in the comforting circle of his arms. My mind exploded with happiness, emotion swimming beneath my hot skin. As I snuggled closer, Oliver stiffened, then dropped his hands and stepped back, his face a mask in the darkness.

"Can I get a ride home?"

"Sure." My face flushed red. I couldn't look at him as I turned and walked to the rental car on wooden legs. My hands shook as I opened the passenger door, the jangling of my keys loud in the silent clearing.

Once we were on the road, I sent furtive looks his way, drinking in the sight of his handsome face as it glowed in the light of the dash. When they said something was a sight for sore eyes, they weren't kidding. Being this close to him soothed my frayed nerves.

"It will take weeks to get over the heart attack I had when I saw Sybil's text."

Oliver looked out the window, his lips tight. "It wasn't a sunset sail, that's for sure."

We drove silently for a while, then he looked at me and said, "I've been getting therapy. It's working, at least a little. I didn't come unglued tonight, so that's progress, right?"

With a grim smile, I said, "If you'd had your powers, you might have." His lips drooped and he looked out the window, his shoulders stiff. I frowned at my misstep, flushing red again. Tension swelled in the small space between us. I filled it with nervous chatter.

"Where did you go during that shit show? I looked over at the car, and you were gone."

Oliver didn't answer, his eyes going to his lap where his hands twitched nervously. Finally, with a grim look, he said, "I hid."

I'm not sure why I laughed, but I did, perhaps a little too long because Oliver's face tightened. "Well, if I wasn't armed, I would have hid too. That was some pretty scary witchy woo-woo."

His head twisted to look at me, his guilty expression disappearing. "Really?"

"Hell ya! I wanted to hide, too. That witch has more power in her little finger than I do in my whole family—for ten generations!"

"Well, I have to say, seeing that side of you was pretty terrifying," he said with a soft smile. "I was proud of you, Pheebs."

I looked out the window and bit my lip, not wanting to cry. To keep the conversation light, I asked him if he wanted some Dion's chicken. He shook his head. "No, but thanks. I have to get back to the sailboat. Can you drop me there?"

The realization that I had nowhere to stay hit me, and I almost swerved off the road. *Shit*. Gabe. By now, he must have read the note about leaving tomorrow. I didn't tell him in person. I couldn't very well show up at his hotel begging for another night.

At my sudden speed wobble, Oliver asked, "What's wrong?"

I bit my lip. "Nothing. It's fine."

Oliver stared at me for a while, then glanced into the backseat. "Going somewhere? The note on my fridge said you were leaving."

When I didn't answer, he poked me. "Phoebe, what's going on? Why are you still in the Keys?" At the guilty look on my face, his expression softened. "Tell me."

"I can't," I whispered.

"Do you have a place to stay tonight, at least?"

Chewing my lip, I struggled with what to tell him. I opted for the truth. "No."

Oliver sighed. For a long time, the only sound was the road beneath our tires. As we crossed the Cow Key Channel and turned toward Garrison Bight, he said, "Would you like to stay over? I can take the dinette foldaway."

At first, I didn't answer. Our relationship was a disaster—you couldn't even call it a relationship.

"It's more of a disastership," I mumbled.

"What?" Oliver stared at me, frowning.

"Nothing. Sure, I'd love to stay over. Thanks."

I didn't mean to sound ungrateful, and I sure didn't want to sleep on a beach. It was kind of him to offer. But this hellish ride was getting old. I loved him. But there were so many—*things.*

A string of curses raced through my head, but I didn't give them air time. I sucked it up, and I managed like I always did.

CHAPTER 12
~ PHOEBE ~

"How in the world do you get yourself into these things, Phoebe?"

A full moon glowed brightly above us as Oliver and I sat on the bow of his sailboat, having a nightcap and decompressing. He drank scotch, and I sipped a half-pint of Dr. McGillicuddy's Fireball Whisky. Yes, the bottle was old enough to still have the inaugural name. And after the night we'd had, it tasted like heaven.

I stretched my legs, grateful that Oliver gave me the more comfortable chair.

"I don't get myself into these things, Oliver. Trouble finds me. It's a skill."

He laughed and wiggled his ass around. His beach chair held his butt six inches off the deck. Secretly, I looked forward to watching him get out of it.

I couldn't help noticing his erection pressed against the side of his shorts. I groaned under my breath as heat pooled between my thighs at the sight. Longing for him flushed through me. He caught me looking, and I blushed, glad it was dark.

"Yeah, it's still a problem," he said, his face tight.

"Do you sit out here every night?" When he nodded, I sighed. "It's a lovely view. The lights on the water are beautiful. It's so calm—like a glittery black mirror. I love the smell of the ocean, too. They should bottle it."

Taking a long pull on his drink, Oliver smiled. "It has its moments."

For over an hour, we talked about the crazy things in Key West: the tourists, the beaches, the boats, the price of groceries—everything except *us*. I finished the half pint and laughed about the taste of cinnamon and how the whisky numbed my lips.

Oliver chuckled. "Well, don't fall overboard when you get up. Speaking of which..." Oliver hauled himself to his feet while I stared at his firm butt cheeks and hoped he didn't notice. Swaying slightly, he helped me up from my chair.

He guided me carefully across the slippery bow, jumping to the cockpit and lifting me down behind him. As I slid down the front of his shirt, for a moment, time stood still. Our faces were close. So close.

I reached up, my fingers tracing his lips. Oliver didn't move, letting me caress the edge of his strong jaw. Longing swelled in my chest, squeezing my lungs. I wanted to kiss him. He was right there, inches away. Beautiful silver eyes shimmered so close—but his expression, nervous and remote, stopped me cold. When I dropped my hand, he sighed. My heart stuttered when Oliver rested his forehead against mine.

"Phoebe—" His husky voice whispered over my skin. I fisted my hand against my belly, willing myself not to touch him.

"No. Don't. It's fine," I breathed.

Oliver reached down and grabbed my hand, bringing it to his lips.

"There's never been anyone else but you. I swear." His thick, muffled words warmed my hand, his silvery eyes peering down at me. *Longing*. I saw it, and my heart raced.

"There's something I need to tell you." *Yes, Phoebe. Now is the perfect time to tell him about your handsome new love interest.*

Sighing, Oliver said, "Tomorrow. At breakfast. Ok? Tonight was nice. Sitting with you was … *nice*. Can we leave it at that?"

His voice broke, the pleading note of those last words a dull knife sawing through the connection between us. I nodded, following him down the ladder to the belly of the sailboat as hope crumbled to dust inside me.

Oliver changed his sheets while I protested, and soon, I slid between them. I listened to the quiet sounds of him in the kitchen, putting down the dinette table and making himself comfortable.

Lying in Oliver's bed, even the clean sheets carried his familiar essence, stirring an agonizing ache for his touch. A heavy blanket of memories suffocated me. We had enjoyed so many happy moments before our lives splintered into ruins.

I breathed into his pillow, the scent a cruel torture I couldn't resist inhaling, over and over. My hands fisted, the desire to bust through the door and grab him into my arms almost unbearable. I couldn't sleep. I tossed and turned, then cried softly into his pillow to muffle the sound.

When the sliding barrier opened, I jumped. Oliver stood in the doorway in his boxers, the faint light in the cabin shadowing the strong curves of his bare chest. With a sigh, he came to me, the mattress dipping under his weight as he sat.

"I can't sleep. Your crying is killing me, Pheebs. What can I do?"

"Cuddles. I need cuddles."

It was an old game we used to play. Before he went missing. Before the torture. He'd sense I was upset about something and would ask me that very question. I would hold up my arms and say, "I need cuddles," and he would pull me into a bear hug.

Oliver chuckled. "I think I can manage that. Move over."

I wiggled sideways, and Oliver slipped under the sheets, wrapping me in a comforting embrace.

"Is this going to hurt your—situation?"

Oliver chuckled, a soft sound against my ear. "Oh, I can pretty much guarantee it. But it's fine. I'll manage. Now go to sleep. And try not to wiggle, or I might not make it through this."

I rested my head on his firm chest, snuggling my chin to breathe in his scent straight from the source. He groaned, his arm pulling tighter. If there was a heaven on earth, it was right here in this cabin as he held me close. I drifted off to sleep, comfortable that for at least the next few hours, I could be happy.

***

~ CHARLESTON ~

Stephen laughed, his glasses flashing, his brown hair almost black in the dim light of the lab. He and Layla had come down to take me for a spin. I didn't care. Layla had juiced me up good. I hung from the ceiling, my arms stretched tight. At least they didn't pull out the mask today. Again, I didn't care. I was high as a kite on her magic and eager for release from my constant arousal.

Normally, Layla's magic sent her playthings to a foggy place with no idea of what went on. I'd endured the thick essence of her power for so long that I now remained conscious for most of their playtime. High as a kite, but conscious. And I felt every burn and every lick of the whip.

It didn't matter. I didn't care. I'd learned to enjoy it. Every strike reminded me that I was filthy. That the black film coating my skin was here to stay.

Layla's long blonde tresses tangled around my cock as she sucked it into her mouth, running her tongue along the swollen head. Her red, skin-tight cocktail dress lay across the back of a chair next to Stephen's lab coat. I didn't look at her. I never looked at her. I knew a monster lurked beneath that pretty skin.

"Yummmmm," she moaned, drawing the word out so that I felt the vibration all the way to my aching balls.

Stephen, his bare chest shining with sweat, stepped behind me, cranking the winch a few more turns. The chains above my head clattered as I jerked higher, my shackles pinching tighter as I swung. Grabbing me by the hips, Stephen tossed the lube aside and seated the head of his shaft against my opening, rubbing it up and down. Layla smiled up at him from where she worked my cock, her eyes glittering a faint red in the gloom.

"He's not screaming tonight, darlin'. Can you get out the torch for me before you finish there?"

Letting go of my cock with a pop, Layla grinned, then climbed up my body to grab the small Chef's torch from the counter. With a flick, it lit up, the hiss an angry sound in the quiet of the room. She flicked it off and handed it to Stephen.

"I think there's enough in there for tonight, anyway," she purred, giving me a sultry smile. Sliding down my front, she grabbed my cock again, and I moaned, my balls tightening under her touch. As she slid her lips all the way down my shaft, my hips thrust into her suction. Fuck. *Fuck!*

Through the fog of Layla's magic, I often dreamed of killing them. As bloody images and imaginary screams flitted through my mind, so did power from the Talisman of Tenebris. Hanging around my neck during every fuck session, there was no escaping its blood oath.

The black horse figurine, normally cool against my chest, stabbed wildfire through my skin at every deadly thought that crossed my mind. The ancient artifact forbade me from harming them, its power ripping into me as punishment. Last time, I dreamed so big that I rendered myself unconscious and woke to broken ribs. They didn't like it when I passed out.

Behind me, Stephen pushed himself home, and my head flopped back as sensation exploded through me. My chains rattled, the ache in my balls intensifying. Layla's magic swirled around me, adding another layer of black to my skin as she ravaged my cock with her mouth and laughed at my excited thrusts.

"I've been meaning to add my initial to our masterpiece. Tonight's the night," Stephen mumbled, sinking his teeth into my shoulder. After a few more deep thrusts, he rolled his hips playfully and paused, panting into my neck.

"Boris, I know you're there, you sick fuck. Do you mind doing the honors while I fuck him senseless?"

The vampire stepped forward from where he watched in the shadows, his erection a promise of things to come. He took the lighter, and flicked it until the bright blue flame popped free.

"My pleasure," he snickered.

***

Oliver thrashed, screaming, and woke me from a dead sleep. I sat up, shaking him, but he didn't rouse. "Ollie, wake up."

Whimpers came from his throat, and he moaned my name, but didn't respond. I shook him harder. He sat up with a gasp, his eyes wide and sweat beading his forehead. My first thought was to touch him and comfort him. But I held back, unsure. His body coiled tight, ready to explode.

The cabin was dark, lit only by a distant lamppost filtering through the porthole. I watched his chest heaving, unsure how to help him. Fear trickled down my spine for an instant, then I clenched my teeth and reached out to take his hand. He tensed.

Quietly, I said, "Oliver, it's ok. You were dreaming. Lay down."

His chin trembled as he stared through me, his unseeing eyes wide with distress. Then he looked at me, focusing. Panting, he flopped back on the pillows and covered his face with one arm.

I lay down on my side, facing him as I snuggled closer. He hissed in pain and stiffened at my touch. "Ollie, do you want to go back to the kitchen? I'm alright now. I promise I won't cry again."

Swallowing thickly, he dropped his arm and, looking at me, shook his head. Even in the darkness, I saw the terror on his face.

Cautiously, I reached out to touch him, running my fingers through his hair like I used to. With a groan, he rolled to face me. Staring into my eyes, he whispered, "The nightmares are really bad."

"I see that. Do you want to talk about it?" When he shook his head, I went back to stroking his hair, and he closed his eyes and moved closer. His arousal brushed along my thigh, hard and unyielding.

"Your breath smells like cinnamon," he huffed. "Now I want a drink of Fireball."

I chuckled, and he opened his eyes. We were so close, scant inches apart, but his stiff, nervous tension made it miles. Then, something changed.

Electricity streaked between us, and our eyes locked. I slid my hand along the ridge of his shoulder, my fingers drifting over the edges of his scars; his eyes widened with fear. When I smoothed my hand down to his chest, Oliver's muscles softened beneath my fingers, and with a long, slow release of his breath, he met me halfway.

His fingers slipped into my hair, gripping a handful to pull me closer. Our lips sealed together in a ragged, desperate kiss. At my pleasured sigh, Oliver's firm sweeps of exploration faltered; he hesitated. I encouraged him in, my tongue meeting his with a hot swirl of excitement. Longing seeped through every cell of my body, my chest aching with it. I pressed into his warmth, eager for the feel of his heated skin.

His hand shook as it brushed down my back, pausing to grasp my buttocks with a tender squeeze. With a moan, Oliver's hips pushed into me, his thick shaft rubbing between us. Breaking the seal of his lips, I looked down, hesitating. Oliver panted into my hair, his body trembling.

"Touch me," he whispered.

"Are you sure?" My voice was soft. Worried.

"Touch me."

I slipped my hand over the tip of his rigid shaft, my touch gentle; softly, I teased him, rubbing my thumb through the bead of moisture at the tip. He hissed, and his hips jerked. The grip of his hand on my ass pushed toward pain as his fingers dug into me.

"Harder," he gasped, his body stretched tight with need.

Not wanting to hurt him, I rolled my thumb around and around, sweeping up every drop as it welled, then painting him with it. His hisses and sighs heated my blood, the sharp jerks of his hips starting a blaze between my legs. Encouraged, I slipped my fingers into my mouth to gather more moisture, my wet fingers sliding smoothly down his shaft.

He moaned and covered my hand with his. Guiding me, Oliver closed our fists around his hard length and stroked with me, firmly and gently. He shuddered, his hips rolling into my touch as his eyes eased shut, his lips parting on a sigh.

The sight of him melting in my hands sent a surge of lust through me. But nothing compared to the flush of contentment at finally being in his arms—skin on skin, drinking in the smell of him, feeling him move against me.

I tried to push myself lower, but he stopped me, shaking his head. Panting, his wild, fearful eyes shot open, staring into me. I kissed him, gently exploring his mouth with my tongue. I stroked him again, and Oliver guided the pressure. Harder and harder, his hips thrusting, he groaned into my mouth.

"Gods, Phoebe!" he hissed, jamming himself into my grip. His whole body shook, his eyelids crushed together as if he was in agony.

With a curse, he came, thick jets of white striping his belly. Over and over, he jerked in my hand. I kept up my strokes until he stopped me, his chest heaving. Oliver sagged, pressing his forehead into my neck, his body wet with sweat.

He sobbed, a quiet sound between pants, and I pulled him close, whispering in his ear that everything would be fine. His sobs turned to tears, and his tears turned into a tsunami of pain, his shoulders heaving as he cried into my neck.

I held him, torn between the happiness of touching him and the agony of hearing him cry. My eyes wet with tears, I soothed him through the wracking sobs. After a time, he settled, his breathing slowed, and finally, he slid from the bed and went to the bathroom. He returned with a warm cloth for me.

"I'm sorry," he said tightly.

That hard, distant voice. I hated it.

"Are you coming back in?" I lifted the covers.

He shook his head, slipped out of the room, and, not stopping at the kitchen, climbed the steps to the cockpit. When his footfalls passed by my window, my heart sank.

I fell into a restless sleep, and in the morning, Oliver hadn't returned. I waited as long as I dared, then headed to my rental car, returning it to the downtown drop-off with a sagging heart.

My bag dragged behind me, heavy with unfulfilled hopes and shattered dreams. I called a cab and waited on the corner, watching the tourists come and go. They were so fucking happy; it turned my stomach.

Bistros dotted this section of Duval, and to my surprise, I noticed Griswald sitting in the glass window of the cafe across the street. He met my gaze, raising his cup of tea at me with a sly grin. At his creepy smile, I didn't know whether to wave hello or scream for help. We stared at each other, my lips turning down as fear fluttered through me. *What the hell … ?*

When I heard Gabe's voice, I flinched. Turning, I watched him jog up the sidewalk, wearing a pair of dry shorts and a tank. He looked like he'd been out running.

"Phoebe. Where did you go?" he asked, his face troubled.

"Like I said in my note, I'm heading back to Augusta today."

He frowned. "There's nothing I can do to make you stay, is there?"

I shook my head. "I can't. I've been gone too long. My business will be in shambles if I don't return. I've done all I can do here. Things will take care of themselves after I'm gone, I guess."

Images from my fleeting moments of happiness this morning steeled my resolve. Oliver left when I wanted so desperately for him to stay. I was tired of chasing him. It was well past time to go. When Gabe frowned at my expression, I reached out to touch his cheek.

"I'm sorry," I said. "It was wonderful getting to know you. Our time together was ... well, it came right when ..." I stopped, then took a deep breath and gave it to him straight.

"You came along when I needed to feel better about myself. It was wrong of me to see you. It wasn't fair to string you along while my heart was wrapped up with someone else. I'm sorry."

"I get it, Phoebe. Will you call me if you ever need my help? I don't want to lose touch completely if that's alright with you?" His hopeful expression sent a wave of guilt through me.

I nodded, and he wrote his number on a receipt from my purse and handed it back to me. Then we said our goodbyes. Gabe helped me into the cab, sadness dragging me down as my ride pulled away from the curb. Another relationship that crashed at takeoff. *Way to go, Phoebe.*

Sighing, I checked my wallet for spare change to buy snacks for the long bus ride home. Thank goodness for credit cards.

***

This time, I made it as far as Marathon, the halfway point along the tropical archipelago. When the bus stopped at the airport to pick up another load of passengers, I peered out the window to see a young couple I recognized.

Her small athletic body swallowed by an enormous bulge, a very pregnant Eddi waited under the shade of a palm tree beside the tarmac. Her short platinum hair shone with sweat; silvery eyes found mine, and she waved, her face lighting up.

Ronan stood beside her, his eyes cataloging everyone as they came and went from the bus. I'd never met him officially, but he was a looker, his short dark hair shining in the sunlight. I hadn't seen either of them since we busted into Charleston and freed Oliver.

Eddi was part Djinn, and meeting her and her friend Cal seven months ago in Key West had turned my life on its ear. A genetic twist in my family tree meant that when the sun set orange, I was able to recognize Djinn. The light refracted in such a way that I detected a faint glimmer around their bodies—but only at sunset. Eddi's shimmering halo drew me to her that evening in Key West so long ago, and we'd been friends ever since.

When the Enforcer's team stormed the facility in Charleston, Eddi and Cal gave me the heads up. I found a way into the lab, and met them to help free Oliver. Gideon wasn't impressed, of course. But getting Ollie back, even in deplorable condition, was worth the Enforcer's anger.

Ronan, Eddi's mate, was a full-blooded Syreni male. Right now, it was hard to imagine that he was normally quite ferocious and, when in the ocean, sported a tail. The bright pink t-shirt went with his tanned body and intricate green leg skin. Somehow, the tiny scales looked enough like fancy dive skins that humans never noticed they were real.

I smiled and scrambled off the bus, then hurried over to receive an awkward bear hug when Eddi's belly got in the way.

"Oh my God, it's so good to see you!" she laughed. "We had a visit from Gideon last night. He asked us to meet you and give you this message." She handed me an envelope and hugged me again, overjoyed to see me.

Happiness flushed my skin a bright pink, but when Ronan slid a muscular arm around Eddi and placed a protective hand over her baby bump, I stiffened. Shoving away the petty twinge of jealousy, I opened the envelope and read the elegant scrawl.

"The Sovereign has need of your services. The payment is generous, and I'm certain that your unique skills will help us greatly. We can take care of any ongoing issues with finances regarding your shop in Augusta. Enclosed is an advance in the event you wish to come on board. The key is for the door of our Guest lodgings. We use it when we have need of outside talent. The directions are below. I can meet you tonight on Sombrero beach — Gideon

PS. I came to present this last night but did not wish to interrupt your stargazing. I'm hoping this is a sign of better days ahead for both of you."

Eddi watched, her eyes wide and her expression cautious. Looking into my tight face, she asked, "Is everything alright?"

I nodded, wiping the moisture from my eyes and trying not to smear my makeup. "It seems as if I was meant to be here. Every time I try to leave, someone stops me."

Eddi grabbed my arm and squealed. "Does this mean you can come for a visit!?" When I nodded, she freaked out.

While Eddi joked about her current state, Ronan grabbed my luggage, and the three of us trundled from the runway. The amount of cash that Gideon advanced was more than enough, including paying down my credit card bill. Thank goodness.

The suite was a short walk from the airport, and close to Eddi's apartment. We stopped to drop off my things and check it out. As we climbed to the second story of the walkup, my mood lifted. The modern building was brand new. Even the newly installed red carpet in the hall had a fresh, clean scent.

I changed into shorts and a t-shirt—sundresses were a lousy idea when hanging with Eddi's gang. Trouble followed her like a frisky puppy. It was no wonder Ronan watched over her so fiercely.

As he investigated the small living room, Ronan reminded me of a police dog, his brows furrowed above his tanned face. I watched him snoop into every closet, the cupboards, and the fridge, his glittering emerald eyes sharp with curiosity.

"Does it get your stamp of approval?" My smile widened when his cheeks flushed red.

Ronan ran his fingers along the shiny surface of the black dinette, his eyes narrowed on the small balcony beyond the sliding door. "This is far nicer than I imagined. Gideon must like you." He shot me a generous grin.

Seeing them again was a balm to my soul. I'd barely seen my feisty friend while running back and forth between Augusta and the Keys to be near Oliver. Now, they were expecting. Knowing their wild history made the big event even more exciting.

Eddi relaxed as I changed, the air conditioner blasting across the back of her neck. "No one told me I'd feel like a beach ball with legs. Things would have gone differently had I known it would be this damned uncomfortable." She grunted and shifted her weight. "My God. The kid is using my spleen as a football."

Ronan slid over and sat on the loveseat beside her, holding her hand with an anxious expression. She laughed and gave him a quick kiss. "It's not your fault, Ronan. Pregnancy is hell for all females. Stop fussing. I'm fine." When he pulled her hand to his lips, pain lanced my chest. I was happy for them, even if it was hard to watch.

"Ok. Good to go," I said. "I have enough cash for a cab if you want a lift home from here?"

Eddi shook her head. "No, the doctor said I'm ok to walk as long as I don't overdo it. I've had lots of rest. I'm only six and a half months pregnant, so I still have a ways to go yet. At least, I think I do."

"What do you mean?" I darted a look at Ronan, who still looked guilty.

"The doctor that the *Others* use can only guess at the timeline for a Djinn-Syreni baby. It could be nine months, the term for Djinn, or six months, the normal Syreni gestation. So, we're on a *wait and see* schedule. Tons of fun." She rolled her eyes and laughed.

That explained why Ronan hung on her like he was afraid she might burst. I smiled inside, then sighed, rubbing my chest.

After we got Eddi back to her apartment, up the stairs, and situated in her favorite chair, we had a wonderful visit. I learned that the survivors of the Charleston battle were doing fine and settling into Keys life, which made me feel much better. After a simple fish dinner, I headed back to my suit.

Tormented by thoughts of Oliver, it was impossible to enjoy the walk home. Where was he now? Was he thinking of me? Did I imagine the connection between us this morning?

I tried not to be angry with him for running. When we slept together, I knew his issues were far from over. As always, it came down to time, and our timer dinged when I left Key West.

Spinning my wheels for so long had exhausted me. It was time to let fate take the wheel. I would leave Oliver in peace. It hurt like hell, but I would manage.

Kicking off my shoes and turning on the TV, I watched the news and rested. It had been a hellish couple of days. I still didn't understand what the hell Sybil was up to with the demon's gemstone. I would ask Gideon about it tonight. I needed to come clean on a few things before I took him up on his job offer.

CHAPTER 13

~ OLIVER ~

If I could kick myself in the balls, I would. Getting close to Phoebe had been a mixture of terror, comfort, and dizzying pleasure. When the dust settled, I felt raw. Exposed. *Guilty*.

I let Phoebe touch me. Let her beautiful hands roam the parts of my body that Layla defiled for so many years. Let her caress the parts of me that enjoyed the touch of monsters. A sour sickness rose from my stomach to clog my throat.

Pulling my hand into a fist, I pounded it against my temple. Asking Phoebe to stay over had been a horrible mistake, and now I hurt her. *Again*.

As I walked down the beach, trying to get my head on straight, dawn pushed at the horizon. My path had taken me to the waterfront behind Munchies, and as I watched, the vampire staff came through the door on their way home.

"Cutting it pretty close, aren't you, Priscilla?"

The bartender turned at the sound of my voice, then, using her vampire speed, she was on me in a flash. At the expression on my face, she patted my back instead of hugging me.

"Ollie! So good to see you. I'm so glad you're alive!" My skin prickled at her touch, and I growled softly. She yanked her hand back with a sad smile.

"Yeah, sorry about that," I said, smiling weakly. "I'm glad to see you. I'm banned now."

She pouted. "I heard. Have you tried the Vampire club in Marathon? I heard it's pretty good."

"Thanks, but I'll pass. I'd have to move, and it took me so long to feel comfortable here. I'm managing. *Just.*"

"Do you want me to put in a good word with Luther for you?"

Shaking my head, I said, "No, I don't think so. There was a time when I didn't think I could live without you guys. But I'm getting better. I'm a little less desperate these days."

She cast an eye at the sky and kissed my cheek goodbye. Before she could disappear, I stopped her with a hand on her sleeve.

"Would you mind telling Stan I'm sorry? These are for you guys."

She looked at the tickets I handed her, then exploded into a toothy smile. "You got tickets to Pink?"

"Yeah. I want you and Stan to use them. I planned to ask someone, but the concert was too soon, and now it won't happen, I'm afraid. You both deserve it after putting up with me."

"Pink!" She screeched, thanked me profusely, and was gone in a blink. I always admired Vampires and their super speed. I was faster, though. When I wasn't cuffed.

Looking down at my wristband, I wondered about Sybil. What was she up to? When she trussed me up and returned me to Phoebe last night, she removed the ward from the band. I had no clue until moments ago when Priscilla almost hugged me and my power surged against her touch. I had no idea why Sybil released me, once again leaving the bright pink glow to hide the fact. Color me happy.

With a big smile on my face, I continued along the beach. When I came to the end, I clambered over the rocks and sat down on the bench at the end of the pier. The view of the water was glorious, the dawn breaking behind me in the east, casting a pink glow over my head. I spent so much time looking at the sky that it bordered on obsession.

I didn't see the sky for almost a decade. Even now, looking back, I wondered how I managed to survive my captivity. When they found me, I was insane. I nearly killed my rescuers. I would have, had I been able to get my hands on them. My bear saved all of us.

Looking at the glowing band, I remembered the day Phoebe put it on me. She cried as she snapped it over my wrist. She'd been so hopeful while at the same time, absolutely terrified. Everyone was frightened of me at the beginning.

They were right. I couldn't be trusted with my Djinn powers. Not at first.

***

~ THE SPECTRE ~

The Spectre yacht was a beaut—a top-of-the-line Italian-made piece of genius. But it had one minor flaw the Witch never considered when she penned me in.

Oh, Phoebe covered most of it. The windows. The door. Even the air vents. Every single crack in my room glowed with a pink seal. All except for one very tiny thing that she missed. The drain.

When Hex had the yacht custom-built, the makers planned for all the gruesome side effects of the demon's hobby. The torture. The blood. The bodily fluids. She had the builder install drains and, over them, industrial carpet. No one noticed, not even the clever Witch.

When the Spectre arrived back in Marathon, Gideon parked the yacht and left me in the medical bay until he made other plans. On the tenth day in my new digs, I found the drain.

I waited until everyone went to sleep—Gideon, Phoebe, the crocodile shifter Cleatus, and the Djinn assassin, Galahad. Their job was to contain me in comfort. They got one part right, anyway. I would miss the gray leather recliner in the corner of my cell.

My balls ached with Layla's magic, but my strength had returned, so the rug ripped easily under my hands. When I misted into my Djinn form, I almost gave myself away by laughing at the exhilarating idea of freedom.

With a whisper of power, I was gone, tearing through the drains until I found the exit. I was glad smells didn't register in Djinn form—and thank God excrement didn't stick to mist; there had been an unfortunate detour through the bilge pump and holding tanks.

Shooting through the night, I swept around the ship's outer hull, high on freedom and itching for action. I came across the slumbering croc on the rear swim platform. He wasn't worth the effort, but feeling playful, I took the time to snake into the water, snag a fish, and crush its skull, leaving it on the end of his long nose. I almost gave everything away by giggling.

I slipped back through the patio doors, visiting every room on the vessel. Stopping outside his door, I mulled over killing Gideon tonight or waiting until later. Getting busted by the Enforcer would end my fun, so I moved on.

Phoebe was next. Slipping under her door, I silently returned to human form. Holding back an appreciative gasp, I crept closer, my eyes tracing the dark shadow of her nipples through the lovely pink lingerie. My brows furrowed when I realized the lacy thing was my present to her on our only Christmas together. We had plans for a ski trip, and she blushed a pretty shade of pink when she opened the gift.

Warmth buried the cold in my chest. The corners of my lips turned up at the memory. Then I remembered Layla wearing delicate red lace. She came to the door of my cell and taunted me, whispering to me with Phoebe's voice. Wearing Phoebe's face. Running her hands over Phoebe's body.

A snarl bubbled in my throat. I took another step, wondering if killing the Witch in her bed would ease the pain in my chest. If she was gone, I couldn't hurt, right?

Lowering my face next to hers, taking quite a chance that I might be discovered, I breathed in. Oh, so quietly, I tasted her essence on my tongue. Cinnamon hearts—tangy and sharp, but sweet. She loved those damn things.

When she mumbled in her sleep, I backed away, fearful of losing my freedom again. This was my one chance to flee. But first—the Djinn. He'd worked for Hex. If anyone deserved to die, it was Galahad.

I misted and slipped away, the spicy scent of cinnamon fading behind me. Down the hall and under another door, I found Galahad in his berth.

Sucker. I stayed in mist form and swept closer, careful to remain silent. Inside the nanoparticles of my cloud, I held a knife I'd picked up during my kitchen tour. Like me, it was invisible.

Holding something inside the mist was easy. Manipulating a solid object in there, not so much. I got into position, ready to drop to human form, fist the knife, and drive it into Galahad's black heart. I stifled a giggle, then counted down, just for fun.

One. Two. Three. I dropped onto my human legs with a thump, flipped the knife, and stabbed downward—straight into an empty mattress.

Fast bastard.

Mid-turn, a punch to the gut sent me flying, and the dark-haired Djinn had me around the throat and lifted against the wall. Dammit, my reflexes were shot to hell.

Being a Djinn himself, the assassin's powers canceled mine out, and with his hands on me I couldn't mist. If he let me go, though—

I struggled like a wild thing, kicking and scratching at the Djinn bastard. The door burst open, and Phoebe rushed in, her eyes wide. She held a bracelet that glowed pink like the doors and windows of my room.

I was a fool. She'd awoken and feigned sleep, the cinnamon bitch.

Tears streaming down her face, Phoebe bravely approached even as Galahad weakened. I increased my efforts, my face red from lack of oxygen.

"Hurry, Phoebe! I can't hold him forever!"

My foot connected with a set of balls, but instead of releasing me, Galahad grunted and squeezed harder, shaking me in warning.

"I'm sorry, Oliver. It's for your own good." When Phoebe reached for my wrist, I flipped my hand and grabbed hers, squeezing it like a vice. She dropped to her knees, crying out in agony. Undeterred, her opposite hand swung up, slapping the ring home with a click.

Gideon appeared in the doorway and leapt into the fray, his lips tight as he pried at my grip on Phoebe's wrist. I refused to release her. When I squeezed with all my strength, Phoebe cried out but held on tight, whispering a spell under her breath.

Heat warmed the wristband, and the assassin squeezed my neck harder, my choking snarls turning into frantic, gurgling screams of rage as my power began slipping away. Galahad thumped my head against the wall and I saw stars. He hissed, "Let her go, or I'll kill you right here."

As my power faded to nothing, the fight drained from me. I dropped Phoebe's hand as Gideon slammed into me. The two males stretched me between them and carried me, kicking and screaming, back to my cell.

Before Gideon slammed the door shut, I said, "Watch your back, Gryphon. You can't keep me contained forever. Next time, I won't hesitate to slit your throat."

The Enforcer shook his head and closed my door with a grim nod of acceptance. When the lock clicked, Phoebe's pale face appeared in the window. I snarled, my lips pulled back and my eyes drilling into her with hatred.

When tears poured down her cheeks, and she raised a hand to the glass, I hurled myself face-first into the furthest corner with a strangled scream. The lights flipped off, and I grumbled to myself, rocking on my heels and rubbing at the foul black film coating my skin.

I couldn't get it off. It would never come off, no matter how hard I rubbed.

***

As the memory faded, I wondered again why they bothered to help me. It would have been far simpler to kill me and be done with it.

"I'm a softie, that's why."

I jumped to my feet, my hands flying before me. When the Gryphon padded into view from behind a cluster of palms, I relaxed. I guess that answered the whole reading minds question. *Sneaky Bastard.*

"Don't do that. You scared the life out of me. I'm beginning to think you do it on purpose, Gryphon."

A chuckle rumbled from Gideon's feathered chest as the space between my ears tickled—*fucking eavesdropper.* I pictured taking a dump, and the Gryphon's golden eyes sparkled.

"I will admit that startling you has become a guilty pleasure, Oliver."

Pausing beside my bench, the Gryphon sat down, tucked his feet, and coiled his tail around them. When the arch of one wing brushed my shoulder, he mumbled an apology and tucked it closer to his ribcage.

"How are things going? I came by earlier and saw the two of you stargazing."

"Phoebe deserves better than me. She's leaving this afternoon. I encouraged her by walking out when I shouldn't have." My ears burned with shame.

"Do you want her to leave?"

"No. Of course not. I wish we had all the time in the world, but we don't. Phoebe has a business to run back in Augusta, and the rent here drained her bank account. Now I feel worse than ever."

Gideon tilted his head to look at the stars, rumbling softly to himself.

"Has it ever occurred to you that things might come together if you stopped putting up roadblocks? Phoebe has been your cheerleader for far too long. It's time to pick up the pom-poms yourself, Djinn."

"That's easy for you to say. You didn't spend years in a basement—"

"I've been alive for five thousand years, Oliver. Don't presume to preach to me about pain and suffering."

He had a point. That made me curious. I knew next to nothing about the Enforcer.

"Who do you talk to when you need advice or a bit of company?"

"A very snarky parrot." The Enforcer's mental laughter tickled through me, and I shivered. Seeing my frown, he cocked his eagle head. *"The Sovereign is a friend. I am*

not completely alone in this life. But there are times I would give every year I have lived for one true love."

Reaching out, I poked his shoulder. "How very romantic of you, Gryphon."

Gideon shot me a disdainful look and ruffled the feathers where I touched him. Prickly bastard.

"What will it take, Oliver? Will you wait until Phoebe has found another male? Or perhaps you'll hesitate too long, and an angry Witch will kill her while summoning demons."

My head whipped to face him, my mouth gaping. What the—?

"I know everything, Oliver." He stood, ruffled his wings, and padded out to the rocky edge of the pier, the tiger-striped fur of his massive legs rippling in the breeze. Turning his head over one shoulder, Gideon nodded. *"Never turn your back on love, Oliver. It's a gift given freely by the Gods. They don't indulge us very often."*

The Gryphon crouched, and with a mighty thrust of his haunches, launched himself into the night sky. I watched him rise, his wings flapping until he reached the air currents above and blinked out of sight.

The sky bloomed a rosy pink, and I stood, winding my way back to the sailboat. *Caught in the Wind* bobbed quietly in its slip, but Phoebe was gone when I padded softly down the stairs. I stopped in my berth and breathed in the smell of cinnamon hearts. I knew she would leave. I was counting on it. Because, at the end of the day, I was a coward at heart.

"You're not a coward, Oliver."

I whirled at the sound of the voice. The small space was empty.

"Who's there?" The faint smell of peaches drifted to me. "Quit stalking me from the shadows and show yourself!"

There was no response, but I felt a presence come closer and heard something slide onto the bench of the dining booth.

"You're safe. I promise I won't hurt you."

Though I sensed no malice, I opted to stand, backing into the corner where the fridge hummed, the small kitchen light showing that I was indeed alone. *Was I losing my mind again?*

Laughter reached my ears, soft and subtle. *"No, you're not crazy. You know who I am, don't you?"*

I shook my head, and as I stared at the empty space, that same scent wafted past my nose. Ripe peaches on a sunny afternoon. I knew that smell, and now that he'd spoken, I recognized the disembodied voice. I'd lived in the cell next to the owner for eight years—*before he died.*

"Ezen?"

"Indeed. I've watched your struggles from afar. You've been granted a boon, Oliver. The Upper Circle has declared I leave the Eternal Sands to guide you. They have deemed you ... salvageable."

I snorted. "Well, that's comforting. Since when did the Djinn Gods care a whit about me? Look at the hell they let me—*and you*—endure."

Ezen sighed. *"Gods have reasons we will never understand, Oliver. But before we go any further, answer this. Is the love of your life worth fighting for?"*

At the dinette, the air shimmered, and the Djinn's long, lean form appeared. His shoulder-length silver hair and near-white eyes shone in the gloom. He wasn't solid, the wall faintly visible behind his athletic torso. He smiled, and his handsome face glowed with health.

I barely remembered his daughter Eddi and her mate saving us from Charleston, but I could never forget the Djinn shimmering before me. I'd have lost my mind far sooner had he not spent hours talking to me through our cell doors. I tried not to think about him these last months. I was the lone survivor.

"You look better than the last time I saw you, Ezen."

He pursed his lips and shook his head. *"Do you love Phoebe?"*

"Yes." I whispered.

Ezen nodded at the note from Phoebe still pinned to my fridge. *"She still loves you. There is hope for you yet, Oliver."*

I turned to look at the familiar handwriting, a lump forming in my throat. She left me. That note represented the end—not hope. When I looked back, Ezen faded away. His voice trailed like fingers down my spine.

"Alright then, my boy. Let's begin."

Every muscle in my body tensed, but nothing happened. The fridge grumbled to life, and the tap dripped, but I heard nothing else.

"Ezen?"

There was no answer. He was gone.

***

~ PHOEBE ~

Sombrero Beach was lovely, with a long stretch of sand, palm trees, and well-maintained grounds. The seagrass could be a smelly challenge along the coast even when picked up regularly. I didn't mind the familiar odor. It was a reminder of where Oliver and I reunited, for better or worse.

Waves lapped gently on the beach as I waited for Gideon, the crescent moon throwing enough light to watch the glittering waves of the sea. The salty air was a balm to my shredded nerves. Knowing Oliver was only an hour away helped ease the stress of leaving him.

I heard the heavily padded footsteps and a subtle ruffle of feathers before Gideon came ambling into view down the beach. A majestic creature, his eagle head swiveled as long, tufted ears lifted to scan his surroundings. Huge padded feet flipped balls of sand as he strutted toward me, his tiger-striped body easily visible in the darkness. Something resembling a purr rumbled from his chest as he stopped before me.

"I've been meaning to ask. Why do you have stripes, Gideon? I always thought Gryphons were eagle-lion creatures?"

Baritone laughter echoed between my ears. *"My mother enjoyed frolicking with tigers in the jungles of Borneo."*

I hid my smile with one hand. "Frolicking. Alright, then."

Gideon sat beside me, the two of us staring out over the water together.

"So, about the job—"

"There is no job." Gideon's growly answer startled me.

"What? What do you mean there's no job?"

"Just as I said. I wanted you off the bus, and it worked." Gideon's huge golden eyes blinked at me. *"You need to be here for Oliver, Phoebe. I don't think he can do it without you. But Key West was too close."*

Anger stirred. The audacity of the *arrogant bast—*

"I've been called far worse."

The fleshy corners of his beak turned up as he cocked his head in my direction.

"And you read minds, too. Great," I snipped. "So what now? I can't take all that money, Gideon. It's needed elsewhere, I'm sure."

"The Sovereign arranged for the sale of a multi-million dollar yacht confiscated during the recent fiasco

with the demon. It will pay for you and many other deserving paranormals who need a helping hand. Oliver deserves a second chance at life. The Sovereign—and myself—mean to guide his recovery to a manageable conclusion."

"You sold a yacht. What the hell ...?

"Did you never wonder how Oliver could afford to live on a sailboat in Key West? Why he always has money in his pocket? The finances of the Southeastern seaboard are set for quite some time, thanks to the demon dipping a greedy toe into our waters. Hex is gone, and we are cleaning up the mess. Oliver—and you—have suffered due to our inability to control our islands. I hope you will accept our offer and stay a little longer."

I listened, my mouth hanging open in shock and a tiny bit of excitement. A little help would certainly go a long way. I nodded. "But before I agree, I have something to get off my chest."

I went on to tell him about the gate, Sybil's behavior, the Incubus, and the gemstone the Witch took from the creature. I didn't mention Oliver. Somehow, I didn't get the impression that the Gryphon was surprised by any of it. *Sneaky bugger.*

He turned to face me, his golden eyes glowing brightly in the moonlight. *"You were wise to tell me, Phoebe. I will admit that this is not exactly news to me. But I didn't know the Incubus was in town, and I will look into this Mr. Griswald. Under the circumstances, I don't believe you deliberately caused problems for myself or the Sovereign."*

He turned to look at the stars as if thinking over my punishment. My jangling nerves made the pause seem an eternity. Finally, he looked at me.

"Oliver is Oemar, a royal Djinn of the Ancient Dunes clan of Mesopotamia. He has renounced his family ties because of a—previous situation. He has no one, Phoebe. Oliver is alone in the world."

When I stared at him, my mouth hanging open, he added, *"I left someone stranded on their own once. It was a mistake I will never repeat."*

Quiet filled the space between us as I heaved a sigh of relief, and digested what he told me. Oliver needed me. Even the Gryphon knew it. But it wasn't just the lack of funds that forced me to leave the Keys. It was the excruciating pain of seeing Oliver doing horrible things to himself. I wasn't sure I could handle it any longer.

Opening my mouth to say exactly that, I realized the Gryphon's eyes had been focused on me the entire time. The corners of his eagle lips drooped.

"Shit. Your mind-reading thing is freaky as hell, Gideon. I hope you don't take this personally, but can you stay out of my head, please?"

Laughter brushed across my senses, deep and throaty. *"I'm sorry. It is a habit. I will endeavor to give you more privacy in the future."*

Why didn't I believe him? With a groan, I stood and brushed the sand from my shorts. I held out my hand to shake Gideon's and realized who I was addressing.

"Thank you for bailing me out financially. It will make staying in Marathon much easier."

Out of nowhere, something screeched, and I jumped. A parrot clambered around the Gryphon's shoulders, hanging from his long pin feathers and glaring at me.

"Uh ... what is that?"

"Not what. Who. This is my parrot, Mr. Darcy. Sometimes, I take him on my little adventures."

With a cautious stare at the evil-eyed creature, I backed away. "Alright then. Nice chatting with you, Gideon. Will I see you again?"

He nodded but said nothing further. When I made it across the sand to the paved stone walkway, I looked back to see his parrot sitting on the sand beside him, staring up at the stars.

"Freaky," I whispered.

CHAPTER 14

~ OLIVER ~

Sleeping all day had some perks, but right now I stared down the barrel of one of the disadvantages. It was dark and I was wide awake—and completely alone.

The stars were out, and my chair on the bow was the perfect spot to watch them. Garrison Bight was flat calm. The colorful twinkling lights of the vessels filled with happy people lit up the dark bay with a festive vibe. The cheery visual turned my heart to lead; the gaping maw of loneliness swallowed me in large chunks.

Sorrow hung around my neck like an anchor. Restless, I wandered back and forth on my sailboat, stargazing, then cleaning, making ice cubes, attempting to read, and failing miserably. Phoebe was gone.

When the bottle came out, I knew it was a foolish move. I didn't care. I'd fallen so deeply into my miserable self that even a hangover sounded good.

I fully expected to sit in my chair drinking until I capsized and took a nosedive into the Bight. Been there. Done that. What I didn't expect was a splash at the stern followed by two young faces peering down at me. I'd gotten a decent start on my bottle, so the white and green of Felix's eyes merged together into a weird chartreuse.

"Can I get you boys a drink? We need some glasses." I tried to stand.

Felix grabbed my arm and settled me back in my seat. "Yes, but I'll go get them."

Jovi refused my offer of a chair, plunking down on the bow to face me. Peering up at the stars, he said, "I never get tired of staring at them. They're so beautiful. So full of promise."

I smiled into my drink. "At least something is."

Jovi frowned. "You do a lot of that, don't you?"

I raised my eyebrows. "Do what?"

"Hating yourself. It's not wise, Oliver. I read once—"

Holding my drink up, I said, "Let me stop you right there. I'm enjoying this evening just fine without any Reader's Digest therapy. Can we change the subject?"

Jovi frowned. "Alright. My apologies." He brightened. "Maybe this will cheer you up. I saw Phoebe today. She's staying in Marathon."

My glass fell from my numb fingers, the ice cubes skating across the plastic deck and plopping into the ocean, closely followed by three bucks worth of Jim Beam. I did manage to save my rocks glass.

Coughing back the fumes of a near choke, I rasped, "What's she doing in Marathon?"

"Working for Gideon. He's got a project for her. I imagine she's also catching up with Eddi and Ronan."

Felix returned with two wine glasses. I rolled my eyes, then poured him a drink. When the muscular male took a sip, I got a cheap whisky shower.

"What's in this, seagull piss?" Felix coughed and sputtered, then stared into his glass and sniffed.

"To be fair, it probably tastes better in the right glass." I wiggled my tumbler as Felix frowned.

"So, back to Phoebe. How did she end up in Marathon? Do you boys know?"

Felix sat down with a plop, spilling his drink. "The Enforcer had Eddi and Ronan pull her from the bus. She's staying at the Sovereign's guest lodging. At Gideon's instruction, we stopped today to ask if she needed any assistance."

"Wait. How did you get here? You don't drive."

Jovi wiggled his eyebrows. "No, but we swim. *Fast*."

Right. Their tails. I hadn't seen them in the water for so long I almost forgot.

After a long visit, the two of them felt the effects of the seagull piss, and soon, the laughter and the jokes got louder and more bawdy. Jovi and Felix had sown some wild oats in Key West, and apparently, Felix was quite the stud.

His eyes sparkling, Felix snorted, "And then she said, 'Take your pants off,' and I said, 'I can't,' and she said, 'Why not?' and I said, 'Because they're tattooed on!'"

Felix and Jovi rolled in a pile laughing like a pair of Hyenas. I smiled, not getting the joke but happy that they found a way to exist outside the Charleston facility.

Jovi looked at me with wet eyes and said, "Don't you get it? *Tattooed?* Those artsy things—the ink they jab into human skin—we can't hide our leg scales, so he told the girl it was a tattoo—" His lips pressed together. "Oh, never mind." Tapping his head, he winked. "Servus humor."

The two males stood, swaying slightly, and Felix said, "We should return to our island. We'll see you soon, alright?"

I nodded, and Felix shuffled toward the edge of the bow. Before he could step off, he lost his balance, landed on his butt, then fell face-first into the Bight with a booming splash. His heavy body tore the ropes from my railing on his way to the water. Jovi roared, then jumped in after him, helping untangle the mess. They waved before diving out of sight, the only sign of their departure a trail of flat swirls from their tails.

I sighed. Well, that killed two hours. Looking up at the stars, I realized it was still early and I wasn't quite there blood alcohol level-wise. I stood up, teetered down the steps, and grabbed my money clip. Chubby raged at being disturbed, and a burn started in my balls, making me hiss.

I managed to get down the docks and over to Handy's store, and had the new bottle at the till before realizing how drunk I was. I couldn't go back to the sailboat. Phoebe's perfume lingered in the cabin; spending time there was unbearable.

With a growl, I headed down to the small beach behind Munchies. Halfway through the second bottle, my problem subsided, the pain returning to a dull ache. Somewhere in the middle, I decided flying sounded like fun.

Hunching over, I managed to mist out, the feeling of taking to the air adding to the effect of the alcohol. At the last second, I sucked the bottle into my cloud, glad that I'd capped it.

"I might need you," I slurred. Then, I was off.

The thing about traveling in Djinn form was that time and space had no meaning. A talented Djinn was invisible to the naked eye and could go anywhere with impressive stealth and not a care in the world. A Djinn who had consumed a ridiculous amount of alcohol was clumsy, and his mist became visible upon close inspection.

And so I found myself drifting at a high rate of speed down Duval, barely missing lamp posts, people, and pink golf carts as I made my way north; a wake of shrieking humans disappeared behind me. When I hit the bridge off the island, I paused under a palm tree to consume the second half of my bottle, hoping it would help fuel my journey.

Unfortunately, all it did was make me easier to see. Misting across the parking lot of the Hurricane Hole, I waited until I found someone turning North on the highway and slipped in through the car vent to huddle on the back floorboards.

For an hour, I lay there, breathing as quietly as possible—not that easy, given the drunken pant I had going. When the vehicle stopped, my mist stirred as I rose to leave. I looked into the rearview and noticed, too late, the outline of my human head and shoulders. The driver screamed, I hissed, and the shell-shocked woman nearly broke my ear drums.

I may have screamed a little, too, but when she opened the door and bailed, I followed, shooting upward into the night sky before I got myself in trouble.

Marathon was a happening place during the day, but quiet at night. Unlike Key West, life was relatively normal here, with families going about their business alongside droves of tourists. I liked it instantly. It reminded me of my old home in Georgia.

Hovering in the air over the Publix parking lot, I opened my mind to search for Phoebe. It took only a moment to find her pink ball of energy squirming with the faint scent of cinnamon. So Unique. *So Phoebe.*

Excitement made me giddy, and I streaked across the distance between us, roiling to a stop outside her window. Gideon had outdone himself; Phoebe enjoyed a lovely suite of rooms.

Eagerly searching along the wall, I found a vent and slipped soundlessly into her living area. She wasn't there. I dropped to the carpet, stretching myself into a ground-covering mist.

I'd played this game many times before. Somehow, she always knew when I crept up on her, hoping to startle a scream from those lovely pink lips so I could kiss it away.

Tonight, I didn't want to scare her. I'd ruined her as it was. So I spread my mist along the floor to conceal my slightly visible form, and snooped through her place.

At the bathroom, I paused, sucking in a cloudful of her familiar smells. Even the minty scent of her toothbrush warmed my heart. I heard a noise, and my cloud contracted, then spread toward the bedroom. Whisking along the floor, I rose to enter at the ceiling. The clock read two in the morning; Phoebe was restless.

Too intoxicated to feel creepy for stalking her, I spread over the ceiling above the bed. Her nightie was new. The flimsy white lace had slipped from one shoulder, exposing the tiniest sliver of her nipple, and I nearly gave myself away with a husky groan.

Freshly washed, her hair smelled of apples. With the makeup removed, her beautiful face glowed beneath the dark brown lashes feathering her pale cheeks. Her sleeping form bathed in the moonlight filtering through the window. God, I loved her.

I sighed and slipped down the wall to hover next to the bed. I needed to get closer. I waved my arm and my hand was only a faint outline. The alcohol had dissipated slightly. Good enough.

Phoebe roused as I settled beside the bed, her soft, breathless mumbles making me smile. I thought she said my name and I smiled harder.

Curled against the edge of the soft covers, I sighed, my face hovering to watch her and marvel at the soft scents that were uniquely *hers*. Not just cinnamon, but the divine smell of—*home*.

This close, I saw the tiny mole beside her lip that she covered with makeup. The piercings in her ear, two on each side. The gentle curve of her brow, a slash of hair missing where she cut herself skating as a child. I loved that scar and kissed her there every night as I whispered my love to her.

My squeezing anxiety eased, and as the alcohol finally caught up with me, I drifted away on comforting thoughts of happier times.

CHAPTER 15

~ PHOEBE ~

My dream didn't scare me. It made me angry. A demon with blue gems for eyes chased a child. I *had* to help the poor thing. As fast as I ran, I never reached her. She was so close—

Something woke me. Did the bed move? I wanted to look. I prayed to the Gods above that Gideon's guest suite had no ghosts, then slowly opened my eyes.

A cloud hovered beside my bed, mere inches from my face. As downy as a gosling's feathers, the transparent entity wafted like smoke, appearing to sleep. For a moment, I wondered if something caught fire in the kitchen, but it was a face. I recognized it.

Oliver? Was I dreaming?

I longed to reach out and touch the apparition, but would it disappear? I watched instead. A pair of lips moved in and out as if breathing. The details of the shadowed eyes were blurred, but I knew they were closed. The cloud moved, and tiny wisps of what could have been hair tumbled forward, partially covering the face.

If this wasn't Oliver, it was a helluva dream. His bracelet kept him from misting; it couldn't be him. *Unless somehow he ...?* I pushed the thought aside.

Was it bravery, or my insatiable desire to touch the male I loved? Slowly, I reached for the thing. My fingertips tingled when I touched it. The cloud moved, and I pulled my hand back; the mist settled, and I reached forward to touch it again.

My fingers followed the hint of an ear and what could have been a jawline. The thing moaned, and it sounded like Oliver. Had he finally come to me?

Holding my breath, my heart swelled with joy; I could barely contain it. I leaned closer, ever so slowly, to avoid disturbing the sleeping entity. It was madness, but I placed a kiss on what I assumed was his cheek.

Eyes popped open and the cloud swirled, then shot straight into the air, slamming into the ceiling hard enough to make a subtle sound like distant thunder.

"Oliver?" I whispered, watching the cloud spread over the ceiling. "Is that you?"

It paused, and I knew. Oliver had come. At first, I thought he would bolt for the door, but instead, he drifted back down to my level and, with a gradual transformation, solidified. Oliver stood before me, tears staining his face.

"Oh, Ollie." I reached out, and he came to me, ignoring my hand and sliding into the bed, half beside and half on top of me. His face tucked into my neck as he sobbed.

"Shh. It's alright. I'm here." A bittersweet ache filled my chest, choking me. An overwhelming bliss at his presence turned into unbearable sorrow at the pain of his sobs.

Sinking into the soft pillows, I cradled him to me, stroking his hair and letting him cry. His arm inched around me until we twined together. Tears threatened; I held them back with steely control.

The smell of alcohol spiced his breath, no doubt causing an emotional kickback from the liquor. I didn't care. He was here. Somehow, after hellish years of pain and suffering, and God only knew what horrific tortures, he'd found a way to take that first step back to me. He still loved me. That was enough for now.

Eventually, Ollie pulled back, and his wet eyes gazed down into mine. I brushed his tears away. He spoke, his voice husky with emotion.

"I'm sorry, Pheebs. For everything."

"I know. You don't have to apologize. You'll find your way, Oliver. I'm still here, and I'm not going anywhere. Even when I'm away, I'm still with you—here." I pointed at my forehead, and his soft huff of relief tickled my face.

A long moment passed while his brilliant gray eyes glittered down at me; their silver flecks shimmered from the shadows with an ancient light; his soft gaze touched every atom holding me together; Oliver slipped into the very heart of me and grabbed on tight.

Slowly, his lips descended, and time swept backward as the old Oliver sank his weight into me. A confident brush of his mouth and I was in knots, his tongue gently exploring to find the seam of my lips before sliding deep, tugging a moan from my chest.

I slid my hand into his hair, my fingers tangling tightly into the soft strands. I pulled his lips closer, and he deepened the kiss, pressing his body into mine as if starved.

Lifting his lips, he traced them along my chin and nibbled down my neck, finding my collarbones and kissing them before raising a trembling hand to brush aside my nightie. He tasted the hard pebble of my nipple, and I arched against him. I held my breath, then gasped, my grip tightening on his hair.

My free hand smoothed over his back, hesitating when I felt his thick scars. I ran my fingertips lightly over the long ridges, and he stilled, panting into my neck; I moved on, grabbing his buttocks and squeezing. I hauled him close and he devoured me, his breath coming in rasping pants as he changed sides, nibbling and sucking. His hands squeezed and kneaded, tracing every contour of my skin. It felt—*I moaned*.

The moon went behind a cloud, and the room plunged into darkness. Oliver forged on, popping my nighty free with a yank on the buttons. I smiled as they pinged off the night table and fell to the floor; then he was down there, his tongue sweeping along the aching seam of my arousal. Muscular fingers gripped my ass, lifting me to his ravenous mouth.

Tasting, probing, his hot, wet tongue filled me and retreated, circling the firm nub that blazed to life under his flattened strokes. My legs tightened with a spasm of delight; my hands tugged his hair as I filled the air with tense, huffing gasps. His muffled groan razed up my spine and tingled behind my ears.

"Ollie," I whispered. *"Oh God."*

His fingers joined his lips, entering me and finding all those places we explored so many years ago. I cried out, and he increased the intensity, driving me wild with the ache of it.

"Stop," I whispered. Oliver looked up, his lips glistening, his hair tousled, a look of absolute hunger on his face. "Come up here. *Please.*"

Oliver answered my whispered plea with a smile, creeping up my body, retaking my lips as he kissed me into the stars. I wanted him. *Oh,* how badly I wanted him.

I hunted for the hem of his shorts and tried to slide them down, but a masculine hand latched onto my wrist. Oliver's face appeared above mine; his sweaty chest heaved as the scent of whisky rose between us. His silvery gaze wavering, Oliver's panicked eyes flicked between mine.

"I want you," I whispered. "*Please* don't say no."

The air stilled, Oliver's heart thumping wildly in his chest. Then, his lips covered mine and he lifted his hips. I yanked down his shorts; he grabbed my ass and pulled me up, then entered me with a swift glide of his straining shaft.

His head fell into my neck and Oliver rocked into me, moaning softly as he filled my body, mind, and soul. As his gentle strokes eased in and out, the thick groans and sighs coming from his lips pebbled my nipples, and his deepening thrusts pushed me into the mattress.

I rose to meet him, our bodies coming together in a sea of ecstatic sounds. Tangling arms, grasping hands, urgent lips—every shattered piece of us spiraled together into a cloud of feeling, his breaths becoming frantic when I called his name.

With a guttural moan, he drove into me, his body seizing as he came. The force of his grinding thrusts sparked a spiral of heat at the base of my spine that climbed, then blasted outward in an explosive detonation of bliss. My hips shoved into his as I groaned, the hot curling tension drowning me until slowly, my rapturous sighs trailed off.

Panting filled the room as Oliver settled onto me, his face wet against my neck. I tucked my fingers into his hair and encouraged him to relax, the two of us still joined. We lay there until his breathing slowed, then settled into a peaceful rhythm. Oliver cuddled close, his fingers tracing along my side, plucking gently at my torn nightie, then sliding beneath it to feel my skin.

I smiled. My body burned, a furnace stoked by happiness, the horrors that had torn us apart driven away by our connection. We were together. For even a speck in time, right now, that was good enough for me.

***

I woke to the sun in my face. My alarm said it was noon. Oliver was gone, but his lingering scent of citrus and sunshine filled my bedroom. My mood swooped low until, through the open door, I spied a note pinned to the fridge.

Terrified to read it, I headed to the kitchen with reluctant steps. Relief flooded through me at his words.

"Phoebe. Please forgive me for not staying. I know you have no choice about fixing my bracelet. Last night was wonderful. I will return for my penance, I promise. There's something I need to do first."

The note would have angered some women, but it was a sign to me—we'd turned a corner. The little heart Oliver added at the end had a smiley face inside, like so many of his past notes. Was it solid progress? Or would he slip back into hiding again? Only time would tell.

After a coffee and pastry I'd picked up the day prior, I dressed and headed to Eddi's for a visit. The five-minute walk was wonderful, the afternoon sun filling the air with the tropical scents of the Keys. The cloudless sky above glowed an incredible blue, and at the end of Eddi's street, the ocean put on a turquoise show. When I got to her apartment, I found her sitting on the sidewalk in a pink plastic chair reading a book.

"Hey! Why are you sitting down here?" I asked.

"Waiting for Ronan. He went for a swim." Her eyes traveled to the end of her road, where a break in the steel barrier led down a path to a short sandy beach. "Since we decided to keep the apartment, Ronan needs to recharge several times a day. Syreni are used to a damp environment," she sighed.

"Well, it sounds like you guys are working things out." The aroma of fresh bread from the bakery behind us filled the air. I'd be as big as a house if I lived here. When Eddi motioned to the second chair beside her, I sat as she groaned and adjusted her position.

"What are you up to, Phoebe?"

"I had a visit from Oliver late last night."

Her eyes went wide. "Seriously? How did he—?"

"His bracelet is dead, and he misted all the way from Key West. He promised to let me recharge the band later. Anyway, things were ... *good*. Should I tell Gideon about his wristband?" I chewed my lip and blushed.

Eddi's face split into a huge smile. "Well, that's great news! I'm so happy for you, Pheebs!" She leaned over and gave me an awkward hug around her stomach. "And no. If you trust Oliver, take care of it yourself. The Enforcer doesn't need to know *everything*." She winked, and I laughed. Her battles with Gideon were legendary.

We chatted for a while, but we didn't mention Charleston again. She'd lost her father on the return trip, and I didn't want to remind her about that terrible time in her life. When I got to the part about meeting Gabriel, she bit her lip as if holding something back. I frowned.

"Spill it, Eddi."

"Well, I'm wondering how you manage to be so loyal to him. Oliver, I mean. You've carried the torch for so long. Maybe you should allow yourself to move on. It's not my life, so I can't judge, but this Gabe fellow sounds promising."

I shrugged. "Gabriel is lovely. But almost too perfect—you know what I mean? Money, charm, incredible good looks ..." I waggled my eyebrows at her, and she laughed. "But something is missing. I don't know, maybe it's because Oliver and I were so good together before he—"

I quit before tears escaped. Eddi's eyes filled with sympathy.

"Did I ever tell you how we met?"

Eddi shook her head.

"We met on a beach. I vacationed at Tybee Island near Savannah and met him during a morning walk looking for shells. The tide was out, and I came across something odd—"

***

TYBEE ISLAND
~ PHOEBE ~

Stooping, I dug the sand from around the piece of driftwood, wondering about the golden color. When I worked it loose from its prison, I was surprised to find it wasn't completely rotten. Digging my nail into the shining wood, I chuckled. Paint. I pulled my arm back to toss it into the surf when a voice startled me.

"Don't!"

I turned to see a handsome guy with platinum blonde hair standing behind me.

"Why? It's a piece of driftwood."

"Ah, but you're wrong. Do you know what you're holding?"

His eyes twinkled when he smiled, and my stomach fluttered with tiny wings of excitement.

"I have no idea. What is it?" I handed the wood to him.

"It's a piece of a figurehead. In ancient times, wooden ships all had one, but they weren't only for decoration. Most of the population couldn't read, and if someone had business in the harbor, they'd never find the boat they sought. Figureheads solved the problem."

His silvery eyes smiled into mine, and he added, "Seamen are a superstitious bunch. Women weren't allowed on board, so they often used female figureheads—for good luck."

"That's fascinating!" I glanced down at the wood in his hands. His long fingers brushed over its contours as I struggled to focus on his words. His blonde hair whipping in the wind was sexy and kept distracting me.

"Personally, I think the seamen used female figures because they were terrified of their wives, and wanted to placate them." His teasing expression made me laugh.

"What part of the figurehead do you think this is?" I asked.

The guy grinned, his dimples lending him an endearing charm. "A breast. See?" He rolled it over, and I blushed as I saw the faintest suggestion of a nipple. At his chuckle, my face flamed brighter.

"Would you join me ...?" He motioned toward the distant parking lot. His sweet smile convinced me. I nodded, and we started down the beach together.

"I'm Oliver. And you are?"

"Phoebe. Phoebe Peregrin. Pleased to meet you. And thank you for carrying my ancient breast."

I joined in at his roar of laughter, and the walk went by far too fast. We chatted about so many things, the two of us falling into an easy banter. The entire way, I couldn't resist peeking at his tanned chest every time the wind teasingly opened the unbuttoned cotton shirt. Even the sandy hair dusting his legs had me gawking. I was awestruck by this handsome stranger, and every time he caught me staring, his warm smile sent shivers over my skin.

At the end of the beach, Oliver handed me back my treasure and asked if I would join him for lunch sometime. When I nodded, he turned to me and very seriously, said, "I have a confession to make. I need to come clean before we go any further."

My heart plummeted. The guy was married. I knew it. I frowned, and at my scowl, he grinned, pointed at my small piece of history and said, "That's not a figurehead. It's a painted piece of driftwood."

I stared at him, my mouth open. Lines curved into his cheeks as he laughed, his eyes sparkling with glee. With a wet thwack, I smacked him with my buried treasure, an embarrassed smile flushing my face.

Oliver looked at me, the wind teasing his hair, his expression soft. "God, you're beautiful."

***

Eddi's eyes softened at my pinched expression. "That's the sweetest story. No wonder you're working so hard to resolve things."

"From the moment I met Oliver, I knew he was the one for me. He worked in Augusta, which was a freaking miracle. We were inseparable, and for months, we saw each other nearly every day. It was so right, you know? I wanted him to move in, and he kept resisting, so we had a little spat about it."

"The day after we argued, he was supposed to come for dinner and never showed up. I was heartbroken. The whole time he's been missing, I fretted about whether I scared him off. But somehow I always knew. Oliver would never deliberately hurt me. I *knew* something happened, but I didn't know what."

Holding in a sob, I stopped speaking and stared out at the ocean. The seabirds calmed me as I watched them hover on the air currents, their high-pitched squawks ringing on the breeze.

Eddi sighed. "I'm so sorry this happened to the two of you. You know I get it, right? I feel your pain, trust me." She reached out and took my hand, squeezing it.

Feeling eyes on me, I watched Ronan trot up the sidewalk, his muscular body slick from the ocean. Eddi's face lit up and a slash of jealousy speared my heart. I brushed it away. My friends had gone through hell to be together. They deserved every second of happiness they could find. I wiped my eyes and steeled myself to think positive from now on.

After saying hello to me, Ronan leaned down, resting his hands on the arms of Eddi's pink chair and kissing her. It went a bit longer than was comfortable, so I looked away.

"Cut it out," she said, giving his arm a playful slap. "We have an audience, remember? Help me up, would you?" Ronan laughed, a wonderfully masculine sound, then put his bare feet over hers, took her hands, and hauled her upright. She groaned as she made it to her feet, but Ronan kept right on going, pulling her into his arms for another deep kiss.

"Ok, you two. Get a room," I laughed. Flushed from his attention, Eddi turned to me and asked if I wanted to come in for lunch.

I declined, telling them I'd return soon for another visit. When I looked back, Ronan was kissing her again, the backdrop of the ocean making me sigh. They were so damned lucky.

Back at my suite, I walked in, dropped my keys on the counter, then screamed when something moved. My hand flew to my mouth. Behind me on the living room sofa was a Koala bear. *A freaking Koala.*

"Oliver? What are you doing?"

The fuzzy little varmint sat notched in the corner of the couch, one arm along the armrest, its cute little double-thumbed hand gripping the upholstery. It stared up at me, the soft brown eyes following my every move. The pupils had slits. *Weird.*

"Oliver, *why...?*"

A cute nose wiggled to sniff in my direction, and something dawned on me. Last night, Oliver was in his mist form. This morning, a cute, cuddly gray Koala adorned my couch. Was he afraid to be himself with me? Was this his way of coping?

Crossing over to the sofa, I sat down, not too close, and said, "I'm so glad to see you. Are you alright? Do you need something to eat?"

The fluffy, slow-moving bear didn't answer. It sat and stared, its little mouth working back and forth under the bulbous, uber-cute nose.

"I must say, this form is even sweeter than the original."

The Koala's eyes snapped to mine. Then, moving slowly from its resting position, the fuzzy thing crawled toward me, its rump wiggling as it ambled across the small space. I leaned back on the sofa, and it curled into my lap. My hand sank into the soft gray fur, a pair of liquid brown eyes staring into mine. After a pause, Oliver eased further onto my chest.

Spreading his arms out, the bear held me close, one furry cheek pressing under my chin and snuggling in. When his claws pinched my leg, I reached down and moved his odd back feet. He nestled into me, unmoving.

I sighed, relaxing into the couch, and enjoyed the feeling of holding him. Sure, it was a Koala. It wasn't quite Oliver, but what a wonderful substitute.

My hand absentmindedly stroked his fur, and I started talking, unsure if he understood me but doing it anyway.

"I miss you. I miss ... *this*."

The Koala made a noise, a quiet rattling grunt, and pressed in deeper.

I laughed softly. "I'm glad you agree."

We cuddled there for a while, and it was so peaceful that I must have dozed off. When I woke up, the Koala was gone. Sad that Oliver left, deep inside of me, a hopeful flame sparked to life. It was far too early to be sure this was progress, but it felt that way to me. Oliver came to me on his own. Twice. Maybe someday soon, it would be as himself. No crutches. No tears. No panic.

The lack of power in his bracelet was a problem, but I didn't have it in me to be angry. I'd never wanted to put it on him in the first place. I'd get it sorted when I saw him again, and if he didn't show up as promised, I'd tell Gideon. In my heart, I was happy Oliver was free.

CHAPTER 16

~ OLIVER ~

Misting along the narrow side street, I left Phoebe's apartment and returned to Key West. It took me three tries, but I finally found a car that went all the way to the island. I lucked out when they took the loop past Garrison Bight.

Exhausted, I slipped into the sailboat and reformed into my human body. I wobbled, weakened from lack of sleep, energy expenditure, and dehydration from drinking. My erection was gone, thank God, but guilt tore at me. I should have been with Phoebe. Instead, I hid in Key West.

Being with her was a mixture of pain and heavenly pleasure, but numbness from the booze was the only reason I managed to hold it together. I was pathetic. Phoebe deserved so much better than what I offered.

I forgot to ask why Gideon stopped her at Marathon. I didn't know the Gryphon well, but I knew he did nothing by chance. But face-to-face conversations were difficult for me, especially with Phoebe. It was hard to imagine that having a conversation would be such a huge hurdle in my life.

The night Phoebe stayed over on the sailboat was an emotional shake-and-bake for me. Suddenly, I went from pushing her away to being too close for comfort. Way too close. There were so many things she didn't know. Things that happened to me in Charleston. But how could I tell her?

I was dirty. Vile. I didn't stay true to her while in captivity. Terror rose every time I imagined opening up and confessing. I couldn't bear to see her expression when she realized I was a sick fuck.

My jagged emotions warred for supremacy. Tell her, and watch her storm away in disgust. Don't, and watch her slowly drift further and further from me. I figured slow would be less painful. I was wrong.

I tried to drive her away, and even now, after all the things I'd done, it hadn't worked. The woman was a pit bull. I smiled at that. Tenacious as ever. Some things never changed.

For better or worse, going to see her in Marathon helped. The Koala was the perfect choice. After Charleston, my monstrous bear would have scared the hell out of her.

Our long snuggle this afternoon had done wonders for the ache in my chest, but guilt was never far away. When Phoebe fell asleep, the walls closed in, and I slipped away.

I needed to work harder on my recovery. Forward was the only direction for us now, yet the thought terrified me.

Determined, I borrowed my neighbor's cell phone and secured a slip at the Marlin Marina in Marathon. It was close to Phoebe's place. As I prepped my sailboat to depart, I smelled peaches and sunshine. I groaned and packed a little faster, but there he was, haunting my dinette.

"Are you sure this is a good plan, Oliver?"

"Hello, Ezen. Not that it's any of your business, but yeah, why?"

"Are you committed to her well-being? While you may recover from your experiences under the demon's thumb, there is still the matter of your past. You must protect Phoebe."

I cringed. "She'll never find out about that."

Ezen's long sigh scraped down my spine. *"Your deceptions will always find you out. Don't you know that by now? After what she's been through, isn't now the perfect time to enlighten her? You two are standing on opposite sides of a doorway. If you step through, it should be with her full understanding.*

"I have no interest in my past. I barely miss the desert. It's well behind me. But thanks."

"Saying it doesn't make it so. Djinn don't have the option to escape their past, Oliver, and yours has certainly not forgotten about you. Do you remember your visitor in Charleston? The mask with the covers over the eyes? Your anonymous friend, 'Y'?"

I froze, unable to breathe. Ezen was there. He knew all about the torture sessions. My terrified screams at every cutting lash from unseen hands. The regular burns and beatings, never knowing who doled out the punishments, *or why*. The sexual violations. My stomach soured.

When I glanced over, his shape was clearer, his silvered, sorrowful eyes drilling into me. The last time I watched Ezen dragged from his cell in Charleston, he was skin and bones, unable to eat or drink, let alone stand. Now, he appeared hale and hearty, as if the past never happened. He was there—did he remember?

"Yes, I know who 'Y' is, Oliver. And if you think hard enough, you do too. He misses the fun he had in Charleston. He's set his sights on Phoebe now—to make you pay for what you did."

With a snarl, I lunged for his throat. My hand passed right through him, and my fist connected with the wall.

Ezen didn't move, and when I pulled away, the wisps of his form followed my fingers like ghostly spiderwebs.

"Tell me who he is!" My scream filled the small kitchen.

"I cannot. The Upper Circle measures the influence I am allowed. I must save my assistance for ... other things. But think, Oliver. Think. Who would want you to suffer most in this world?"

His words hit me like a bus, bile splashing the back of my throat. The desert. The stolen slave.

"Janus," I hissed.

Ezen nodded. *"He loves his games, doesn't he? Yanis is the Greek pronunciation of his name, hence the 'Y'. He was cautious, fearing your retribution should you escape. You must protect her, Oliver. Your past is alive and well. Janus will use Phoebe to watch you crawl at his feet again."*

With a plunk, I sat down across from him and put my head into my hands, my elbows digging into the tabletop. "What will I do? The bastard probably knows my location. Why doesn't he just take me now? I don't care about myself, but if he ever hurt Phoebe ... "

Horror flooded through me. I'd seen firsthand what Janus did to women when it suited his purpose. Tormenting females was his favorite form of entertainment.

Ezen sighed. *"Janus feeds from his games. He's twisted, Oliver. My pain matches yours. Many years ago, I found myself in much the same situation. My daughter was in grave danger ..."*

His form flickered, his eyes wide as he faded. Ezen furrowed his brows in concentration, returning to his usual wispy self with a relieved sigh.

"Speaking of things other than my task is not allowed. I wish I had more freedom to help you." He leaned back against the cushions, watching me with a sad expression.

"I was a master swordsman in my time. I would have destroyed the demon who enslaved us had I not been outnumbered. Imagine how different things might be for both of us had I succeeded in killing Hex. Janus was very well acquainted with the demon."

My skin tightened as his words hit home. "My capture wasn't random. Was it Janus' work?"

He nodded. *"While Janus was not directly involved in Hex's Charleston operation, it was no coincidence you were the Djinn chosen for their breeding program. Though we are rare, there are six Djinn on this continent who would have suited their needs."*

Pain reflected in the glowing silver of his eyes. *"As you are aware, I was their first choice. Driving the Demon mad with my continued resistance kept me sane. But looking at you now, I wish I had relented, allowed her to use me, and spared you the horrors of that place."*

Running my fingers through my hair, I whispered. "I'm sorry I couldn't help you. I could barely help myself. I don't remember half of it."

Ezen's misty hand reached out. Although he wasn't solid, my skin tingled where he touched my shoulder.

"Remember, Oliver. Time heals everything. Djinn may not be Immortal, but you have plenty of time to weave a future for yourself. Don't make the same mistake I did. My futile resistance destroyed my life force, and now there is no going back. I regret that I cannot spend this time with my daughter, Eddi. I will never hold my grandson. I would do so many things differently if given the chance"—his eyes flashed—*"even if it meant letting a monster use me."*

My eyes burned. "I tried to resist. Hex's magic in the Talisman of Tenebris stole my will every time they put it around my neck. How in the world did you manage to avoid its thrall?" I raised my hand to my chest, a phantom memory of the shiny black horse figurine burning my skin.

Ezen smiled, a grim, brittle thing. *"I was far older than you, Oliver. A Djinn's tolerance to blood magic grows over time. I resisted to drive the demon mad, not knowing my daughter would come for me. Sadly, she was too late."*

At my stricken expression, he whispered, *"Do not trouble yourself. It is the past. Leave it there. If you don't, your mind will fester into the madness that lurks for all Djinn."*

When I stood to get a drink, Ezen sighed. *"How is my daughter? Have you seen her? I know she is with child.*

How I wish I could speak with her once more." He hung his head, his form flickering and almost disappearing.

I paled. "Phoebe visited her recently. I can bring you news if we cross paths. Do you want me to tell her about our visits?"

Ezen shook his head. *"No, the reminder would be too painful for her. She is in a better place. When I close my eyes, I see her. That is enough for me."*

As I watched, he faded from view. As he disappeared, I heard the faint sound of sand lifted by the wind. Too late, I remembered that I wanted to ask him if he was able to leave the boat. I still wondered if I imagined his presence. Was I toeing the line of madness, where a nudge would push me across?

I shivered, finished my drink, and crawled onto my mattress. It still smelled of Phoebe, and my cock roared to life. Punching my pillow, I flopped down and, through sheer exhaustion, finally fell asleep.

***

~ PHOEBE ~

As I picked up food and supplies in town, I kept my eyes open for a certain Witch. Sybil disappeared without a trace after the gemstone incident, and now, with things settled down, I pondered her motives. What was she up to?

Oliver said he knew of another gem. I meant to ask him about it, but it slipped my mind. With a sigh, I picked up the paper to check the job listings. I didn't want Gideon footing my entire bill.

Flicking through the help wanted section, a small ad caught my eye. It was a short ad with an email.

Looking for a witch with a strong background in Binding & Grounding. Must have own transportation and be willing to sign a contract. Location: Boot Key. Email sybilmetroyer@gmail.com

What the hell? Surely she wasn't looking to open another tear in our dimension? The Witch was mad. She had to be. No one in their right mind trifled with magic that dark. I grabbed the paper, paid my bill, and stepped out of the air conditioning into the blast furnace of the afternoon. Gideon needed to hear about this.

***

~ OLIVER ~

Darla blushed when I leaned down and kissed her cheek in greeting. Settling into my chair, I crossed my legs and clapped my hands. "So what's it going to be today, darling—I mean, *Darla*?"

She pursed her lips, but her eyes smiled. "You seem in much better spirits today. Are things going well?"

Phoebe's sleeping face flashed through my mind, and I gasped at the pain that shot through my groin. "Yes," I croaked. "I've been seeing Phoebe. We … I … "

When I trailed off, Darla beamed. "Have you found a way to breach your intimacy barriers with her? That's wonderful news, Oliver. I'm so happy for you."

Mumbling under my breath about alcohol helping, Darla frowned. "You were drunk when you had relations?"

Guilt tore through me as I nodded. Darla looked out the window, chewing her pen. She pointed the gnarly tip at me and said, "I see by your expression that you already know it's not the best approach, hmm?"

Another nod, but this time, my face turned red.

"If it helped you take that first step, it won't hurt anything. But you realize that until you can approach her sober, you haven't made the progress you're looking for. Using alcohol to lower inhibitions almost always ends badly. Fights, misunderstandings, bad behavior—they all come hand in hand with alcohol."

"I understand that. Phoebe deserves better." I shot her a hopeful look. "Being with her was wonderful. It hurt like a bitch in here"—I pointed to my head—"but it felt amazing here." I tapped my chest.

"I'm truly happy for you, Oliver. Let me ask you something. Do you trust Phoebe?"

"With all my heart," I whispered. "I don't know why she's still here, but she is."

Darla put down her pen and shoved her glasses onto her head. "I'll be honest with you. Many partners don't make it through treatment. Phoebe is generous with her support, but I hate to say it ... co-dependency can be an issue. It concerns me that she hasn't reacted to your intoxication during interactions."

I frowned. "What do you mean—co-dependency? And I'm not *always* drunk when I'm with her. Maybe some of the time. Ok, most of the time. *Shit,* you're right."

Looking straight at me, Darla said, "Phoebe loves you. That is clear. But there are times when love can become unhealthy."

At my angry stare, she continued, but not before her eyes flicked briefly to my pink bracelet. Luckily, it still glowed with Sybil's spell, and she had no idea I was free to get my freak on.

"You've pushed her away, Oliver. You threw down roadblocks, refused to see her, and tormented her by having only one toenail in the relationship—yet she's still here. Codependency happens when a partner overlooks problems until it becomes unhealthy. Phoebe's self-esteem is probably at an all-time low. She's lost the love of her life. She's struggling to maintain your relationship in the face of unimaginable odds. Tell me, has she been drinking or using drugs?"

"NO!" I shouted. "Phoebe isn't a drinker. She's never ... I mean, I'm not there often, but I've never seen her ..." I sighed. "I don't know what she does when I'm not there.

But I've never smelled alcohol on her breath, and there's never been any in her... " I realized then that I never set foot inside her Key West apartment after she arrived. *SHIT.*

"Perhaps she's a strong female and isn't having codependency issues, but it's something to be aware of. Addictive behaviors can be an issue on both sides during times of intense stress in a relationship."

"Has Phoebe ever tried to manipulate you? Threatened to leave you if you don't change? Is she angry at you or disappointed? Or how about physical tells? Does she have headaches, any unusual eating patterns, or trouble sleeping? Does she blame you, Oliver?"

"NO!" I shouted, jumping to my feet. "Phoebe is a SAINT. She puts up with my crap and never says anything like—what you're suggesting!" The room was suddenly too small, and I started pacing, my hands clenched at my sides. "She's too good for me! She's ... she's ... *fuck!*"

Darla tensed at my outburst, but her voice stayed quiet. Gentle. "Well, then, Oliver. You're the luckiest male alive, aren't you?"

I stopped where I stood and frowned. "You did that on purpose."

Darla sighed. "Not really. Oliver, you're a valued client. You're such a pleasant fellow at heart. What happened to you is beyond horrible. I want you to know that to the depths of my soul, I want only the best for you."

Staring at her, I waited for the other shoe to drop. "But?"

"Until you open yourself up completely to recovery, you'll limp down this road like a car with two flat tires dragging its muffler, its bumper, and with a headlight out. And you'll drag Phoebe with you."

"I've tried! Don't you think I've tried?" I stuffed my hands into my hair and pulled, my eyes wild.

Darla scribbled something into her notebook, and I wanted to grab the pen from her hands and snap it in two. I gritted my teeth instead.

"Would you be open to having Phoebe join us for a session?"

"NO. *Absolutely not.*"

Sighing, Darla said, "That's your right. But give it some thought. Dig deep and ask yourself—is Phoebe your spare tire? She may not be codependent, but eventually, frustration turns to anger, and bonds can break. Yes, recovery is a battle you fight for yourself, but remember, it's not just you suffering through this. Partners are often collateral damage."

After I left, Darla's words tore through me like shrapnel. All this time, I never thought about whether Phoebe had suffered. I was a selfish monster. For the love of God, recovery was hard and sucked ginormous balls.

CHAPTER 17

~ OLIVER ~

Caught in the Wind was an easy sailboat to handle, but today she was a challenge. I had my hands full when the wind picked up halfway to Marathon. I managed to reef the main and lower my speed, but the offshore swells got so big that I headed toward shore and sailed down Hawk's channel. The long trough connected Key West to Key Largo, and the waters weren't as rough.

I heaved a sigh of relief when I finally dropped the sail and puttered by motor into the marina. My hands shook, but the trip thrilled me to the marrow.

After settling into my slip, I visited the office, paid the tab, and hit the showers. Although it didn't have a pool, the marina was pleasant and offered two outdoor hot tubs with a killer ocean view. Sharing one with Phoebe crossed my mind, but the pain between my legs diverted my attention back to settling in.

Thumps on the deck told me I had visitors. Jovi and Felix charged down the steps, their bare chests glistening with seawater. Angry scowls filled the kitchenette.

"You didn't wait for us!" Jovi grumbled. "We wanted a ride on your boat! I've never been on a sailboat before!"

I froze, my flipper dripping grease back into the pan. "You guys wanted to come sailing?"

Felix nodded. "Jovi's been bugging me since we first saw your boat. It's pretty cool." He ran his hand over the wood trim of the stairwell and sighed.

Ok then. These clowns could swim thirty-five miles an hour but wanted to sail. Who'd have thought it?

"Next time, boys. How about something to eat?"

They nodded, and Felix peeked into the pan. "We're starved. What are we having?"

My half-Syreni, half-Djinn friends had a wide range of food preferences, unlike their Syreni damline, which preferred fish. Felix and Jovi inhaled the burgers I put together, the grease dripping down their chests and all over my dinette.

"We have another job," Jovi said around his mouthful of burger. "Another demon." It sounded like he said *WeeWum*, and I had to laugh. I handed him a napkin.

"Another demon? Where is it this time?"

Felix mopped his chest. "Boot Key Harbor. The location is only accessible by water. It's hiding in the kayak trails of the Mangrove island there." Looking me up and down with a frown, he added, "We won't be taking the truck. Do you have access to a motorboat?"

I smiled. Phoebe's friend Eddi was a captain. "I might. How much time do I have?"

The Servus agreed to meet me here the following afternoon. I cleaned up and headed over to Phoebe's. When I got there, she wasn't home. Her suite was in a low-slung apartment building overlooking a canal, so I ducked into the brush behind the building, wisped into Djinn form, and then located her. She wasn't far.

As I swept toward her life force, I realized she wasn't alone. Hovering above the island gathering, I kept one eye on the crocodile shifter sunning itself on the bank. A Sea Sprite sat on its nose, a mass of younglings swarming around the duo.

Nearby, Eddi and Phoebe lounged in the water, wearing swimsuits and floating up to their neck in the ocean. The boat I hoped to inquire about bobbed on its anchor in a channel thirty feet from the swimmers. I moved closer.

"So, do you love him?" Eddi asked. I froze, waiting for Phoebe's answer and feeling horrible for listening.

"With all of my heart. But I often wonder if I've got the strength to see it through." Her eyes shone with tears. "It's been so freaking hard, Eddi. One minute, he's there, and I'm hopeful; the next minute, he withdraws again."

Eddi reached out and touched her shoulder. "Ronan and I almost didn't make it, but I assure you. If he's right for you, he's worth the effort."

I met Eddi once. In Charleston. I barely remembered her frantic face peering through the glass doorway of my cell in the facility basement. At the time, I was lost to rage and the voices in my head. She and her friends broke in to save me, but I would have killed every one of them if I had the chance.

Fury heated my skin. Charleston ruined so many lives. Eddi's swollen belly reminded me of Ezen's sorrow, and I breathed deep to regain control. I needed to stay focused.

Phoebe looked up as if sensing movement, so I retreated to the mangroves. Dammit, I needed to speak to her. And Eddi. But I couldn't randomly show up.

I listened to them for a while, but they talked about Sybil, so I drifted away. I would wait at her apartment. She'd come home at some point.

When I arrived, I slipped through the vent and reformed, checking through her apartment. I knew it was rotten, but Darla made me nervous with the whole drug-alcohol-codependency thing. There was nothing in the suite to indicate a problem. Phoebe managed my mess alone—without crutches.

As I sat on the couch, loneliness darkened my vision as doubt filled my mind. What had I done? Even before my abduction, my presence put her in danger. On the run from my past and Janus, I'd been in the States for thirty years. I always assumed he lost interest and gave up on finding me. What if I was wrong? Where was the bastard now?

Putting my head in my hands, I winced when the scars on my back pulled tight. Janus gave me those scars. Darkness fogged my vision, the smell of metal invading my nostrils.

It was cold against my face, and when Stephen slid the covers over my eyes and blocked my vision, I knew 'Y' was here, and today I'd get the whip. The smell of cedar teased me, a forceful breath my only warning before—

I opened my eyes with a gasp, my scars stinging like they remembered the bloodied strokes of Janus' whip. Memories of his pounding cock assaulted my senses. His muffled pants and hissing laughter reached from the past, freezing my blood as if I were still beneath him, his sweaty skin pressed to mine.

Wrenching my thoughts under control, guilt slashed through me. On top of the emotional wreckage, I had to worry about Phoebe's safety. Rising to pace across the living area, I bit my nails.

My cock throbbed in my shorts, my anxiety intensifying the pain. *Fuck.* I wanted to tear the damn thing off to get some fucking relief from it! Rage at my captors and Janus roared to life; they'd done this to me; there was no undoing the damage; the black coating on my skin would never wash off; I would never get better; I was filthy; doomed; and that fucker Janus wanted Phoebe.

Panic snuffed out reason.

Darla's breathing exercises collapsed under the onslaught of my anger, mist rising from my boiling skin. I nearly suffocated in that fucking mask every time he whipped me. My chest squeezed, the mist rolling much thicker now. The smell of a propane flame and burning skin sickened me. The four walls of the apartment closed in. Trapped, I put out my hands to push them away. I was back in Charleston. In my dark cell. Stephen stepped from the gloom in the hall. Smiling. The fucker was always smiling. He flicked the Chef's torch in his hand.

A scream tore from my throat as I misted out, swept through the vent, and blew past a surprised Phoebe. Startled, she dropped her bag of groceries. I whirled to gape at her, and although she couldn't see me, she knew.

"Oliver?" Her soft whisper pushed me over the edge.

"I'm sorry." The words disappeared into the black void of my living hell.

***

When I came to my senses seated in a bar, I moaned. Rubbing my forehead, I looked around me. I was in it up to my asshole again.

Vampires pranced around half-naked on a dance floor nearby, writhing to a Techno beat. I slouched in a dark corner, in a private booth, with a drink in my hand.

Shit. I scrubbed my face, barely feeling my fingers. With a shrug, I took a sip of my whisky, the burn of the liquor stronger than I expected.

I glanced around the room, wondering where I was, and then I remembered. Priscilla told me about the vamp bar in Marathon. A pink, green, and blue neon sign on the wall gave me the name.

"Delirium." Perfect. Three hours in town, and I'd found one of my greatest weaknesses. Delirium didn't have a back door club, though. It was all out front, and it was neither shy nor subtle.

The sounds of sex filled the air. Bamboo partitions screened the booths lining the outside of the dance floor, but no one used the privacy curtains.

Kitty corner from me, a vampire sprawled on an ottoman, a girl in a skimpy skirt sliding up and down his rigid shaft. Moaning, she leaned down for him to bite her neck. Pain stabbed through my cock at the sight, and I looked away with a snarl.

I was sober enough to know it was time to get the hell out of here. I picked up my drink to finish it. As I got closer to the bottom of the glass, it seemed further away. I blinked, swaying in my seat and staring into the empty tumbler for who knew how long.

A pretty waitress in a mini skirt and high heels stopped by, her curls bouncing as she bobbed her head with a giggle. "Another house special, honey?"

I mumbled, "What the hell is in this stuff?"

"I told you, silly. It's Delirium. That shit messes you up, but it's super popular." I frowned as her body went in and out of focus. Watching her pretty lips moving, I narrowed my eyes. I couldn't think of a single reason not to say yes to her question. In a heartbeat, I nursed another house special.

How long I sat there, I don't know. Dimly aware of being joined by another couple, I ignored their fuckery, sipping my drink with great focus. At some point, one of their male friends stopped by. I watched the threesome and nursed my drink, my mind swaying back and forth between Phoebe's pretty hazel eyes and the debauchery going on before me.

The waitress brought me another drink, and the world faded; when the pricks of two vampire teeth brought me around for an instant, I gave the male vamp a stupid grin. I couldn't feel my aching cock any longer. I sighed and settled into the rush of his venom.

My world became a sea filled with warm cotton candy that stuck to my skin, covering the blackness of it and lifting me into the clouds.

A few bites later, I couldn't feel my toes or fingers. A silly smile plastered my lips; I let the male devour me. My weightless head lifted from the cushions to kick away an aggressive female with a rabid snarl.

When someone resembling Phoebe appeared in my face, I cocked my leg back to boot her in the gut. I stopped when those pretty pink lips said my name.

"Oliver?" The beautiful face drifted in and out like an angel, a strange blue light glowing behind it. I lifted my hand but couldn't feel the skin under my fingertips.

"You look like someone I knew once," I mumbled. "She's not dead—yet." Tears filled my eyes, and I whispered, "I'm going to kill her."

Someone took the drink from my hand. I didn't need it. I flew with pink elephants and didn't have a care in the world.

After loud voices and a flurry of activity, I found myself staring at the ground, something hard pushing into my guts. Struggling to keep my *house special* where it belonged, I breathed through my nose. Cool air brushed my cheeks, then there was nothing.

I woke up in the berth of my sailboat, my body and brain on different planes of existence. My eyes rolled as I looked around the small room, then paused on Phoebe sitting near my berth. She clutched a cloth in her lap, staring at it. Feeling my gaze, she looked at me, her eyes rimmed with tears.

"Hey," she said, leaning forward to dab my forehead with the cloth. "Are you alright?"

"What happened? One minute, I waited in your apartment, and the next …" I frowned. "Delirium. I ordered a drink called Delirium, and they spiked it with something."

"Vampire venom," she said, her voice cold. "House specialty. Very popular. They told me all about it right before I punched the manager in the face."

"How did you find me?" I slurred.

"Ronan's brother Bacchus. He's quite the party boy and frequents the bar next door. Do you remember him from Charleston?"

I shook my head, vaguely registering a massive body with long hair and glittering blue skins.

"He was outside and recognized you. You seemed—*off*. He was worried. He went to Eddi's, and she called me. You're very lucky, Oliver. *Others* have died from that stuff." She frowned, then dabbed my face again. "Gideon is shutting down the bar as we speak. He was livid."

I turned to face the wall, hoping the room would stop spinning. "I blacked out."

"You're still having blackouts?" Phoebe frowned.

"Not as often anymore. While I waited for you, I got worked up about something and lost control. I nearly ran you over on my way out the door."

"I thought I felt you. Why didn't you stop?"

"I don't know." My voice came out a rasping whisper. I reached up to take her hand. "I'm so sorry. God, I'm constantly saying that to you these days, aren't I?"

Phoebe looked down into her lap, her expression strained. "I knew what I was getting into, Ollie. You don't have to apologize."

Staring up at her, barely able to focus, the crushing weight of my guilt pressed me into the mattress.

"This is why I tried to push you away in Key West. My life is an ongoing nightmare. Tonight was tame compared to some of the shit I've done recently. You don't need to see it, Phoebe. You should be with that other guy."

Her head snapped to face me, her eyes wide. "How did you—?"

I stuttered, suddenly unsure about what I should say to her. I was so busted. I lowered my eyes in embarrassment.

"I saw you. At the bar near the docks. The day you saw my bites, and I chased you off."

She groaned and covered her face. "I'm so sorry, Oliver. I didn't mean to take up with him, but Gabe came along right when it seemed we wouldn't make it through this. I felt so guilty this whole time …. " Her voice cracked, her eyes filling with tears. I reached up to brush them away.

"See why you shouldn't be with me? There's been way too many of these lately. You don't have to apologize. I had no claim on you, Phoebe."

She began crying in earnest, and I pulled her down with me, tucking her into my shoulder.

"My therapist, Darla. She made me realize something, and I'm glad she did. Never, in all the time I've been stewing in my own mess, did I understand how much you suffered too. I have no idea why you're still here. But I'm glad you are."

Phoebe cried harder, and I cuddled her close. My mind was still in the clouds, but holding her grounded me. I let her cry, my eyes closed as I listened. I stroked her soft hair, pressing kisses into it, and wallowing in her unique scent.

When she settled, her hand came up and played with my chest, her fingertips brushing over my skin. As I knew she would, Phoebe found the lumpy scar Hex gave me after biting in a fit of passion. I remembered that one because it hurt like a bitch for weeks.

"You're mine, and you're delicious," the Demon hissed, its beady eyes glowing red. That night was a bad one, more bites following the first. I shivered and shoved the memory away.

Phoebe's tears clogged her throat, her voice husky. "*Oh, Oliver.* What are we going to do?"

She asked the wrong person because I hadn't a clue.

"Keep going forward. Keep working toward stability. I'm sorry, that's all I've got, and I got that pearl of wisdom from my therapist."

She laughed, a wet, weak sound, then snuggled tighter against my chest.

I dozed off, but when I woke up, I felt clearer. I also had a hand tickling across my belly. My cock filled to the point of pain, and I took Phoebe's hand in mine.

"As much as I'd like to go there, I don't think it's a good idea. If we have sex again, I should be sober." Phoebe rose on her elbow, her brown hair cascading down her face. "You what?"

"In case you haven't noticed, love, I have to be intoxicated to be with you." I frowned. "I'm still hiding. I want to be sober the next time we … "

I stopped when I saw her scowl in the darkness. "Wait. You're mad?" Now, I was confused.

"Oliver, your therapist is great, but I don't care if you're drunk. Don't you see? It's a step forward, not something permanent. If that's what it takes for you to relax with me, why shouldn't you?" I chuckled, but Phoebe wasn't finished.

"A few months from now? Yeah. If you're still doing it then, I'll kick your ass. But right now I want you and I don't care about anything except being next to you." She settled back onto the bed with a grumble and undid the buttons on my shirt. When her hand slid over my chest, I moaned.

"I've wanted to ask you this for so long. Why don't you—*you know?*" She looked at my groin.

"Jerk off?"

Red flushed across her face. Gods, she looked lovely in the moonlight.

"I can't. Trust me, it was the first thing I tried. No matter how hard I—" My face burned. "It gets raw because I ... *I can't finish*. Booze works sometimes, but until now, it took vampire venom to relax me enough to climax. But I didn't want another female to touch me, so I only let—"

She put her fingers against my lips. "I know," she whispered. "I went to the club. I talked to Polly."

Well, that was news. Somewhere inside of me, a boatload of tension sank beneath the waves. All this time,

I was afraid to let her see I was a weakling. That I was sick. That I wasn't the male I used to be.

Phoebe tucked herself closer and resumed her gentle strokes over my chest. If anything happened to her ...

I thought about Janus and knew this was the perfect time to warn her about my past, and the danger she was in. Ezen was right. Phoebe needed to hear the truth.

Turning my head, I whispered, "Pheebs, I have something to tell you. It's important, and you need to listen carefully before we go any further."

She answered with soft snores, and inside, I cursed. Time was running out, disaster racing toward us like a speeding train. Ezen wasn't here by accident. Janus was a threat, and Phoebe was the perfect bait. Where was the bastard?

CHAPTER 18

~ OLIVER ~

Sitting on the bow of the *Wanderlust* with Ronan, Jovi, and Felix, I tried to ignore the furious stares Ronan sent our way. Growls rumbled from his chest every time I met his glittering green eyes, and my two pals weren't helping.

"Ronan, your female is a wonderful driver." Felix's bi-colored eyes glittered with mischief. "It's a large and powerful boat for such a small woman, is it not?"

"If anything happens to my female, you're all dead." Another dangerous sound rippled from the Syreni's chest. Putting their hands up, Felix and Jovi rethought their teasing.

I glanced over my shoulder and smiled at Phoebe sitting beside our very pregnant captain at the helm of the Grady-White Explorer. Eddi focused on our route, her lips curled up with an enthusiastic grin. She promised to stay on the *Wanderlust* with Phoebe during our hunt. My witch was fully prepared to defend her if necessary.

If a demon hid in the maze of mangroves, Eddi was in no condition to fight. It would sense her weakness and go straight at her. Then, after tearing the demon limb by limb, her Syreni mate would turn us all into chum. Well, maybe not Phoebe. He seemed to like her well enough.

Sighing, I said, "Ronan, I told you. Eddi can drop us off and pull back to watch from a distance. She'll be fine. I promise. Plus, I brought the Ringling Brothers with me. Felix and Jovi are fully trained at Hex's school of world domination. They'll crack the thing's head, and we'll be off."

I shot a look at Phoebe, and frowned. "On second thought, maybe I should stay on the boat and protect the females." The bristling Syreni scowled, his eyes tracking over my physique. I appeared small next to the well-muscled sea creature. Vaguely, I registered the ten pack on his stomach, and shuddered.

Ronan grumbled but settled down a tad. Felix and Jovi smirked at me, and I wanted to kick their Captain America asses.

"Yeah, yeah," I growled. "You're bigger and badder than me. Gideon insisted I join you for some unknown reason. Trust me, it wasn't by choice."

"Sorry, Oliver, but I think the Gryphon may be getting soft in the head as he ages. I cannot see what use you are in a demon fight."

Coming from Jovi, that hurt. I rubbed my chest and shot him a dirty look to cover my frustration. Once I could reveal my Djinn powers, I'd show them how tough I was.

I felt Phoebe's eyes on me, and when our gazes met, she mouthed, "You know what to do." Biting her lip, she added, "Knock 'em dead, stud."

My face flamed red, but we'd arrived at Boot Key. Eddi nosed in, dropped us off on a sandy spit near the island, then backed the *Wanderlust* away, the twin Yamahas grumbling with power. She would circle the island and try to stay close enough to pick us up if things got crazy.

Thigh deep in the water, I looked at the ten-inch narrow blade in my hand, then slipped it into the sheath on my belted shorts. Remembering the sword slicing into my forehead, I decided to leave the knife right where it was unless I was desperate. Thank goodness Ronan and the two Servus knew how to use the short swords they carried.

Jovi and Felix failed to mention that the damn island was a mangrove swamp. I wasn't a great swimmer, so a kayak would have been lovely.

My companions could quickly morph from tails to legs and back again. They swam leisurely beside me as I splashed my way toward our destination. The green water of the wide tunnel into the gnarled mangroves didn't give me the warm fuzzies as I swam closer.

"I can carry you," Jovi said with a grin. He offered his hand, but I shook my head, swimming into the gloom. The water wasn't deep, but it was gross.

Thankfully, we didn't have to go far before the wide tunnel narrowed, and it was shallow enough to walk. My water shoes didn't help because I sank over my ankles in sandy vegetative muck. I lost them in the first hundred yards. Gross. Points to the demon for choosing the perfect hiding spot.

The mangroves closed in, and I eyed the little crab things clinging to the slimy branches above my head. Glancing over his shoulder, Felix followed my nervous stare, smiled, and shook a branch. One of the damn squigglers fell off and landed on my shoulder.

I couldn't help it. I screamed, frantically slapping it off. That earned me an angry hiss from Ronan, who led the way. I shot Felix the finger, and he looked at it, confused; I rolled my eyes.

We hit a wider channel, and the brackish water deepened, so we swam again, soon reaching our destination. It was a dead end piled with the wrecks of old boats.

The bottom was sludgy and filled with roots but deep enough to tread water. I yelped when something long and thin brushed past my leg.

"*Shh,* Djinn!" Mumbled curses followed Ronan's warning, and my ears turned red. I was fairly certain he called me a whining infant in Syreni, but couldn't be sure.

We fanned out, carefully scanning the assorted wrecks. There were a half dozen boats scattered at the end of the tunnel with little room between them. Some were large, their helm half submerged, with slime-covered seats and steering wheels jutting from the water. On one wreck, an iguana sunned itself beneath a break in the canopy.

"Gideon said it was here," Jovi whispered. "Do you see anything?"

The closed-in mangroves blocked much of the sunlight, and the whole place was horror movie creepy. It looked like the perfect place for a demon to—

"Look out!" Felix screamed. Water boiled inside one of the half-sunken boats, and a long tentacle shot out, wrapping around Felix's arm. Dragging him forward, the monster let loose a spine-chilling hiss.

Felix yanked up his shortsword and lopped off the rubbery tentacle, the creature's shrieks filling the air. Green blood spewed as it withdrew, the stump slipping back into the sunken boat as the water bubbled furiously.

"How the hell are we supposed to get that thing out of there?" I asked. Treading water, I was completely exposed.

Ronan disappeared, swirls marking his passage as he dove and approached from below the waterline. There must have been a hole in the bottom of the vessel. Seconds after his eddies faded, the water swelled inside the boat, and a struggling creature burst into view, squeezing through the missing windshield. Its massive frame a writhing tangle of limbs, it fled the stronghold, Ronan dragging behind it. The Syreni hung onto one thick tentacle, stabbing at it with his sword.

Felix and Jovi dove into the fray but quickly wound up wrapped in enormous tentacles from neck to balls. Arms clamped tightly to their sides, the duo's gleaming swords dropped uselessly into the water, their snarls now whispered grunts. The demon's thick limbs contracted, tighter and tighter, squeezing as they wriggled like worms. They struggled to breathe, and their legs stopped kicking.

Writhing and splashing sheets of water into the air, the demon seemed unstoppable. Ronan disappeared, the water roiling as he was wrestled beneath the surface. It was trying to drown him.

Rising from the water, the monster revealed its sheer mass. The elephant-sized blob expanded into the canopy, the torso capped by a neckless head covered in twisting feelers of every size. The thing's flat gray face glared at its prizes, the fangs snapping together with a hollow clunk.

At my terrified squeak, golden eyes focused on where I hovered up to my chin in the swamp, my mouth hanging open. That was when I noticed the blue gemstone glowing from the center of the hump behind its head. My eyes shot wide, and like a dumbass, I pointed.

Felix grunted, unable to speak, his oxygen-starved face a bright red. Dimly, I was aware that Ronan had yet to reappear. Jovi, wrapped even tighter than Felix, tried to murder the thing with his eyes. I was the last one standing. *Shit*.

The demon's slitted gaze narrowed, and it hissed a snakelike laugh. Its mouth opened, the jaws gaping toward Felix first. Without thinking, I misted, streaking across the distance to hover before my friend, turning the blade inside my cloud to point toward the monster.

"You dare, Djinn ..." The thing hissed a warning, but before it snapped, I changed to human form, dropped into the mucky water, and stabbed upward into its bulbous body.

It bellowed, dropped the two Servus, and swung, lifting Ronan into the air to swallow him instead. The Syreni dangled by one muscular arm, water streaming from him as his snarling face morphed into something terrifying. Ronan's eyes burned chartreuse with rage, his long fangs dripping with viscous strands. I shivered, hoping he remembered I was a friend and didn't take my head off.

Jovi and Felix dove, came up with blades in hand, then scrambled up the sides of the thing. Snarling, they buried their swords in its skull, and with an ear-piercing shriek, the beast threw Ronan at me.

The Syreni's heavy body hit me like a Volkswagen, forcing me under the water. When I came up sputtering, the thing had tentacles wrapped around the blades in its skull, pulling them free with a wet crack. Ronan bobbed up beside me, his eyes back to a sparkling green.

When my pals morphed to their tail form, I knew it was time to go. A streak of blue shot past me, and Jovi's arm snaked out, grabbing my wrist as he shot through the water. Ronan and Felix were right behind him.

Brackish water blasted my face with the speed Jovi traveled; sticks, leaves, seagrass—I coughed and sputtered under the onslaught of vegetation. If it was in this swamp, it was in my mouth at some point. When we got to the shallow sections, Jovi didn't hesitate, switching to leg form and tossing me over his shoulder.

Bouncing as he ran, I lifted my head to see the damn thing right behind us, blood tracking down its face as it scrambled, its tentacles twisting to pull it along. Branches cracked, and mud churned as it pursued, its glowing yellow eyes screaming for revenge. *Fuck*. This was bad. Very bad.

Back in deeper water, Jovi shot towards the light, hauling me to the end of the mangrove tunnel, the dragging branches washing away with the speed we traveled. We were back in the ocean seconds before I drowned from the relentless tonsil washing. It made no difference because we'd pissed off the demon and it wasn't giving up. Ronan and Felix appeared, and we widened the gap, signaling the *Wanderlust* for pickup.

In the middle of the bay, we stopped and faced the creature. We had mere seconds; the beast was thirty feet out and closing fast, water spraying over its half-submerged body. I braced for impact, and as the demon paused to snarl, I realized that my erection had disappeared. Good to know.

With a roar, it coiled to launch—then disappeared under the hurtling form of the *Wanderlust*. Eddi was here, and she was *pissed*. I caught a glimpse of gritted teeth, flying silver hair, and a protruding belly. The *Wanderlust* came about, its twin Yammies roaring like angry bears.

Throttles forward, her eyes wild, Eddi ran it over again, then dropped to neutral, threw it in reverse, and backed over the bubbling mess of green blood and globulous chunks. A face floated briefly to the surface, two lifeless eyes telling me what I needed to know.

Ronan surfaced beside me, his face beaming. "That's my female." His eyes shone as he watched the boat return, slowly easing up to where we floated.

Jovi and Felix dove to search through the disgusting mess, then popped to the surface with happy shouts. Jovi held the blue gem, which faded before our eyes.

Phoebe's relieved face hung over the vessel's railing, a hand extending to help me on board. My finned friends gave a sweep of their muscular tails and splashed over the side, dragging green slime and earning a frown from Eddi. Phoebe helped haul me up, then threw her arms around my neck, shaking as she hugged me tight.

"Don't do that again!" she grumbled. "I nearly had a heart attack!"

"You had a heart attack?" I rolled my eyes.

"You were more afraid of those little crab things," Jovi sniggered.

Eddi turned to me, circling her finger as she eyed the twigs and slime dripping all over her deck. "Rinse hose is at the back, my smelly friend."

I looked down and cringed. As I showered off, at least three creepy crawly crabs fell from my clothing and scuttled across the deck. I danced away with a yelp, throwing the hose.

Sighing, Eddi bent over with a groan, retrieved the nozzle, and sprayed. "You're funny, Oliver. They're mangrove tree crabs and quite harmless."

My miniature nightmares sluiced through the rinse holes, and soon, the boat was clean. Our captain throttled forward to head home, and I sat down, my legs still shaking.

I'd misted into Djinn form, and none of the males said a word. I was sure I'd hear about it soon enough. Phoebe's worried gaze covered every inch of my face, her eyebrows raised in question. I shrugged. My time was up, and there was a glowing pink cuff in my future.

CHAPTER 19

~ PHOEBE ~

Gideon came to me that evening in his human form. His knock was sharp and to the point. Gideon declined a drink, then stood stiffly near the dining table while I sat on the sofa.

"Phoebe, I realize we did not initially require your services, but I find myself in a difficult situation, and I need your help."

The breath left me in a rush. He wasn't here about Oliver's powerless bracelet.

"I'll help any way I can, Gideon. What's up?"

"We had someone do a fake interview with Sybil. We believe she's looking to open another rift, and we must stop her. The creature you recently killed came from hell, and our rogue Witch is likely the culprit. We could detain her, but we suspect there is more at play here. I would like you to offer your services to her. We need someone on the inside of this thing."

Struggling with a healthy dose of fear, I considered his words. The entire fiasco had been a nightmare I didn't wish to repeat.

"How will I keep Sybil from opening another rift, though? I wasn't exactly successful on my own the last time."

"It will never get that far. Once we have the location of Sybil's next gateway, we can set up a surveillance operation and pick up whoever is helping her—*or hiring her*, as the case may be."

Nodding, I made a decision. "I'll help. Even though that Witch scares me to the marrow, I sense she's not a dark Witch. Something is off about this whole thing."

"She didn't kill Oliver, so I believe you are correct," he said.

"Wait. You *knew* about the kidnapping? *How the hell ...?"*

Gideon smiled, starting for the door. "Utilizing information is my job, Phoebe. Nothing happens in the Keys that I don't know about." As his hand slid over the handle, he turned and said, "We will endeavor to protect you throughout the operation. As I am sure you are aware, you will be walking into danger."

As the door clicked shut behind him, I wondered why he didn't mention Oliver's bracelet.

***

~ OLIVER ~

The expression on Felix's face said it all. They were about to bust me for the bracelet. As we sat together on the bow of *Caught in the Wind*, I sighed and vowed to change the name of my sailboat to *Silver Linings,* or even *Rich and Famous.*

Jovi's lips turned down. "I'm sorry, Oliver. We must tell Gideon. We wanted to speak with you first because we owe you for saving our lives. But we vowed our loyalty to the Gryphon. You aren't supposed to be running around free of your restraints, my friend."

Rubbing my jaw, I mentally scrambled for something that would change their minds.

"But I've been fine! I haven't had any issues. I've not threatened anyone—it's all good, guys. Honest!"

When their frowns deepened, I added, "Someone from my past may be after me. I'm worried that he'll attack, and I won't be able to defend myself—*or Phoebe*." I gave them my most pathetic, imploring expression, but instead of relaxing, they stiffened.

Felix shook his head. "That's not the point. We're bound to help the Sovereign however we can, and Gideon wants your powers cuffed. It's out of our hands."

Jovi interjected, frowning at Felix. "We can give you until this evening. Then, we must disclose the truth. It won't be so bad, you'll see. You've got us. We'll protect you."

I rolled my eyes. "Yeah. Well, you'll try, of that I'm sure. You have no idea who I'm up against here."

"Why don't you tell us, Oliver? Then we can make a more informed decision." Jovi's green eyes flicked over my face. He was the softer of the pair. Sharp as a pole spear but sensitive to the things happening around him. Jovi was my best shot at staying free.

"Janus is a Djinn from my homeland. He's been after me for a very long time. The King of our clan received an indentured servant as payment for a debt, and he gifted her to Janus—my great-uncle on my mother's side. A powerful Djinn, he had a terrible reputation for abusing his slaves. Mother hated him."

Jovi snarled, his eyes glowing a brighter shade of green. "Go on," he nodded.

"I saw firsthand the way he treated the poor female. One day, in the local market, I watched him beat her nearly to death for dropping a box of dates. The poor girl could barely lift her head, and he still made her pick up each fruit, brush it off, put it back in the box, and then carry it home unassisted. The dates had to weigh twenty pounds."

Jovi and Felix went utterly still, their eyes blazing. They suffered greatly under the demon responsible for torturing me in Charleston.

"Djinn were reclusive back then. On the desert sands, we were free from those who sought to capture us for personal gain. You've heard the story of the Genie in a bottle? Granting wishes is our specialty. Or our curse, depending on how you look at it."

At my bitter words, the two males shrugged, so I hooked my thumb at myself. "Ya, that's me. At full power, I can make anyone's dream come true, but I can't do squat for myself."

Sighing, I continued. "It's a long story, but Djinn are nomadic. A month after the incident in the market, we moved to the Mesopotamian desert. Djinn don't need camels to move. Traveling in mist form, we get a contact high from the sand storms ... " My voice trailed off as happy memories tugged at my chest. My mother. My father. My little sister Edrina.

"Djinn had few belongings back then, but basic needs meant we kept a few servants and camels for when we traveled. My great-uncle preferred slaves to servants."

***

~ The Great Desert ~

The pungent aroma of burning camel dung wafted through the cold night that cloaked me. Even in my mist form, the scents of the desert were a happy reminder of the joys of living free. Our day's travel had been uneventful, and as the servants lit fires to cook our nightly meal, I explored the area.

I loved the vast rawness of the sand dunes, the seemingly endless mounds of possibility disappearing into the indigo horizon. The sound of camp behind me—water pouring, knives chopping fresh vegetables—the familiar routines filled me with peace.

As I traveled around the outskirts of camp, a shrill scream jolted through me. The sound came from my great-uncle's tent. Cries of pain, the snap of a whip—the sounds raked across my skin. Without thinking, I misted over the ground, wisped through an open flap, and hovered, unseen, at the peak of my great-uncle's tent.

Janus towered over the slave I'd watched him beat at the market a few days prior—her name was Lilith. Her face streaked with tears, the girl struggled to pull her shredded garments over her scarred breasts. I gasped at the newly healed stripes scoring her back, a crimson fury kindling in my belly.

My great-uncle was known for his temper and a terrifying disposition. The King denounced him for various abuses, and disgraced, he took it out on others.

Father hated traveling with him for that reason, but my family's lofty station attracted many hangers-on. As third Prince of the Court of Sands, my father endured him every year as Janus struggled to wiggle into the fabric of the reigning family. He wasn't fit to be a thread in the royal rugs covering the floor of my tent.

I cursed under my breath, and the bastard paused to look up. Satisfied that he was alone, Janus coiled the whip he held and untied his robe. Smiling at the fresh lashes on the girl's buttocks, he hissed, "On your knees, whore. I'm hungry."

Sobbing, Lilith slowly rolled to her knees, cowering as he loomed behind her, stroking his cock with a greedy smile. As he lowered himself to his knees, Lilith cried, clenching her thighs in anticipation of the coming pain. I lost my mind.

I swooped from the ceiling, fell to my feet in my human skin, and swept up a knife from the table. I was on him before Janus could open his mouth, my knife swinging with my usual horrible accuracy.

A red line appeared across his hip, his cock hanging lopsided. As a blood-curdling scream filled the tent, I pulled my arm back to finish the job, but Janus misted, his boiling cloud disappearing through the tent flap.

I stared at the knife in my hand, then looked down at Lilith, who watched me with terrified eyes. I held out my hand, my lips curving downward.

"Come. We're in this together now. I'll take you to safety."

As Lilith stood, I swept into cloud form and enveloped her, pulling her close enough to blend her molecules with mine. In Djinn form, I felt her pain—every remembered slash of the whip and every painful thrust of his many rapes. Before I fell to my knees under the sensory overload, I took to the air, the two of us fleeing into the night.

***

Jovi and Felix stared at me, their mouths open.

"I couldn't return to my family. After a long and terrifying flight across the desert, I made it to Bagdad, convinced a friend to give me a bagful of gold, and sent

Lilith on her way in a clean set of robes. To this day, I don't know what happened to her."

"After what I did, Janus hunted me. The laws of my people are strict. Stealing a slave from its owner was punishable by execution."

"What!?" The Servus gasped in tandem. "How is that possible?"

"It happened a long time ago. Things are different now. At the time, it was the law. I never saw my family again. The friend who lent me the gold helped me escape. I fled to the New World, laid low, and have been off Janus' radar ever since. Or so I thought."

I watched their faces. Jovi hesitated, but Felix, who tended to take everything quite literally, set his jaw, his eyes narrowing on me. While under Hex's thumb, the Servus must have learned nasty lessons about trusting others.

I tried again. "I swear it's the truth. I recently became aware that Janus was the reason I wound up in Hex's cells. The demon had connections to a Djinn court—The Court of Seas—and was often hired for their dirty work. Monsters attract each other."

"Janus and Hex probably met at a court function, and my great-uncle would have offered me up with a happy smile. Being a Djinn who had his 'honor' threatened, killing me wouldn't have been good enough. Retribution by extended torture would be a good fit. He visited me in

Hex's cells, hiding his identity. At least I know now that he didn't lose his cock."

My hands shook as I lifted a bottle of water to my lips, dark memories snaking beneath the surface of my consciousness. Shoving them down, I gave the pair of Servus my most beseeching look.

"No. I'm sorry, Oliver. As sympathetic as I am to your plight and what happened to you, I can't go against the Enforcer." Felix set his jaw, his white eye glittering at me. Even with his pained expression, I knew he wouldn't budge.

All the air came out of me at once, my shoulders drooping. "If Janus gets hold of me, I can't defend myself. And you two won't be able to do a thing. He's an incredibly powerful Djinn."

It was too late. Felix had made up his mind. Jovi shot me a sympathetic look as they climbed the stairs to the stern. A pair of mismatched eyes met mine as Felix poked his head back down the hatch.

"Tonight. I'm sorry, Oliver. I really am."

After they left, I stewed. I was well and truly fucked if I didn't find a way to keep my powers. Damn the Gryphon for sending me after the demons. Why the hell would he do that? He must have known by now that I was a flat tire when it came to fighting—*I narrowed my eyes.*

"You scheming bag of feathers!" Gideon knew the entire time. I thought back to the beach, that first night, and pretty much every visit since. That buzzing between my ears. The bugger had read my mind every time. I climbed onto the bow to gaze up at the stars.

"What are you up to, Enforcer? Why not just lock me down right from the beginning?"

When the stars didn't answer, I sat in my chair and unscrewed the bottle I held. The whisky burned all the way down and tasted sour on my lips. Tipping the bottle, I read the label. It was a middle-of-the-road brand, and the name had rubbed off. When I read the fine print, I laughed.

"Aged eight years. You went into that bottle on the day I was captured, didn't you? No wonder you're pissy."

I settled into my depression, thinking back to the moment that destroyed my life. That fateful day in Augusta, when I took a wrong turn. My stomach churned. Another swig didn't help.

Opening my mind to the past was a bad idea, the memories coming fast and furious. All those years in Hex's facility, trapped in a dark cell with no way out, I wondered why I hadn't just said yes to Phoebe that day.

***

~ AUGUSTA, GEORGIA ~

Guilt rode me as I stepped into the corner shop to buy Phoebe flowers. Roses, a deep red, mixed with white. She asked me to move in with her, and I said no.

"We're together all the time, Ollie. I miss you so much when you stay at your place. Can't we just say to hell with it and take the next step?"

I wanted to say yes. But I couldn't, and we argued. At that moment, I had no way of knowing it was the last time I'd see her. During my long captivity, I'd recall her tears that day and cry into my pillow like a baby. Even then, I'd been hurting her.

Picking up flowers was my way of apologizing. She didn't know about Janus or my fears that he would find me. There were so many things she didn't know about me. I never told her much, glossing over it whenever the subject of my past came up. She didn't question or push. Typical Phoebe, letting people do their thing and then suffering through the fallout.

I gripped the neck of my whisky bottle so hard that the glass gave way with a rippling crack. Janus got to me before those roses ever made it to her apartment. Of course, back then, I had no idea it was him. It was sad how simple my capture had been. I'd grown weak after leaving the constant drama and intrigue of the desert clans.

Things were more peaceful in the States. Walking down the streets of Augusta, Georgia, was a safe bet. We lived in a nice area. The town's little shops had beautiful window displays that drew in tourists and locals. When I heard a feminine scream from an alleyway, I immediately ducked into the darkness to intervene.

Two men carrying knives cornered me near the darkest end of the alley, and a female with a pistol stepped out from behind a dumpster. When the males attacked, trying to overpower me, I knew immediately that they were Djinn. The fight got ugly, and before they got their hands on me and canceled my power, I changed to my bear form.

Djinn didn't change forms like Shifters. There was no popping or breaking of bones. With a targeted thought and seconds of spooled power, I became anything I wanted. My mist reformed in that alley in seconds, and my bear charged.

The massive creature lasted five seconds. The woman raised her gun, darted me in the shoulder, then smiled when I fell at her feet with a groggy snarl. Whatever they used was strong, and I was out in seconds. I woke up in a cell with Stephen standing at the door wearing a lab coat, a nasty glint in his eye and a cattle prod in his hand.

I shuddered, nearly retching at the image. Darla didn't know about Stephen's games yet. Edaline and Ronan knew all about Stephen. So did Jovi and Felix. But no one spoke of him. He was dead and needed to stay that way.

With a shudder, I shoved the memories away. Janus could be sitting in our homeland, planning nothing. But Ezen's arrival and his words of caution told me otherwise. My great-uncle had plans for me. I'd been free for six months. To Janus, that was probably six months too many.

Staring up at the stars, I contemplated running. I could set sail and travel anywhere I wanted in a few weeks. I'd been sailing since female figureheads adorned ocean-going vessels. But then I pictured Phoebe.

The pain my disappearance would cause her. The worry, night after night, that I'd been taken again. She'd held on for me far too long, and I wouldn't make her go through it again. As long as Janus lived, I would never be free. Running was pointless.

Was it selfish for me to want her? I didn't need anyone else. Phoebe was everything to me. The roses that day should have been handed to her from my knees while I begged her to have me.

Setting the bottle down on the bow, I sighed, then misted over. As I watched the thin streams of my Djinn form lift from my skin and waft upward into the darkness, I knew this could be my last night of freedom from that cuff. I needed to make it count.

I found Phoebe sitting on the small balcony of her guest suite, her brown hair tumbling forward over her face. Peering over her shoulder, I read the words as she typed. It was an email to Sybil Metroyer, arranging to meet with her. I recoiled, my molecules spreading across the ceiling.

What the hell? Why would she do that? My cloud roiled so hard that Phoebe darted a look over her shoulder, her eyes wide. Finally, she relaxed and resumed typing. I had to talk her out of this foolishness, then warn the Gryphon.

There were so many things I needed to do and so little time to do them. I swept over the railing and headed straight to job number one. If Janus captured me again, I had unfinished business that couldn't wait.

CHAPTER 20

~ PHOEBE ~

Sybil's quick response to my email was a surprise. Her agreeing to meet me immediately was a shock. I was on high alert as I waited beside the mermaid fountain at Burdie's restaurant. At least I had the fabulous smells of some of the best food in the Keys to keep me company. There was no time to stop and eat today.

"Hello, Ms. Peregrin."

I whirled, my hand instinctively shoving outward in defense. A blast of breath left me as I glared at the Witch. To my surprise, Mr. Griswald stepped from the darkness to stand beside her. He looked down his hawkish nose at me, his saggy eyes as creepy as I remembered.

"Lovely. We're off to a good start, then. Is scaring me entertaining to you, Sybil?"

"What do you want from me, Phoebe? I haven't got much time to spare."

"The demons. You've been collecting gemstones. Why?"

Sybil's mouth opened in shock, but she didn't answer. I tried again. "As we discussed in my email—"

With a frown, Sybil said, "Yes. Your very suspicious email. Why do you suddenly want to help me?"

Direct as always. "Because I have an excellent shit-o-meter, Sybil. You're dabbling in dark magic, yet my gut tells me you aren't a dark Witch. I believe you have another reason for doing this, and I'm curious. So tell me. Why do you want those blue stones?"

Sybil went quiet as she weighed my words. Normally stoic, her hands moved nervously at her side. Beside her, Griswald watched through his spectacles, saying nothing. His eyes flicked at the shadows creeping around us, the orange of the sun well below the horizon. The old fogey reminded me of an over-the-hill guard dog watching for his next victim.

"Those gems are a personal matter," Sybil muttered. She looked down her nose at me. "I don't trust you, Witch. Why would you help me now? You nearly cost me the whole enterprise."

Drawing from my grade nine acting class, I tipped my chin up and sent her arrogant stare straight back at her. "Because I'm broke. I need some money. You have money—but this time, I have different conditions.

"And what are those 'conditions,' pray tell?"

"When we finish, I get my money, and I walk away." I almost left it at that but added, "And you never hurt Oliver again. What you did to him was reprehensible." I glared at her.

Griswald laughed, his expression sending fingers of dread fluttering across my shoulders. I tensed at Sybil's wry smile.

"Things are not always what they seem. Remember that," she said.

With a haughty once-over, Sybil said, "Meet me tonight at the end of Long Beach Drive near Coupon Bight. Park and follow the path. I'll be waiting on the beach. And as they say in the movies, come alone. If you don't, I will rescind my promise, and Oliver will be my first stop after killing you." The expression on her face hardened.

I nodded, and Sybil turned to disappear around the side of the building, Griswald right behind her. For an old man, his step was light, and once again, I shuddered. Something wasn't right with the freaky old fossil.

"Did you get all that?"

Gideon blinked into view in his birth form, making me yelp. "You did well, Phoebe. Your acting is exemplary. Thank you."

"Ya, well, I'm hoping I don't need to do that again. That was terrifying."

Gideon frowned. "We'll have a plan in place for your protection, and the two gemstones she seeks are securely warded on my boat at Davy Jones Locker. This will all be over soon enough. Was that the Griswald character you spoke of?"

"Yes, he's a mystery to me. I keep seeing him. I don't know why but he gives me the willies. What do you think—?"

Turning to look, I found myself alone. "Gideon?" When he didn't answer, I wasn't surprised. The Gryphon was gone. I hoped he left to secure the location for my meeting with Sybil tonight.

I glanced up the restaurant stairs, trying to decide if I could shove a piece of deep-fried Key Lime pie down my gullet. When a familiar face appeared, and a tall, athletic guy in shorts and a button-down shirt trotted down the steps, I bit my lip.

"Gabe?!" Air rushed into my lungs; it was good to see him.

"Phoebe." He joined me by the mermaid fountain but didn't seem happy. Right now, he looked stressed. My eyes shot in the direction Sybil had gone, wondering if I should be worried about this huge coincidence. Was he somehow connected to her?

I reached in to hug him, but he stiffened. "What's wrong? I'm so surprised to see you here."

"Can we sit down?" Gabe motioned to the bench near the fountain.

The trickling sound of the water seemed loud in the quiet evening, the voices of the diners above reassuring me somewhat. His tension grated on my nerves, making me feel jumpy.

"Phoebe, there's something I must tell you."

"Wait. Did you come here looking for me? How did you know—?" I glanced after Sybil again, stiffening.

He shook his head, then took my hands as he sat facing me. "I'm not sure how to say this, so I'm going to spit it out and pray that you don't shoot me."

"What did you do? *Gabe*—?"

After a quick look over his shoulder, he stared into my eyes, and his expression turned my blood to ice. "I care about you, Phoebe. Remember that."

I watched his face in terror as it shimmered, and between one breath and the next, a familiar face stared back at me. His blonde bangs tickled by the breeze, Oliver's eyes glimmered in the darkness.

Every hair on my body stood on end, and heat flashed across my nerve endings. Hot as the fires of hell and then ice cold, I forgot to breathe. Images flashed, horror hit, then I shook with barely controlled fury.

"You bastard." My quiet voice, thick with unshed tears, barely made it past my numb lips.

I stood, backing away, ignoring Oliver's hand trying to hang onto my frigid fingers. I yanked free of his grasp, my face a cement mask that weighed me down, rooting me to the spot.

"You didn't. You couldn't—"

When Oliver looked down at the hands rubbing his thighs, something supernova'd inside of me, whiting out the world for a moment. The flare receded, returning my world to shadows, pain, and the sound of a trickling fountain.

Slowly, I turned and walked toward the parking lot. Oliver rose to follow, but I spun on my heel, rage deepening my voice.

When I stormed back toward him, Oliver's lips turned up slightly, hope filling his expression. I reached for his hand and pulled it to me. When he heard my mumbled words, hot, fast, and ferocious, Oliver's lips curved down. The light faded from his eyes.

Pink flared to a new brightness level at my shove of power into his band. Oliver looked down at his wrist as I retreated, stopping at the edge of the darkness. I turned to face him.

"I don't deserve this. I had no idea you were so *fucked up* that you'd purposely destroy the last shred of *whatever the hell* bound us this long. Congratulations, Oliver. You win."

Before he saw the tears in my eyes or the tremors of my hands, I turned and disappeared into the night.

***

~ PHOEBE ~

"Do I have a big fat 'L' on my forehead?"

Eddi handed me another tissue, and I flopped back on her couch with a pathetic whimper. "I'm a fool. I thought ... I tried ... I wanted ... *FUCK!*

Taking my hand, Eddi sent Ronan an apologetic smile as he slipped out the door. I'd run for the ocean, too, if I were him. I was glad he left because, Lord help me, seeing them together would shatter the heart trying to beat in my chest. And Eddi didn't need me raining on her parade by frowning every time Ronan rubbed her belly or brought her a drink.

"Phoebe, it's not your fault. No one tried harder than you. I'm not sure why Oliver did what he did, but remember, he's in a dark place right now."

Tears poured faster than I could mop them up. An evil laugh preceded my whining mimic. "*Poor Oliver. Oliver is hurting. He's so sad. Oliver's trying. Poor guy.*"

Every time I tried for the 'O' sound, long strands of goo strung between my lips. I blew my nose with a wet honk, the tears refusing to quit.

"What about *me*, Eddi?" It came out as a whisper. "When do I get some sympathy?"

"Do you know what you need right now? A drink."

I snorted as Eddi struggled to her feet and returned with a pineapple margarita in a can. I laughed sloppily when she hugged it to her chest, then made a huge display of giving it to me, refusing to let it go when I tried to take it.

She sighed dramatically and released the beverage. My mood lifted at her pouty lips. And damn, that drink tasted wonderful. Eddi watched, envious, as I swigged it back.

"So, while you're enjoying the fruity beverage meant for my post *explosion* celebration, tell me—what's your plan?

"That's the thing. I don't know. I have no idea where Oliver went or what he'll do next. I'm afraid, Eddi. What if he hurts himself?" I sobbed into the can as I took a sip.

"You can't control him, Pheebs. That's the issue here, isn't it? You're like the love child of the Energizer Bunny and Mother Teresa. You'll run yourself into the ground to help others while you sink out of sight with a burp. Don't do it. You need to look after yourself."

I sobbed, knowing she was right. "I've been like that my whole life, you know? Ever since my father died, I've been the cheerleader for everyone. It's exhausting."

Eddi smiled, her eyes glittering with tears. "I'm so sorry this happened. But I know one thing. Ronan and I made it—so happiness can happen for you, too. You need to have faith." She shrugged. "Who knows? Maybe if you let Oliver go, you'll find out he's ready to stand on his own two feet."

"Yeah—*doubtful*." I sobbed, finished the drink, and wiped my eyes with a hiccupy sigh.

"Well, if Oliver's not ready to step up, then you shouldn't be with him anyway. He has shit to deal with. Let him deal."

"I don't want to let go. It hurts like hell." I rubbed my chest, my lips pulled back in a grimace.

Eddi leaned forward, pulling me into a hug. When her belly pressed against me, I felt the baby kick, and she pulled back with a laugh. "Ouch. Pipe down in there, Flipper." She hissed and rubbed her stomach.

"You're the best person I know, Phoebe. You'll get through this, I promise." She looked deeply into my eyes and said, "I hope you're around a while longer. Then you can hold my hand when this thing comes out with six legs and two heads."

I slapped her, and we laughed together. For a moment, the weight lifted from my shoulders. I glanced at my watch. I had more than Oliver to worry about at the moment.

***

Jovi and Felix would watch from the ocean after I got to the beach. Gideon hovered above us, cloaked in his Gryphon form. There were two cars besides mine, so the party had already started. And Sybil picked one of the only remote spots in the Keys. Great.

As I worked my way down the path through the dead mangrove shrubs, I saw a light ahead. Someone had started a fire. Two males chatted beside the small blaze, and when I stepped onto the beach, I recognized them. Sybil stood a few paces away, looking up at the stars. When I approached, she nodded sharply, her expression grim.

The skeevy asshole from the Bat Tower looked up, his black curls swinging as he shot me a dirty smile. Charles seemed a tad angry tonight. I guess he didn't appreciate the trachea full of sand.

Beside him stood Griswald, his lips a tight slash in his wrinkled face. An eerie feeling crawled up my spine as I glanced over his perfectly tailored clothes. Tonight, a strange power emanated from him, the energy snapping against my skin like a rubber band.

Sybil stepped forward, the firelight raising a shine in the dark pools of her eyes.

I looked around, confused. "Where are we doing this? Right here on the beach? A little too open for a demon summoning, isn't it?" When no one spoke, the hairs on my neck rose. Something wasn't right, a feeling that was confirmed when Charles' Incubus magic reached for me, the slimy tendrils of it tracking across my skin.

Crossing my arms, I clenched my fists. "You never learn, do you?"

Dark eyes glimmered with malice as Charles stared at me. "Oh, I learn. And so will you. That was merely a taste of the wanton delights that await you, my sweet."

My eyes rolled, but my stomach twisted with tension. I wanted to run back the way I'd come but knew I wasn't alone. My friends were nearby. I tried to relax and have a little faith.

Sybil cast a rabid glance at Charles and stepped forward. "Your hand, Phoebe?"

Tucking both of my hands into my armpits, I narrowed my eyes. "Why?"

"I need to read you. If you've got someone with you, it won't go well for your Djinn friend."

Sybil was powerful enough that she didn't make idle threats. We stared at each other, and I mouthed the words, *you bitch,* then held out my hand. I kept my ring hand under my arm, power spooling in my fingertips.

I resisted looking at the sky and giving myself away. If she picked up on the creatures watching us right now, I was toast.

Sybil took my hand and energy buzzed between us. My brain did laps as I worried that she would discover my protectors hovering nearby. Surprise rocked me when she stepped back and nodded to the two males beside her. I prayed that my friends covered my ass if this went south. Something was off.

Charles reached into a cooler and pulled out a drink. He offered one to me, but I shook my head, my mind on fire as I waited for the other shoe to drop.

Sybil began pacing off a square in the sand, murmuring as she swept her fingers together, pulling pinches of white powder from a pouch at her waist. Charles handed Griswald a drink, and the pair sipped away, chatting quietly.

Instead of relaxing, my nerves tightened like guitar strings. Charles' eyes never left my face, and his nasty grin made me a little queasy. Griswald stared at the sky as if he knew Gideon stalked us from above.

Sybil was a methodical, precise spell caster. After a few laps around the square, she motioned for me to join her in the center. I stepped over the path she'd made in the sand and froze. I couldn't move.

Griswald stared down his hawkish nose at me and narrowed his eyes. Gone was the unassuming man from my interview. A triumphant, nasty smile creased his face, and he nodded to Sybil, still standing beside me.

"I'm sorry," she said, coming closer. I still couldn't move. "Don't be afraid. The spell won't hurt, but it will immobilize you." I tried to speak, but my lips had fused. To anyone watching, it would appear as if we stood on the beach having a lovely chat and watching the fire.

Charles stepped forward to the edge of Sybil's spell and smiled at me. I sucked in air and tried to spit at him, but with my lips sealed, it came out as a dribble of drool down my chin.

"Feeling more comfortable, Phoebe? Oooh, can't cast a spell? Hard to do if you can't speak. What a shame. Well, I'll put those lips to good use later." He grabbed his bulge, but at an angry rumble from Griswald, he stepped back.

Sybil pulled her hand from her pocket and opened it slightly. "I know your friends are watching, Phoebe. If you're wise, you'll relax and go with it."

Something darted from her hand to hover before my mouth. A smooth, round object drilled against my lips. I pinched them tight, but the pressure increased, and something hard shot into my mouth. I almost choked when it hit the back of my throat. I rolled the thing with my tongue. It was a pill.

"Swallow it." The compulsion that followed the words hit me like a slap to the face, and my throat convulsed against my will.

In seconds, there were two Sybils, then four. My face came unglued, and I could move my fingers again. My lips curled upward into a smile when I saw that each of Sybil's faces had a different expression. The one on the right was the grim one, so I addressed it.

"Yrg n rassole. Wad n giv may." I tried again, but the second attempt made no sense whatsoever. Griswald's chuckle caressed my skin, the beach a psychedelic blur of pinks and blues. Sybil's face came closer. When she was close enough that I smelled the berry scent of her skin, she whispered, "It's Delirium, condensed to pill form. Don't fight it, and I won't give you any more."

Sybil put her arm over my shoulders and turned to face the men, pretending to chat with them. As the pill hit my system, I wondered how the hell these assholes would get me off this beach without Gideon attacking from above.

Sybil must have sensed my thoughts. She smirked and whispered, "Have you never heard of a cloaking spell? I have a dandy one that hides emotion, too."

Inside, I kicked myself, my brief glimmer of hope fading as Sybil took my hand and led me from the beach. My cavalry never arrived.

At the cars, I fought back, raising my ring hand to cast a spell. Someone stuck a foot behind my ankle and lowered me into the rear seat of a sedan. When I slumped against the leather, another pill drilled between my lips. I drooled, and the world melted away.

***

~ OLIVER ~

Rage wasn't a good thing where Djinn were concerned. Impetuous at birth, dangerous into the teens, and briefly homicidal as young adults, it took the better part of a century to assume complete domination over our power. Tonight, rage held me in its thrall, reducing me to a glowing red cloud simmering inside a human body. The fucking bracelet glowed happily on my wrist.

After she left the restaurant, I went looking for Phoebe at her apartment. I waited, but she never returned. Without my Djinn senses, I couldn't track her. So when I finally gave up there, my next stop was Davy Jones Locker, a marina at the edge of Marathon. Felix let it slip once that Gideon kept a boat there. I had a hunch he knew all about Phoebe's meeting with Sybil. I would strangle him if he got her into something dangerous.

Nothing stirred when I got to the marina, but a dim glow lit the living quarters of a new Ranger tugboat at one of the slips. When I got closer, I watched Jovi, Felix, and Gideon searching the vessel for something.

As I stepped into view, Gideon slid through the sliding door, a sword appearing in one hand. His bare chest glistened with sweat under the moonlight.

"You seem nervous, Enforcer. Anything I should know about?"

Gideon lowered his sword, but when Jovi's head popped up from behind the couch, the Servus shared a nervous look with Felix. A tidal wave of fear hit me at the expressions on their faces.

When neither of them said a word, I snarled. "What did you do? Where is Phoebe?"

Gideon looked down at the extra bright pink glow on my wrist and sighed. "I see your magic is bound again, so you'll be no help whatsoever. Stay out of the way." He motioned to Felix, and the two Servus resumed tearing the cabin apart.

Inside my head, something dark clamored for freedom. The bracelet on my wrist trembled under the force of the rage building beneath my skin. "I'm only going to ask you once more. *Where's Phoebe?*"

Felix stepped closer to the Enforcer, but Gideon put up a hand to stop him. "The connection between the two isn't clear yet, but Sybil has a partner. Griswald is lean, old, and has a hawkish nose and light gray eyes. Do you know him?"

Holding my breath, I counted to ten, then let it out with a long slow hiss. "I know him. He's here for me. What are you looking for?"

"The gemstones. They're missing."

"The two gemstones we cut from the demons we killed?"

Gideon nodded. "I assume Griswald is a Djinn, and overheard their location. I underestimated the power of the witch's cloaking abilities, and while helping us tonight, Phoebe disappeared. While we searched for her, someone matching Griswald's description broke the wards on my boat and stole the gems. I am truly sorry, Oliver."

Rage coiled inside of me, dark, dangerous, and itching to break free. When I stomped toward him, Gideon's sword came up, and he took a fighting stance. Stopping, I glared at him and held up my hand.

"Take the bracelet off so I can find her."

Gideon shook his head. "Only a witch can remove it."

We stood there for a moment, frozen in time. I searched the Enforcer's hazel eyes, which stared back at me.

"Congratulations, Gideon. Your little mistake just killed her." I turned and stalked into the night.

CHAPTER 21

~ OLIVER ~

Janus wanted me? He could have me. He had Phoebe and the gemstones, so he'd come for me soon enough. The sailboat rocked gently in its slip as I changed into jeans and a t-shirt. While I laced up my boots, Ezen's voice was no surprise.

"You know what he wants. Will you give it to him?"

"Who are you, the Ghost of Christmas Past?"

When Ezen stared at me without speaking, his expression grim, I answered. "Yes. The answer is yes."

"You know that will be a senseless death and a great loss for your house."

I scoffed. "I let my family down long ago. I broke our laws. My actions started this mess, and I won't allow Phoebe to suffer like I did. I'll find a way to free her and let Janus have what he wants—me crawling at his feet like the dog I am."

"What will it take, Oemar, to make you realize you have value?"

My eyes blazing, I turned to glare into his semi-solid face.

"She is worth a thousand of me. It's a fair trade."

When Ezen followed me into the cockpit and hovered at my side, I looked at him with surprise. "Can you leave the boat?"

"I can. Not in corporeal form, mind you. That takes far too much of the energy I must conserve to assist you."

He wafted over the railing onto the dock and promptly disappeared. When I asked him a question, he didn't answer, but when I climbed off the sailboat, I felt the tingle of a palm on my shoulder. It was better than nothing. At least I wasn't alone.

"You would walk back into the mouth of the monster with me?" Another tingle pulled a grim smile from me as I remembered something. "I met your daughter, by the way. She's a spirited one, that girl. Mowed down a demon with her boat." Faint laughter drifted to me through the darkness, and another tingle confirmed that he heard me.

Right. Enough of that. Stomping to the parking lot, I didn't have long to wait. A sedan pulled up, and Janus stepped from the passenger seat. Charles' head popped up from the driver's side, and the smile the Incubus sent me was gift-wrapped evil.

"I've missed you," he mouthed.

"You're dead," I smiled.

"Enough!" Janus snapped. "Get in the car." His glasses glittered beneath the street light, and I chuckled to myself. His cock may still work, but his eyes didn't. Small victories.

I slid into the back seat to find Sybil staring at me, her expression cold.

"They've certainly found a good use for your cloaking powers, Witch. I hope you're happy." It was all I could do not to strangle her on the spot. Sybil ignored me, staring out the window.

That answered whether the Gryphon would rescue us tonight. The magic of one secretive Sorceress brought down the mighty Enforcer. Everyone had underestimated Sybil's power.

After a quiet ride down Highway 1, we pulled up to the elaborate, unfinished concrete shell of a mansion on Craig Key. Thousands of people drove by every day, wondering why no one finished the project. The cement walls and arched windows were the only thing completed on the building overlooking the Gulf of Mexico. The etched concrete was a reminder that the wind never stopped trying to reclaim land in the Keys.

On the outside, it appeared unfinished, but it was a lie. A powerful glamor cloaked the luxurious mansion beneath the falsehood. Beauty glowed within the abandoned facade.

As we stepped through the front doors, ornate finishings and solid oak floors gleamed in the light of extravagant wall sconces. The three-level interior of the mansion was a thing of unrivaled luxury, filled with Persian rugs and artwork from periods across history. A granite horse's head balanced on a white pillar in the entrance. At the furthest end of the foyer stood a black onyx statue of three tall, slim figures walking beside an elegant camel.

Stepping into the living room, I saw a portrait of Janus hanging proudly over a mantle of polished oak. I smiled at his family saber resting in an ornate cradle beneath the painting, vowing to use it later to take off his head. The expansive living room of white leather furnishings featured a matching polar bear rug. I ground my teeth.

Janus smirked. "Killing polar bears has become one of my favorite hobbies." He chuckled, stepping aside with an overly gracious sweep of his arm and a depraved smile.

I froze, my heart stuttering to a stop. An open-concept kitchen drifted from the edge of the living room. At the glass island, Sybil stood beside Phoebe, who slumped in a white leather barrel chair. Her head hung limply on her neck, a foggy smile on her lips.

A sob begged to escape, but I bit it back. Think, Oliver. Think. My eyes darted around the space, and Janus laughed, his lips curling.

"You're finished, *Oemar*. Your time is up. I require your *services* in a newer, more secure facility. We cut the ribbon on it yesterday, so it's time to reel you in and put you back where you belong." He leered at me. The bulge behind his zipper made me snarl, and I stepped toward him.

"That's close enough," Janus snapped. I stopped and waited, biding my time and cataloging everything in the room. I was well and truly fucked, but I would go down fighting.

Charles strolled to the kitchen island, and Phoebe raised her head, her eyelids drooping. She frowned and spat at the Incubus. With a chuckle, he poured a drink for her and shoved it into her hands.

"Here you go, love. Have another. Someone hasn't seen to you properly." Charles frowned at Sybil.

When I saw the label on the bottle, I recognized it. *Delirium*. I narrowed my eyes at Charles, who grinned back at me, cocky as always. My bracelet vibrated as fury struggled for freedom.

Phoebe smiled, her expression a lopsided mess. Looking down into the glass, she brought it to her lips and drank. Charles encouraged her with one hand on the base. When she finished it, the tumbler fell from her hands, Charles catching it before it hit the floor.

"Whoopsie. There you are now. No harm done."

Phoebe's head rolled as she tried to look at Charles. When he saw her struggling, he leaned down into her face and whispered something. She giggled.

Red filled my vision, my bracelet hot against my wrist. Janus chuckled.

"You are a disgrace to your bloodlines, *Oemar*. Even your father backed my request to find you. No one wants you. Except me, of course."

With a snarl, I rounded on him. "My only mistake was having bad aim that day, you swine. I'm glad I saved your slave from beneath your whip, and I'd do it again tomorrow without question, you sack of shit."

Sybil straightened, her full lips pulling tight. Her head turned, and she stared at Janus, her narrowed eyes trained on his face.

I pinned her with a hot glare. "What? You didn't wonder why a power-sucking Incubus like Charles followed him like a hungry puppy? My great-uncle loves wringing the pain and anguish from his victims—more than enough for a hungry Incubus. I sure hope it was worth it, *Witch*."

Sybil stepped away from Phoebe, her chin high.

Janus chuckled. "Oh, Ms. Metroyer and I go WAY back. In fact, she helped Charles and I set up the facility in Charleston to contain you, Oemar. I didn't want you slipping through my fingers, now, did I?"

My mind skidded to a stop, and I narrowed my eyes. Sybil refused to look at me. I stared, the skin of my face frozen. I knew the wards in my prison were unbreakable, but I never clued in the Witch before me was the source. I was a fool not to put it together when she messed with my bracelet. Especially with Savannah being only two hours from Charleston.

"Well, here I am, ready and willing." I spread my hands out, palms up. "Now let her go."

"No." The Djinn smiled, a cold, cruel thing. "You owe me a replacement slave, *thief*. This female is mine by rights. And after I'm through enjoying both of you, I'll break your mind and send you to the Eternal Sands. Perhaps I'll keep her as a memento of our time together, Oemar."

He turned his cold eyes to Phoebe, who struggled to focus on me. Seeming to recognize my voice, she lifted her hand, but it fell back into her lap, her chin tipping to her chest.

"I'll die before I let you put one finger on her."

"Oh, you'll die alright. And I have the blessing of your own house to do it. No one wants you, Oliver. You've embarrassed your family for the last time. Your father wanted me to give you a message."

Janus pulled a piece of paper from his pocket and read it to me with a smug smile.

"Oemar, my son. As I am the third Prince of the King, I regret that your actions have tied my hands. Our laws decree that your life is forfeit, and I must follow them. Your mother's family bears no ill will toward you. You have been forgiven, and she bids you rise to your next life with no shame. Your friends, Rashid, Sufian, Qisas and Kiran join your mother in sending prayers for your swift trip to Glory."

A snarl tore from my throat, my fists white. My eyes found Janus; my lips twisted with a vengeful fury.

Charles traced a fingertip over Phoebe's foggy smile. "Janus," he purred. "You said I could bed this one before you took her back to the new prison." At Janus' nod, he grinned, then lifted her hand and sucked one finger into his mouth, his eyes boring into me with triumph.

I launched toward the kitchen, but Janus' arm lifted, and a sharp mist shot across the distance to wrap my throat. The strands of his power pulled tight, cutting off my air. Choking, I fell to my knees, my face swelling. Phoebe's wristband erased my magic. This was a one-sided fight, and the bastard knew it.

Sybil stepped forward and her hand sliced toward Janus. He gagged and, with a cough, released me to put his hand to his throat.

"You bitch!" Janus wheezed.

"Allow me." Sybil's dark eyes calmly watched the Djinn before she turned to me. The deep pools of her brown eyes captured my thoughts. I swayed on my knees as she smiled.

"Relax, Janus. I owe this one for almost ruining my plans. I will immobilize him for you. Then you can take your time and enjoy yourself more fully."

Sybil strode forward as Janus massaged his throat, his cold eyes tracking the Witch. I tried to move, but my body refused, the billowing force of the witch's power swallowing me whole. I stopped breathing, my face heating from the lack of air.

I kneeled before her as Sybil gripped my wrists, lifting my arms over my head. Leaning down, her eyes drilled into me. Power raced through me, sharp and brutal, pulling a gasp from my bruised throat. Her hands squeezed my wrists, and with a snap, shards of pain dug into my skin. I screamed, collapsing in her grip.

Sybil dropped my hands as Janus laughed. Frozen where I knelt, I whined as tears of pain spilled over my lids. Blinking through the moisture, I watched Charles lift Phoebe from the chair and slip her arm over his shoulder. I struggled to move but couldn't. Inside, I raged. Against the pain. My failure. Charles, his hands all over my girl. As I knelt there, completely powerless, something snapped inside of me.

Turning to Janus, Sybil said, "It is done. You have your prizes. Now my dealings with you are complete. The gemstones."

Holding out her hand, Sybil whisked forward to stand before the Djinn. With a nod, he pulled the missing gems from his pocket and handed them to her.

Looking them over, Sybil slipped the two blue stones into a dress pocket, whirled on her heel, and stalked to the door, her hard eyes finding mine as she passed. The oak door slammed behind her.

As the door closed, the pain ebbed, and sensation returned to my body. It took me a moment to realize I could move my fingers. Janus stood tall, his pale eyes gloating.

"Your family should have taught you to mind your business, Oemar. A lesson learned far too late, unfortunately for you."

Charles crossed into the living room, awkwardly dragging Phoebe's weight, her arm slung over his shoulder. As they passed behind Janus, she lifted her head to look my way.

"Oliver?" she slurred. Charles hissed something at her, but she dragged her feet.

"That's Oliver," she said to Charles, her expression happy. "Wait. I need to apologize to him."

The Incubus pulled harder, but Phoebe resisted. "Don't you see him? He's there." She tried to point, but Charles slapped her hand down.

Rage poured through me, the floodgates opening as my body filled with power. I stood, and Janus' eyes shot wide.

"Janus, there's something you should know. Those friends in Father's note? They weren't real. Apparently"—I sent him a mocking smile—"my family *does* want me."

I took a step closer, my power spooling beneath my skin. "My father and I played a game when I was a kid. Did you know that *all names* have meaning?"

Janus recovered and tensed, a snarl coming from him as he raised his hands to gather his power.

Picking up speed, I strode toward him, my voice rising. "*Rashid*—rightly guided. *Qisas*—retaliation. *Sufian*—be quick. And *Kiran?*' Beam of light, *motherfucker*."

I screamed, every ounce of spooled power punching through my body. My mist exploded outward, arcing with a blast of light that blinded Janus. His arms flew to cover his eyes and I moved. The light snuffed out, and before him stood my eight-foot-tall polar bear, mouth wide and lips curled back in a ferocious snarl.

Janus screamed.

With a roar that rattled the lights, I slashed, my enormous paw swiping at nothing as Janus misted. Landing on all fours, I whirled on my haunches, my bear's bloodshot eyes narrowing, hunting. If I could get hold of him ...

From my right, a knife sliced across my face, then disappeared; blood trickled from a deep gash on my muzzle. Again, from the left, but this time, it rammed into my shoulder, sinking to the hilt and retreating. I bellowed, slapping at it, but the pain was background noise, a heavy throb I shoved from my mind. I crouched, my predator's eyes searching for telltale shadows. There. On the glass kitchen island. The napkins in the holder stirred. My bear coiled on his haunches, completely still. Thick white hair quivered as he watched for the next clue.

Air rushed toward me and the knife appeared, stabbing for my eyes. This time we were ready. My bear's enormous paw punched out, sending the knife careening across the open space. A yowl, and specks of blood splattered across the tile floor. Still, my bear didn't move. Stealth was his calling; he crouched, his eyes focused.

A whiff of cedar—above him. Twisting, the polar bear launched straight upward, his mouth wide. He snapped, connected, and Janus wailed in agony. Landing with a board-cracking thump, the bear choked down a small, semi-solid hunk of his prey with a satisfied growl.

Blood poured from nothing, a jagged red trail zagging across the living area. The bear lunged to follow, his neck thrashing back and forth, his jaws clunking together, once, twice. His thick claws struggled for purchase, clacking on the hardwood floors. With a final, meaty snap, heavy jowls latched onto Janus' weakening form. Screams rent the air.

The bear's teeth met with a sickening crunch, and Janus blinked into existence, his wrinkled face frozen in shock, his spectacles hanging askew. Flinging his head back and forth, the bear shook his prey, his enraged snarls mingling with screams as Janus bellowed in fear. A bite-sized piece of thigh tore free, and the ancient Djinn tumbled through the air, landing across the room. Shaking with shock, Janus dragged himself to one knee, gasping as he stared down at the jagged, gaping wound in his thigh.

"You lovesick fool," he spat, his face white with fear and blood loss. "The King will see you dead for this assault on me!"

My bear growled, deep, and predatory, stalking forward to finish the job. Janus smiled and pulled on his power; nothing happened. The bear lunged, and the Djinn's eyes shot wide with a horrified shriek as an enormous paw swung, claws outstretched.

Janus' head came off with a wet pop. The rolling mess flew through the air, touched down in the kitchen, and rolled across the floor, coming to rest against the fridge.

Lost to my fury, I grabbed Janus' now solid remains in my mouth, lifting his torso and whipping it back and forth like a bloody rag. Muffled tearing sounds filled the room as hunks of flesh flew, blood splattering the walls, the ceiling, and the white leather furniture. Dropping the carnage with an angry huff, I surveyed my handiwork, panting as blood drained from between my teeth. Then, a dangerous snarl expanding in my chest, I turned on Charles.

Phoebe, roused by the sight of my bear, stood before me, her mouth hanging open as she struggled to stay upright. My bear thumped to all fours, his red, dripping muzzle swinging toward her with delight. Distracted, I didn't see Charles as he charged across the living room, a sword in his hands—the sword from the mantle. With a terrified scream, the Incubus ran at me, the saber's tip pointing straight at my bear.

Time slowed to a stop as Phoebe stumbled into Charles' path and screamed, "*Mortem Tibi!* Death to you!" Her arms came up to clap the spell, but she was too late.

Charles couldn't stop. A bright flash of power outlined Phoebe as the sword burst through her, the tip shining red. Crimson flooded down her back as she reached toward her chest, then slumped to the ground with a weak cry.

An unholy roar filled the room, the furniture flying as I charged. Charles disappeared underneath me as every claw, tooth, and two thousand pounds of angry polar bear reduced him to a pulpy mess under my feet. I dug, slashed and tore, the splashing sounds soothing me as my enemy disappeared beneath my fury.

A feminine moan snagged my attention, and I spun, blood splashing from my drooping lip. With a fizz of mist my bear dissolved, and I ran to her, my feet slipping in the crimson mess coating the floor. Blood streamed from my wounds, but I saw only her. Broken. Dying.

"Phoebe! No! *NO!*"

She'd fallen on her back, the sword twisting to form an even bigger wound in her chest. With trembling hands, I lifted her to me, my face twisted and ruined as I cried down at her.

"No. You can't. I won't do it without you. *Don't leave me!*"

Her eyes half closed, Phoebe smiled up at me, unseeing. She tried to speak, but crimson bubbled into the gap of her lips. Blood smeared my cheek as I pressed my face to hers, my hands shaking. Blinding fear and pain replaced the blood in my veins and the air in my lungs.

"I love you," she choked.

"Oh my God—*fuck!* Phoebe! Don't go. I'll get help! *PLEASE! Wait ...!*" My voice trailed off as sobs stole my air. I saw the moment her life force slipped from her body, a nearly invisible mist rising from her skin. She was leaving me.

Her eyes brightened for a moment, and her lips moved. I leaned close to hear her whisper.

"Worth. World. To ... *me.*" Her last word slipped away like crumbled leaves on a slow-moving breeze, her body drooping in my arms.

Rocking, I pressed my forehead to hers, curling close. No tears came. She was gone. I was alone. I'd never see her smile again.

Rage, horror, and heartbreak flayed me, the fluttering strips of my consciousness drifting away. My power surged outward, trying to fill spaces that could not be filled; I embraced the mushroom cloud of grief that consumed me.

My skin turned to dust, a faint crackling sound reaching my ears as I vaporized, rising to spread through the room. My Djinn soul, lightly tethered by its very nature, disconnected into a suffocating cloud of gray motes. I swelled into the space around me, the life force beneath my skin hanging by the finest of threads.

The world spun into nothingness; I held her; she drifted through my fingers; I followed after her, begging her to return. Then she was gone. My light disappeared beneath the dust.

I don't know how long I hunted the departing wisps of my one true love, but tingles began in my fingers and toes, biting at me. Irritated, I shrugged them off, but they persisted.

Sharper and sharper, a harsh reality attacked every nerve ending until finally, a bellow tore from my lips. I struggled against the pull, but it was useless; I returned without her, empty. The cloud of dust filling the room slowly wafted to the ground with a muffled sound. I blinked, my lashes coated with gray.

Ezen hovered before me, frowning, his gentle eyes reproachful.

"You cannot go, son. It is forbidden to follow the dead into the Eternal Sands."

I stared down at the lifeless body in my arms, now coated in a layer of ash. "I don't care. I have to follow her. She can't leave me. Phoebe gave everything to me, and I never deserved her."

Shaking his head, Ezen whispered, *"That's simply not true. Think. What is the one law that a Djinn must abide by, no matter the cost?"*

I looked up at him, my wet face smeared with ash and twisted with grief.

"We have a limited number of wishes to give, and none for ourselves."

Ezen smiled. *"Oliver, today you will finally see your worth. Because I find you worthy."* Touching my shoulder, he said, *"All these years I've carried wishes for others, but I saved one, meant for my grandson. Sadly, it will never come to pass."* The Djinn's face flared with grief, then he smiled.

"I gift it to you, Oliver. Use it wisely."

Shocked by his words, tears streaming down my face, I watched him fade. The last thing I saw was the white of his smile, then Ezen was gone.

Phoebe stirred, her gasp of breath loud in the dust-filled room. When I looked down, her eyes flickered open. The sword was gone; there was a hole in her blouse and a crimson stain soaked the garment from top to bottom. My frantic fingers felt for her wound, but it was gone as if it never happened.

Blinking against the ashes on her lids, Phoebe swallowed, her throat bobbing. She coughed, and dust sifted from her cheeks, whispering to the ground.

"Oliver?"

Her croaky voice sent goosebumps across my skin. Unseeing through blobby tears, I pulled her to my chest, crushing her to me. I slid my arms around her slight frame to grip her tighter. Phoebe's hands trembled against my sides.

I kissed her forehead, unable to speak. I could cry, though, and the tears poured, my messy sobs painting both our faces with streaks of wet ash.

"*Shh,*" she breathed. "Making me feel bad."

Laughter joined the tears, and although I wished I could slip through her skin to get closer, I didn't. She was ticklish and always hated it when I teased her with my power.

Instead, I kissed her, and my heart detonated with joy. I vowed never to fail her again.

CHAPTER 22

~ PHOEBE ~

"I'm getting up, and you can't stop me."

I pushed Oliver's arm away, laughing off his efforts to hold me down in bed. Staring at my nightie, he swallowed and stepped back. I glanced at my pretty pink lingerie and smiled.

"This is the one you bought me for Christmas."

Oliver nodded, his throat working. I sighed and grabbed my bathrobe, then padded into the kitchen. I wasn't sure how he could blame me for getting up, knowing the irresistible scent of coffee and caramel creamer made me drool. Grabbing a cup, I retreated to the soft chair near the picture window and sat back to enjoy my morning indulgence.

"How do you feel?" His quiet words filled the room, and I drank in the sight of him. Freshly showered and wearing a pair of my jean shorts, I almost laughed out loud at the feminine style on his manly ass. I didn't want to embarrass him, though.

"Where are your clothes?"

"They were covered in ash. I rinsed and hung them in the bathtub to dry."

"How domestic, Oliver. I like it." I chuckled. "How did we get home?"

"Barely, that's how. I used the mansion's phone to call Felix on his cell phone, and thank the Gods, he figured out how to answer the damn thing. Then Jovi got a crash course in learning how to drive a truck. Almost literally. Twice."

Huh. I had no idea they even had a truck. What the hell had they been up to these last few weeks? I tucked my feet beneath me as Oliver poured himself a cup of coffee, then sat down on the couch opposite, his face long and broody. Quietly, he sipped, his eyes watching me over the rim.

"Oliver, we need to talk."

He nodded, his eyes widening slightly as his lips turned down. He looked so tired I almost didn't have the heart to do this right now.

"Why, Oliver? I just need to know *why* you pretended to be ... *Gabriel*."

He swallowed, put his cup down, and stared at me, rubbing his tanned thighs. Damned if I didn't watch, fascinated, as the blonde hair bounced back into place.

"I don't know. I guess I figured you deserved better—than me." He looked down at his hands. "I couldn't be near you at the beginning. God. There are so many things you don't know, and I don't know how to tell you. You wanting to get closer scared me to death, but being away from you nearly killed me."

He usually wasn't a nail-biter, but Ollie lifted his hand and nervously started chewing, his eyes pleading for understanding.

"It was *fucking* stupid. I see that now. But I wanted you so badly. It hurt like hell." He rubbed his chest, his brows pulling down. "I tried to push you away because—Well, I knew it wasn't good for you to be near me, especially with my past …"

I held up my hand. "We'll unpack that later. Stick to telling me about *Gabriel*."

"Gabe was everything you deserved in a man. Loving. Attentive. A great sailor." A wry smile softened his features. "I wanted to see you. Be near you. See you smile again, and kiss you. I couldn't do those things in this body—as myself—and you needed someone in your life. If it couldn't be me …" Oliver dashed his hand through his hair, frowning.

I pointed my finger at him and circled it. "There's a lot in there you aren't telling me, Ollie. What am I missing?"

Biting his lip, Oliver gazed out the window. "Conflicted. I was conflicted as hell, Pheebs. Don't you remember how dangerous I was at the beginning? And then once I got better, I felt dirty. Even now, sometimes it's like there's a black slime covering me. I couldn't be with you. Not like—*that*. I was so scared to hurt you. I felt guilty about the things I did—*horrible things*." He trailed off, then took a deep breath.

"Things happened in Charleston, Phoebe. Things I'm not ready to reveal. But I swear, I never cheated on you." He pointed at his temple. "Not up here, anyway." The desperation and fear in his eyes almost undid me.

"Did it ever occur to you that I would feel guilty for dating another man? As if I was cheating on *you?*" I tried not to sound harsh, but it came out colder than I intended.

Oliver shook his head. "I didn't mean to."

His anguished voice lashed my heart. I was such a sucker for his sad face. We stared at each other, so far apart these days. I hated it. I'd broken my fuckit meter, anyway, so why the hell not?

I stood and crossed the room, and when I sat down with my thigh squashed against his, Oliver's arm came around me. He pulled me in, and I rested my head on his shoulder, careful not to spill my coffee.

"Oliver, there's only one person on this planet I deserve, and that's you. I love you more than anything else in the world. You're sweet, you're funny, and I guess it's safe to say that you still love me too. All the shit holding us apart has to go. And if it takes me the rest of my life to claw through the layers of crap those bastards buried you under, I'm going to do it."

A hitch of his breath told me I'd hit a nerve, but I didn't want to see him cry. I wanted to see him smile.

"Now, tell me what happened. The Delirium they gave me— it's all coming back in a wicked blur." I lifted my gaze to the silver specks in his eyes. "That shit is powerful stuff. If I hadn't been seconds from a horrifying death, it might have been fun."

With a weak laugh, Oliver hugged me. After a brief pause to gather his courage, he told me everything. About Janus. The slave. His family sent word that he had their approval to kill Janus. The whole thing was freaking nuts.

"Your bear! I remember now. He has an anger management issue, doesn't he?" Oliver cringed.

I reached up to touch his cheek. "Thank you for saving me, Ollie. I'm not sure how you did it, but we can talk about that later, OK? I'm hungry. Let's get breakfast. We need to see Gideon about what's happening with Sybil and those damn gemstones."

Oliver frowned. "I can take you right to her. I got a good whiff of her last night when she removed the magic from my cuffs." He tapped his nose. "I can find her anywhere, now."

I gasped. "That's how you got free? Sybil did it?"

He nodded. "She whispered, 'I'm sorry,' then hit me with some sort of pain spell to make it look good for Janus. I didn't clue in until after she left that my cuffs were drained, and I had full use of my powers. She saved my life, Pheebs. Yours too."

I sipped my coffee, thinking. "Well, I guess we need to find out why she needed those gemstones and make sure she never opens another rip in the fabric of the world again."

"Shouldn't that be Gideon's job?"

I smiled. "Well, right now, I'm sort of pissed at him. He was supposed to keep me safe. So he can't be upset if I bypass him this one time."

***

After we ate and I convinced Oliver that I was good as new, he led me to a two-story home on the Atlantic side in Coral Key Village. Pillars lifted the beautiful home over an open two-car garage, and Sybil's car sat inside.

The Atlantic shone a vibrant blue, the killer view drawing me in as we cut through the garage to climb the stairs. It was the perfect Keys vacation rental and must have cost her a small fortune. At our knock, Sybil opened the door. She'd taken her braids out, and her long shining hair curled in dark ringlets over her shoulders.

"We have concluded our business." She looked us up and down. "I'm glad to see you managed after I left. Well done." She tried to close the door in our face.

In a flash, Oliver had her throat in his hand, and he shoved her into the home, pushing her back against the wall. Surprised by his outburst, I grabbed his arm.

"Oliver, let her go!"

His face inches from hers, Oliver snarled, "You owe us some answers."

Sybil's cheekbones flushed beneath her ebony skin, but she nodded. Why she didn't retaliate, I wasn't sure, but I heaved a massive sigh of relief. I let the magic unspool from my fingertips as she led us into the living room.

Raising her chin, Sybil said, "That wouldn't have worked, by the way. You're badly in need of some training, my dear."

Today, she wore jean shorts, and I gasped at the fresh whiplike scars covering the back of her upper thighs. Seeing my surprise, Sybil looked down her nose at me with distaste.

"Power comes at great cost. So do exorbitant wishes. Some things are worth the pain."

When she didn't elaborate on her cryptic words, we followed her into the luxurious home, the brand new interior bright from the sun filtering through the windows. The modern kitchen and open living area had a stellar view of the sea. Wow. Just wow. I was surprised when Sybil turned and led us across the living room and down a hallway.

At the end, she opened a door and motioned us inside. I suspected she meant us no harm, but my witchy senses stayed on high alert—until I saw the bed with the child in it.

A machine on the floor droned and hissed, a thick tube running up to a clear mask on the little girl's face. Her dark skin was dull, but her hooded eyes lit up when we entered. When she lifted a hand as if to wave, a children's book slid from her chest to rest on the bed. She tried to pick it up but was so weak she gave up, her ragged breaths filling the room over the clatter of the machine.

"We have visitors, Sofia. Are you up to it?"

The child looked about ten, but it was hard to tell with the oxygen mask consuming half of her face. She nodded, her beautiful lashes lifting as her tired eyes looked us over.

"Phoebe and Oliver are the two who helped me find the gemstones. They wanted to meet you and see if it helped."

Sofia nodded but seemed sleepy, and as I watched, her eyes drifted closed. I glanced through the room, the machine a harsh background noise jarring my nerves. On the side table, blue crystals of various sizes filled a metal bowl—the same blue granules in the reservoir on Sofia's nebulizer. One of the gemstones sat on the table, glittering dully in the shaded room.

Sybil had crushed the gemstones. They were for her sick child. I blanched.

The Witch ushered us out, my heart sinking as we left Sofia behind. It didn't take a person with medical training to see the child was in a desperate situation.

Sybil breezed back into the living room, going to the window and gazing at the ocean with her back to us.

"So much beauty and Sofia hasn't even been able to enjoy it."

Turning to face us, Sybil sighed. "The ocean has healing properties. I rented this home to give her a reason to try a little longer—and to benefit from the air while I hunted for the gems." She motioned to the deck outside the window. "We sit there in the evening when the sun goes down and it's cool enough for Sofia. She loves watching for dolphins."

My heart broke for her child, because I loved dolphins too. "What were the stones supposed to do?"

"Oxygen," Oliver said quietly. We both looked at him. "Gideon told me those demons used the gemstones to travel into the parts of hell with unbreathable air. The question is, how did *you* find out about them? And how did you get the demons to come to the rift you made?"

Sybil huffed a soft, resigned sound. "The Charun are guardians of the gates of Hell. Any rift would bring them running. Quite simple, really." She glanced at us, her lips tight.

"I found out about the stones from a colleague. He discovered the story in an ancient grimoire in the master library of our order.

A hundred or more years ago, a brave Witch named Leopold Bennett ventured into hell to look for apothecarial advancements in the form of living matter."

She raised her chin. "What he got was a death sentence. He returned to this plane, but lasted only two days. In those final moments, he managed to enter the information in his family's grimoire. I hypothesized ..." She stopped, her expression wary.

"It doesn't matter. The gems aren't working. Sofia will die, and there's nothing I can do about it. Especially since my ace in the hole was recently terminated by justice that was long overdue." She stared at Oliver for a long moment, her eyes filling with tears, then Sybil turned to gaze out at the ocean.

"I'm sorry," Oliver whispered. "Even with everything that happened, I wish it had worked for you. I would help if I could." We headed for the door, but Oliver stopped.

"Before we leave—why were those two demons running loose in the Keys?"

Without looking, she said, "Arrogance, and a misplaced belief in my ability to manage the rift alone. The two demons escaped on my first attempt. I barely got the gate closed on my own. I found them, and warded small areas to contain them until I could determine the best way to get the gemstones out of their miserable hides."

Sybil turned to face me. "The truth is, I couldn't stabilize and close a new gate without your help, and I needed three stones. When Janus told me about the two of you, I didn't understand his interest, or his agenda. I should have asked more questions. But I was desperate, and you were my best bet, Phoebe." She glanced at Oliver. "Thank you for killing the other two demons."

After a lengthy pause, Sybil said, "I'm sorry for what I dragged you into. I did it for Sofia, which doesn't excuse it, but I'm hoping it will lend you some understanding of my actions. I know it's hard for you to believe, Ms. Peregrin—but I am a peaceful Witch. Had I known the entirety of their plans for Charleston—"she looked at Oliver—"I would never have agreed to do the warding there. My apologies will never be enough, Djinn. I am truly sorry."

Oliver nodded, and we turned to leave, but as we crested the stairs, Sybil stopped us. "Ms. Peregrin. I have a lucrative business and am paid handsomely for my talents. You have more skill than you realize. You need to increase your pricing to reflect the current market." With a soft smile, she added, "And for the love of God, get some offensive training." She turned and headed down to the hallway to Sofia's room. I watched her go, my heart breaking for her.

As Oliver and I walked back to the car, I paused to look at the ocean. After all that time and so much effort, Sybil and her sick child were right back where they started. I sucked in a pained breath, my chest heavy. Then, a joyous thought tore through me.

"Oliver! You're Djinn. You can grant her a wish!" Before I finished speaking, he shook his head, his expression grim. "What do you mean, no? Why?"

Oliver squeezed my hand. "I'd help her if I could. But my power is so depleted from my time in that damn basement that it would kill me. It takes an enormous amount of power to grant a wish to save a life. In three, maybe four months … "

"Gods. Sofia will never last that long." When he shook his head, I cried.

CHAPTER 23

~ OLIVER ~

"Come on, Darla. I need to know. We've been hanging around for six months, and I still haven't a clue what your animal is. I'm sure it's cute—so why not just tell me?"

I gave her my most charming smile, but her eyes glittered above a tight, professional smile. Ok, that was a dead end.

"It's got a stubby muzzle and nose hair. What could you possibly be? You said it's not a pig—is it a skunk?" I sniffed the air. "Nope, not a skunk."

She frowned, opened her mouth to say something, then closed it again.

"There's a weird monkey with a nose like a ... " I looked down at my crotch. "Well, it can't be that, anyway. Not the right shape."

Tilting her head, Darla asked, "Are you finished? Because if you are, we need to talk about *you*, Oliver. Knowing my animal will not further your recovery, so quit stalling."

I sighed. "Yeah, alright. Things are better, but it's still awkward between Phoebe and me. I did some pretty dumb things." She wasn't outright nodding, but Darla's eyes sparkled.

"It was messed up. I know that now. Looking back from where I'm standing, I see it pretty clearly, but at the time …" I sighed. "I was drunk and probably had vampire venom numbing me most days. Of course I was a mess."

Darla straightened in her chair and jotted something on her pad of paper.

"Quit doing that!" I snapped. "It's making me nervous."

"I'm simply noting that you've made progress, Oliver. The fact that you see clearly that alcohol and drugs worsened your situation is an 'aha' moment indeed. How is that going, by the way?"

I shrugged. "Whisky is still my beverage of choice, and that's not going to change, but I haven't drank for a few days. Phoebe and I have spent time together, but it's awkward, and I don't know what to do about it."

Darla knew nothing about the battle with Janus, or Ezen's gift to me. With all things Darla, I stuck to the fixable parts of my messy life. My therapist didn't need to know I was the son of a Djinn prince—or that my polar bear killed someone a few days ago.

Chewing the end of her pen, Darla said, "Well, I have a suggestion if you'd like. Easing back into your relationship will take some time, but you could work at it in small steps. For instance, going out for coffee. Taking in a movie. A nice dinner on a romantic patio. Think of it like backing up and starting over. If it's meant to be, your love will return and grow. You'd be surprised at how well removing all expectations can work. Less pressure means more time to find a new balance."

I looked down at my lap, where my erection pressed eagerly against my zipper. "And what am I supposed to do about this? I can't be near her without Chubbers creating a level of pain that's difficult to tolerate. As soon as I see her …"

"Still no luck with masturbation?"

My face flamed, and I shook my head. "I end up raw. The only time I can ejaculate is if I use vampire toxin to dull my senses—or if I'm with Phoebe."

"Are intoxicants still required to share intimacy with her?"

I scratched my ear and fidgeted. "Uhh … yeah, well, I was drunk at the time. Both times."

"Oliver, I can't tell you what to do. My heart goes out to you for what must be a very painful situation. While I strongly recommend forgoing the drinking—and most definitely the vampire venom—if alcohol helps and can give you a measure of relief, then do what you need to. But give yourself a firm line and try to reduce its use to the barest minimum. Eventually, if you and Phoebe rebuild your life together, you must ensure that inebriants aren't a crutch. Trust me, they do more harm than good in the long run."

"She deserves better than me," I whispered. "It's so damned embarrassing wearing loose shirts and constantly icing myself."

Darla shook her head. "You're not cured, Oliver. This will take time. You *are* worthy of happiness, and when you realize that, this entire mess will fade away to a tolerable background noise."

"That's all I get? Tolerable background noise?" I frowned. *Fucking background noise*.

She nodded. "I'm afraid so. What happened to you was horrific. But pretending it didn't happen won't work. You must find a place in your head where you can live with it. It's like a pile of shit in front of you that's so big, there's no way around, over or under it. You have to get to the other side of that steaming pile, and the only way is *through* it. I'm right here. I will go through it with you, and I'll be on the other side of it with you when you get there."

I sat there, my mouth hanging open at her words. Her eyes, while kind, gleamed with a fierce light. At that moment, I realized this wasn't a job for Darla. It was a calling.

Still, I couldn't resist it. "You'd swim through crap with me? I knew you were a pig—"

Frustration slid over her features, and the pen started tap, tap tapping. I wiped the smirk off my face.

"Thank you, Darla. I'm sorry for how badly I behave around you." Even my therapist deserved better than me. Scrubbing my face, I leaned back in my chair and looked at the clock. My time was up, but I had to ask one more time.

"So, about your animal—"

Darla's head wagged, and with a sigh, I stood to leave. When I got to the door, I turned around to say goodbye and got the shock of my life.

"Holy. Shit."

Sitting in her place was an Aardvark. Its tapered tail hung through the back of the chair, and it—*Darla*—sat up, her tiny dark eyes glittering in a face that waged the ultimate war between ugly and cute. Cute won out when her long rabbit-like ears twitched forward. The wet, pig-like nose on the end of her long snout tested the air between us. The curly hairs around the nostrils made me run my hand over my own scruff and think about shaving.

As she sat up in the chair, she was bigger than I expected, and her thick, furry forelegs were darker than her grayish body. She reminded me of a fuzzified, oversized kangaroo-piglet with claws.

"I knew you'd be cute as a button, Darls. I guess that explains the nighttime appointments. Nocturnal, right?" I shot a finger gun at her and winked.

Darla raised a furry forearm, the long black claws clicking together as she waved goodbye.

Closing the office door behind me, I immediately began thinking about where I could rustle up an ant farm as a gift. Then I wondered if Amazon sold chocolate-covered ants. Smiling ear to ear, I trotted down the steps into the cool air of a Key West dawn.

***

Wind snapped the sails of *Caught in the Wind* as I squinted against the bright sunshine, reveling in the ocean spray on my face. It was a glorious day, which helped settle my nerves.

Phoebe sat on the bow, wearing a peach-colored bikini that, thankfully, was covered with a lacy wrap. She'd offered to wear shorts and a t-shirt, but I refused. It was far too hot for that, so I iced myself before she showed up. Saluting her choice of suit, Chubby threatened to push over the top of my shorts, so I averted my eyes. I wouldn't say the Succubus magic had faded, but the ache was bearable these days.

We were bound for Boca Grande Key near the Marquesas. It was the perfect trip for an overnight stay, and after a week of coffee dates and movie nights, Phoebe asked if we could go. I agreed.

Nerves rode me for days while I prepped the boat, but when we pulled out of the marina, some of the tension eased. This was Phoebe, and she loved me. I told myself that over and over. The ocean rushed past the hull, washing my cares away, and an hour into our voyage, the mongoose pacing laps in my guts settled down for a nap.

"Hang on tight!" I yelled, hitting a wave that lifted the bow and juddered the hull. Phoebe giggled, raising her hands in the air and howling with glee. She kept letting go of the wooden cleats as we powered through the chop, but after I barked at her a few times about the slippery deck, she agreed to behave. She was a great sailor and never got seasick, thank God. She loved to get me going, though, so I kept one eye on her the whole way.

Every patch reef we breezed over glowed vibrant blue against the darker coral, the mottled colors a balm to my soul. I decided the color blue had healing properties, and today, sandwiched between the sky and the water, excitement and happiness replaced my usual tension.

We made Boca Grande and had the opposing anchors down and a cocktail in our hands in a little under two hours. As we lounged in the cockpit, relaxing after our voyage, Phoebe tugged on my sleeve.

"Take it off. It's too hot for a shirt."

I shrugged her hand away, and she frowned.

"You don't have to hide your scars from me, Ollie. I want to see them."

"They're ugly."

"No, they're not. They're you. Someday soon, I'm going to touch all of you, but I can't if you wear that shirt everywhere."

I watched her eyes, so soft, so Phoebe. They twinkled with magic and kindness.

With a sigh, I undid the last buttons and tucked my shirt into the Captain's wheel, feeling awkward when I turned back to face her.

"See, that wasn't so hard." She went back to sipping her drink with feigned innocence. I grumbled, knowing that it wouldn't be long before she'd have her hands all over the damn ugly things, but I went with it. She was right. I couldn't hide them forever.

In no time, Phoebe's infectious laughter had my cheeks aching, and I gave up thinking about my scars by the time we hopped overboard for a swim.

A postcard-perfect beach stretched into the distance, the water beneath the sailboat the perfect depth for swimming. A short jaunt brought us to shore where we explored for an hour. Phoebe loved shells but never collected them.

"Why do you do that? Why not take a few shells home for decorations?"

She shrugged. "It doesn't feel right to me. If I take them home, they'll gather dust and end up in a drawer. This way, others can enjoy them too."

After a swim and a brief snorkel, we tread water off the bow, our drinks resting on a flutterboard beside us. When a reef shark swam past, I shrieked, but my girl wrapped her arms around my shoulders and promised to protect me.

Floating nearby, Phoebe shot me a sly smile and said, "I feel like I've done this with you before."

I growled. "Not funny."

Wet hair plastering her cheeks, Phoebe swam closer until her face was inches from mine. Bobbing like a cork, she grinned as I struggled to keep my lean muscular frame afloat. I was at her mercy when she kissed me, a brief, gentle brush across my lips.

"Oliver, sometimes I think you don't know me. I can't hold a grudge. I know why you sent Gabe my way." She wiggled her eyebrows. "And just think! If I get bored with *Oliver—*"

Dunking her, I took off for the boat. Pulling myself up, I was halfway to the deck when a hand snaked out and grabbed my swim trunks, pulling them down around my knees. My cock reached for the sky, and Phoebe shrieked, then covered her mouth, giggling until she almost sank.

I lost my grip and fell back in the water as she shoved me aside, scrambling up the ladder with a triumphant shout. I enjoyed the lovely view of her firm cheeks, and the urge to touch them overwhelmed me. I kept my hands to myself, vowing to be a gentleman on this trip. Rebuilding things would take time, according to Darla. I wasn't about to rush this.

We enjoyed a leisurely afternoon and then made dinner, which was *not* grilled shrimp; it was fish tacos. Phoebe loved fishing and pulled in two nice mangrove snappers during what she liked to call *the witching hour* of fishing.

"The sun, Ollie. As it heads for bed, the little fishies, they get hungry." The words barely left her mouth when she screamed, reeling in an enormous mangrove. I let her take it off the hook. And clean it.

A reef shark was kind enough to take our scraps, and when I watched it snatch the floating fish carcass, I decided swimming was off the schedule for tonight.

After dinner, Phoebe mixed us a margarita, and we curled up on the bow with a few cushions as a backrest. Laid out beside me, her tanned body was sheer perfection. If it wasn't for her matching wrap, my hands would—

"You're being very well-behaved today, Oliver. Is everything alright?"

Phoebe's smiling face sucked the air from my lungs. With the sun changing color behind her, an orange glow shimmered over her skin. Her mussed hair, teased by the wind, begged me to comb my fingers through it. My chest tightened at the sight of her.

"Am I alright? Uh, yeah. Fine. Wonderful." A fierce arousal strained against my swim trunks, and there was no shirt to hide it. Phoebe's eyes trailed downward and her tongue darted over her lips. When she took my drink and set it aside, I held my breath and cautiously tracked her movement.

Turning back to me, her face glowed with mischief. I knew that look, and my shaft pressed against my belly in anticipation. Leaning forward, she kissed my chest and I slid an arm around her, tucking her tightly to my side, hoping that she'd settle and not stir me up any further. When her hand headed south I grabbed it with a gentle squeeze.

"This is wonderful, Pheebs, but I don't want to rush. We have time now. I'm in this to stay. You'll see."

Ignoring me, she kissed a little lower, her lips tracing the shadowed muscles of my belly. It tickled, and I sucked in a breath when heat spasmed through my swollen cock. *Jesus. Fuck.*

Phoebe's fingers traced the outline of my shaft through my suit, palming up and down the length of it as a whimper leaked past my lips. My legs stretched convulsively, my toes curling tight.

"Gods. You're killing me—"

In a flash, my shorts were down and my cock was in her mouth. Stars flashed behind my lids. When she sucked, my legs turned to steel rods, the squeak of the deck beneath my heels a reminder not to fall in.

With a breathless groan, I threaded my hand into the waves of her hair, the bobbing of her head almost impossible to watch without losing my mind. She was so fucking beautiful.

Strangled by the sensations she wrung from me, I panted, hissing and grunting through gritted teeth. With wet slides her lips swallowed me, pulling up and plunging down, over and over. I pushed into the pillows as my thighs spread wide, the noises coming from my throat causing a sexy smile around my shaft.

"Gods, what you do to me, *witch*."

My head fell back, my neck turning to putty as she laughed. Deeper and deeper, she took me in as my legs shook. My hand slapped flat on the deck still warm from the sun, and I clenched the fist in her hair, trying desperately not to hurt her. I drifted away on a sea of pleasure, sailing higher with every wet slide of her mouth.

When Phoebe stopped to take a sip of her drink, I struggled to breathe, glancing down at the slippery erection throbbing against my belly. With an evil smile, she swallowed me down again.

I barked as the ice cube slipping around my cock started a chain reaction. Arching my hips, I thrust into her mouth. Released from beneath me, a small cushion shot sideways, hitting the deck and tumbling over the side to splash into the ocean. Sliding off what was left of the pillows, I didn't care when the plastic of the deck pinched my ass.

"Phoebe. *My God.* Fuck. *Fuck!*"

Swirl. Swallow. Suck. Up. Down. My hips reached for her as, faster and faster, she plunged my cock into her mouth, her hand reaching up to cup my aching balls. I roared through gnashing teeth, my feet wiggling as heat lashed the base of my spine and spiraled upward.

With a soundless scream, I came, trying desperately not to yank her hair. My shaft pulsed against the back of her throat, her hands and mouth softly milking me. Drowning under the force of my orgasm, I couldn't help the incoherent, breathy curses that filled the air.

I felt her laughter down the length of my cock, the frisky witch. With a groan, I let go of her hair and lovingly smoothed it down, then pulled her to my chest, squeezing her in my arms.

"Mmm ... " A husky mumble was all I managed. Phoebe chuckled against my wet, heaving chest, then rained a few kisses over it.

"I'm glad you liked it. I love you, Ollie. With all of my heart," she whispered.

"Love doesn't even come close to describing how I feel about you." My quiet, reverent words made her smile; the image of her happy face branded me for the rest of eternity.

We lay there, my limbs doing a passable impersonation of jello as we watched the sun go down. My arousal subsided, and I enjoyed some blessed relief from its incessant prodding. Phoebe noticed but didn't say anything. The satisfied smile on her face said it all. She took off her wrap and draped it over my hips.

"Thanks for protecting my modesty, beautiful," I said with a sleepy grin.

As we cuddled, I played with her hair, finger-combing the knots as she sprawled across my chest. We chatted about the apartment she found for us in Augusta. We planned another month in the Keys so I could work with Darla, then we'd move back to Georgia. Together. When Phoebe asked me to move in, there was no hesitation. From now on, it would always be yes for my Witch.

I lazily rubbed my hand down her back and cupped her ass in my palm, feeling first one cheek and then the other. When she giggled, I squeezed. Her soft slap on my belly earned her a smile and a stretching yawn.

"Sleepy?" she asked.

When I nodded, Phoebe snuggled against my side, one hand sweeping gently back and forth over my chest, the other folded between us. Alone in our private oasis, my mind finally went quiet. Comfortable. Content. I explored her curves with one hand, slipping a finger beneath her suit to trace her slick folds. I almost choked when I got more than I bargained for.

So fucking wet. My God. My cock leapt to attention, aching to be inside of her as I struggled to keep up a gentle, stroking rhythm. All I wanted to do was yank her on top of me, bury myself inside of her, and express my love the only way I knew how.

Slowly I eased a finger into her wet pussy, stifling a groan at how ready she was for me. Adding a finger, I slid them gently in and out, smiling to myself at the sweet sounds I teased from her lips.

Phoebe's heart pounded against my side, her body pressing closer as she tensed beneath my touch. I swept my fingers around her clit on every pass. Gently. Firmly. Steady as she goes. I smiled into her hair when she pushed herself against my hand, straining for more. Her body slowly coiled with the inevitable tension that would bring her release. I kept going.

"*Gods!* Shit, Ollie! Please, more ... *Fuck*!" She grabbed my shoulder with her free hand, squeezing her fingertips deep. Hearing her curse like a sailor cranked my gears. I smiled at the crazy sounds coming from her mouth and pumped slow and steady, circling her clit with a little more pressure. She was ready, and I was going to push her over the edge. I'd forgotten how much I loved torturing her.

I knew how she liked it. We'd learned each other's bodies long ago. Hearing her scream my name had always been such a huge high for me. My mind drifted—thoughts of torture and screaming were a mistake.

With the sun almost set, the rising darkness stuck to me. A seabird screamed, and my body froze, my hand stalling as tingles raced over my skin. Suddenly, I walked down a dark corridor, someone leading me by the cock as magic filled my head with cotton and made me stagger. A choking hiss shot through my lips and I started shaking.

"Oliver?" Phoebe pushed herself up, her eyes probing my strained expression.

She growled, "Stay with me. It's you and me. No one else. We're alone, and we're together. Those bastards are six feet under, and if anyone else lays a hand on you, I'll kill them myself."

At her fierce, protective words, the darkness receded and my lips found hers. She kissed me back, burying me with love and affection as the screams, hisses and smell of burning flesh whisked away. Soon only Phoebe stared back at me, her eyes hooded with desire.

Forcing myself to relax, I smiled at her, swiping the sweat from my forehead.

"I'm ok. I'm ... *I'm Sorry.*"

"It's alright, Ollie. I love you. We have all the time in the world."

I slid my hand over her back, pulling her down onto my chest. Before I could reach for her again, she wriggled her bikini bottoms down and tossed them with a deft flick of her toe. She yelped, and I glanced up in time to see them slide off the bow and join the pillow in the ocean. Phoebe laughed, her happy smile chasing my darkness away.

"I'll rescue everything tomorrow." I grunted as I pulled her up my body, my shoulders sinking into the cushions. She giggled as I positioned her over my mouth.

The salty tang of her sparked a throb in my shaft, but I ignored it. I dove my tongue into her, picking up where my fingers left off, circling her clit with steady, flat rolls of my tongue. Her glossy response and gasps of pleasure sent my poor cock into overdrive.

When I increased the pressure, Phoebe fell forward and slapped her hands onto the cushions. She spread her legs, her thighs shaking.

"Oh God, Oliver ... that's.... *Unnngh.*"

I dug my fingers into her ass, pulling her tighter against my tongue, eager to feel her come undone. As Phoebe's lusty cries peppered the air, my cock pressed urgently against my belly. It was too much. I let go of her with one hand and reached down to stroke myself, desperate to ease the torture even a bit.

Phoebe glanced over one shoulder, then with a worried frown, backed herself down my body. I grabbed her arm to pull her back.

"I'm ok. Let me finish," I whispered.

She ignored me. Phoebe's gaze never left my face, love shining in her eyes as she seated the tip of my shaft against her entrance. I groaned as she slid me home, my legs jerking straight at the grip on my cock.

Holy mother fuck, she was tight ...

Silently, I thanked Darla for the *it's better when you're sober* lecture, because she was right. Man, but Pheebs felt good, strangling my cock as she slid up and down, smiling like a cat after catching a mouse.

"Ok lover boy. Let's see what we can do about your little problem."

The tease took her time. Slowly sliding up and down, she leaned back, pulling my hands to her breasts. I fondled them, gently rolling my thumbs over each nipple as my cock surged inside of her. I called her name with a choking whisper, embarrassed at how deeply she moved me. I needed her closer. I had to show her what she meant to me.

Tugging her to my chest, I rolled over with a smooth motion, pinning her to the cushions. My face inches from hers, I whispered, "I love you so much I can't stand it. I still can't believe you waited for me." I tipped my forehead to hers, trembling as my heart jackhammered against my chest. Tears threatened, and I tried to bury my face in her neck, but she pulled me up to look into my eyes.

"I'd wait until hell froze over to have you with me, Ollie."

Covering her lips with a scorching kiss, I rocked into her, pushing deep and angling my thrusts, knowing exactly where she liked it. Emotion bubbled inside of me. She'd unzipped me, and my soul spilled out, naked for all to see. I closed my eyes, fighting down gasping sobs as we came together, skin on skin, face to face, sharing tortured breaths.

With a stretching shudder, Phoebe hit the peak and threw herself over the edge.

Her orgasm squeezed my cock and I lost control. Pushing her into the pillows with frantic lunges of my hips, I erased every molecule of space between us. Dropping my head, I ground out my release, following her into the abyss. Spasms shook me until, finally, I shuddered to a stop, panting into her neck.

She stroked her fingers through my hair, whispering loving words in my ear. I eased down to stretch against her, struggling to catch my wind.

Curled tightly together, our breaths mingled as I closed my eyes, slipping into the strong, protective cocoon of Phoebe's love. After a long cuddle, she smiled at me with soft, contented eyes.

As the last sliver of the sun slipped beneath the horizon, instead of pulling us apart, the darkness wrapped us together in a warm sea of bliss. I slipped my body to the side and hugged her close.

Feather soft, she kissed my temple and whispered in my ear, "You're mine. And don't you ever forget it."

CHAPTER 24

~ GIDEON ~

Matilda giggled as I dropped a shoulder and dipped, my wingtips stretching to hold a glide. The dark water beneath us teamed with life; I felt it all. The creatures below the ocean were as much mine to protect as the ones above it, and my heart swelled with pride.

Speeding above the flat calm of the sea, I turned my wings, and we shot into the sky. A shriek from the child on my back turned my lips up at the corners.

"Do it again!" she squealed.

"We have business tonight, Matilda. Maybe on the way home."

With an affectionate pat, the tiny body pulled tight to my neck, and I set my sights on Coral Key.

I didn't give rides to anyone; it was beneath me. This child was special in so many ways. Love wasn't something I allowed myself, but she captured my heart when I wasn't looking.

Cupping my wings, I pulled up to land softly on the balcony of a stunning home overlooking the ocean. Lowering myself carefully, I tested it for strength. Set on cement piers, the decking seemed strong, so I folded my wings and dipped my shoulder. Matilda slid from my back. Lifting my head, I watched the Witch step onto the deck, closing the patio door behind her.

"You took your time," Sybil whispered, her eyes flicking to where Matilda stood by my side, her eyes wide with excitement.

"Can you hear me in your mind?"

Sybil nodded.

"You broke the laws of the Sovereign, Witch. Calling demons is an offense punishable by death."

Pulling herself up straight, Sybil's hands trembled as she held them out to the side.

"I won't fight you on my punishment. But I must make arrangements for my daughter before you take me. And for the record, I'm not sorry about calling the demons. I'm only sorry it didn't work."

I narrowed my eyes. *"Matilda needs to use the bathroom. Would you allow it?"*

Sybil looked down at Matilda, then reached behind herself to slide the door open.

"Down the hall on your right. But be quiet, please. My child is asleep."

Matilda nodded, and, catching her lip in her teeth, she slipped inside and disappeared.

"Sybil Metroyer, you are charged with two counts of calling demons for personal gain. One count of kidnapping. Three counts of willful endangerment. One count of conspiring with a known enemy of the Sovereign. Two counts of aggressive action against citizens of the region, and ten thousand dollars in fines for damages."

At her inquiring look, I grunted. *"Eddi ran over one of your demons. She needs two stainless props and the hull of her boat fixed. She will be insufferable until it is repaired."*

Sybil lowered her eyes but nodded in understanding.

"Under the circumstances, the Sovereign is willing to overlook the formal charges and waive sentence in return for certain—favors. Services and ongoing consultations, to be specific. The time period for said services would extend for twenty years commencing today if you agree."

Sybil looked up, her eyes wide. She held her breath and nodded, her gaze meeting mine as if she couldn't believe her good fortune. She opened her mouth to say something, but I snapped a wing to silence her.

"I'm not finished." Glancing over Sybil's shoulder, I spied Matilda through the glass, and at the expression on her face, I nodded to the Witch.

"The Sovereign is a generous soul. He understands your pain and your motivations for your evil deeds. In return for your lengthy term of service, he would like to offer you a boon that he trusts will smooth over the beginnings of what he hopes is a long and mutually beneficial relationship."

The patio door swept open with a whoosh, and Sybil whirled. With a sharp cry, her hands covered her mouth.

Matilda stood in the doorway, her glittering emerald eyes shining with tears. The luminescent, incredibly powerful tears of the Gods. The tears that not so long ago had saved my life, and the life of a dysfunctional Djinn.

Beside her stood Sofia. The indentation of her mask marked the conspicuous absence of it. Her bright eyes shone above a generous smile while smooth, strong breaths swept in and out of her lungs.

With a scream, Sybil fell to her knees, Sofia racing into her outstretched arms. As they clutched each other in wonder, laughing and sobbing, Matilda skirted them, and I dipped my shoulder.

Accidentally plucking out a feather on her way up, Matilda whispered, "Sorry," then settled between my wings. The emotions of the child on my back tickled my senses: joy, laughter, and a deep sense of belonging. Sometimes, life was good. Today was one of those days.

I glanced at the Witch, then at my feather on the deck. Reaching out one paw, I scooped it up and, with a painful stretch, handed it to Matilda.

"Never leave your DNA behind when a Witch is about. Remember that, Matilda."

Matilda giggled. Crouching, I whispered into her mind, *"Hang on tight!"* and shot straight into the air, wincing when I heard a board crack beneath the force of my takeoff.

As I took to the sky, I glanced down at the two shining faces watching us rise. Sybil smiled, her lips moving. I didn't hear her words, but her overwhelming joy whispered down my spine. The wonderful sensation sparked a rumbling purr in my chest.

"Where to now, Matilda? The night is young."

"Can we go see Phoebe and Oliver?"

I chuckled. "Maybe tomorrow. *They're a little tied up at the moment. How about a quick visit with Ronan and Eddi? If I'm not mistaken, we'll have an addition to the Shoal very soon."*

Matilda clapped her hands, and with a playful wobble that made her shriek, I turned toward Marathon.

Did you enjoy Oliver?
CLICK HERE FOR
EDDI & RONAN'S STORY

The completed trilogy prequel to Oliver

~~~~~~~~~~~~

With your support, I will gladly write more epic tales for you!
WHAT CAN YOU DO TO HELP?

LEAVE A REVIEW!

You'll be helping this Indie Author more than you know!

~~~~~~~~~~~~

NEXT IN SERIES

One of my favorite characters
from the Tides Trilogy

CAL'S STORY

~ COMING FEBRUARY 2024! ~

~~~~~~~~~~~

FOLLOW THE AUTHOR!

https://www.amazon.com/stores/Penelope-Austin/author/B0C3YCXSYG

OTHER BOOKS BY PENELOPE AUSTIN

~~~~~

THE MARTYR TIDES

BOOK ONE OF THE TIDES TRILOGY

THE BLOOD TIDES

BOOK TWO OF THE TIDES TRILOGY

THE MOON TIDES

BOOK THREE OF THE TIDES TRILOGY

(FINALE)

OLIVER

A STAND ALONE SEQUEL ROMANCE

Printed in Great Britain
by Amazon